Bello:
hidden talent rediscovered!

Bello is a digital only imprint of Pan Macmillan,
established to breathe new life into previously published,
classic books.

At Bello we believe in the timeless power of the imagination,
of good story, narrative and entertainment and we want to use
digital technology to ensure that many more readers
can enjoy these books into the future.

We publish in ebook and Print on Demand formats
to bring these wonderful books to new audiences.

About Bello:

www.panmacmillan.com/imprints/bello

About the author:

www.panmacmillan.com/author/rogerbax

Roger Bax

Roger Bax is the pen name of Paul Winterton (1908–2001). He was born in Leicester and educated at the Hulme Grammar School, Manchester and Purley County School, Surrey, after which he took a degree in Economics at London University. He was on the staff of *The Economist* for four years, and then worked for fourteen years for the *London News Chronicle* as reporter, leader writer and foreign correspondent. He was assigned to Moscow from 1942–5, where he was also the correspondent of the BBC's Overseas Service.

After the war he turned to full-time writing of detective and adventure novels and produced more than forty-five books. His work was serialized, televised, broadcast, filmed and translated into some twenty languages. He is noted for his varied and unusual backgrounds – which have included Russia, newspaper offices, the West Indies, ocean sailing, the Australian outback, politics, mountaineering and forestry – and for never repeating a plot.

Paul Winterton was a founder member and first joint secretary of the Crime Writers' Association.

Roger Bax

DEATH BENEATH JERUSALEM

First published in 1938 by Collins

This edition published 2012 by Bello
an imprint of Pan Macmillan, a division of Macmillan Publishers Limited
Pan Macmillan, 20 New Wharf Road, London N1 9RR
Basingstoke and Oxford
Associated companies throughout the world

www.panmacmillan.com/imprints/bello
www.curtisbrown.co.uk

ISBN 978-1-4472-2053-4 EPUB
ISBN 978-1-4472-2051-0 POD

Visit **www.panmacmillan.com** to read more about all our books
and to buy them. You will also find features, author interviews and
news of any author events, and you can sign up for e-newsletters
so that you're always first to hear about our new releases.

Contents

Author's Note

Every character in this book is fictitious and no reference is made or intended to any living person. The topographical details of Solomon's Quarries and Hezekiah's Tunnel have been freely altered to suit the purposes of the story.

1. Dawn Encounter

The stars in the eastern sky were just beginning to fade into the grey of morning as Philip Garve rounded the south-east corner of the wall of Jerusalem and faced the Mount of Olives.

He walked quickly, partly because the air was still chilly from the night, and partly because he had not yet lost the habit, formed during the last outbreak of Arab violence, of presenting the briefest possible target to an enemy.

He made a wry face as the putrid odour of the brook Kedron filled his nostrils, and drew a long breath of relief when he had crossed over to the windward side of the stream.

Picking his way cautiously through the incredible debris which littered the track of beaten earth, he reached at last the Tomb of the Virgin Mary, and bearing to the right past the unkempt Garden of Gethsemane, began to climb. He had met no one and heard no sound except the crowing of a cock and the occasional barking of a dog. Jerusalem was still asleep.

As he mounted the hill, he stumbled once over a boulder in the dim light, and once thrust his face into the twisted branches of an ancient olive tree. After some ten minutes' hard climbing, however, he reached the top without further mishap, and peered around in search of the flat yellow rock which had provided him with such an excellent observation post on a former occasion. When he found it, he saw that it was already occupied.

During ten eventful years as Special Foreign Correspondent of the London *Morning Call*, he had often known surprise without showing it, but this morning on the Mount of Olives he could not suppress an exclamation of astonishment as he drew nearer and discovered that the figure silhouetted against the lightening eastern sky was that of a young woman with a most attractive profile and a highly European appearance.

He had approached within a yard or two of her before a loose stone, clattering from under his feet, attracted her attention. When she saw him, her "Good-morning" was as unperturbed and natural as though she were welcoming a member of her family to breakfast.

"How do you do?" said Garve, peering. "I can't see you very well in this light, but your voice sounds English."

"It is," replied the girl without moving.

"H'm!" The disapproval in Garve's tone was unmistakable. "In that case I wager my last piastre that your name is Esther Willoughby."

"Right again," said Esther cheerfully. "How did you guess?"

"Well," said Garve, "there aren't many English women left in Jerusalem, you know—they've wisely cleared out while there's still time—and none of those who are left would venture up here alone at daybreak to commune with nature. I heard yesterday that the famous author, Francis Willoughby, had arrived with a charming daughter —no, don't bother to bow—so putting two and two together I arrived at the inevitable conclusion. By the way, my name is Garve—Philip Garve of the *Morning Call*."

"How do you do? I feel I ought to say, 'No, not really,' and ask for your autograph, but I'm afraid we always take the *Telegraph*, and I've really never heard of you."

Garve grinned broadly. "That's the biggest blow my professional pride has received for years. By the way—if you'll forgive my meeting brutal frankness with offensive curiosity—does your father know you're here?"

"Of course not. He'd be furious. I would have asked him to come too, but I knew he would be writing until the early hours of the morning, and it seemed a shame to drag him out."

Garve nodded and stood silent a moment, listening. It was a consolation to him that no one could move without noise on this stony hill. He satisfied himself that the sombre shadows contained nothing immediately menacing before he gave the girl his full attention again.

"If rumour doesn't lie," he said, "your father is working on a new volume of memoirs which will place him beyond all question among the literary giants. I suppose that means that you'll be on your own a good deal while you're here."

"Well," said Esther demurely, "it all depends. We've brought a young man named Jackson with us to act as chauffeur and secretary for father and escort for me. He'd tackle anything on two legs, but unfortunately he's inclined to be chatty at the wrong time—that's why I left him at home this morning."

"I see—and it wasn't possible to get a guide right away, so you came without. You don't let your enthusiasms die of old age, do you?"

"I just couldn't wait," declared Esther, in a voice so pleading that she made Garve laugh. "We've been out of England all the winter, and I *know* I'm rather a *blasé* traveller; but ever since father mentioned Palestine I've been dreaming of the mountains of Moab and sunlight glinting on the Dead Sea. It sounded irresistibly fascinating."

"I've often had the same feeling," Garve admitted. "I was here for six months last year, when the riots were at their height, and I must have climbed this hill a dozen times, just for the view and the quietness. So I can't really lecture you. All the same, you're lucky not to have had an Arab knife stuck in your back while you were gazing so intently at the horizon."

Esther gave a little exclamation of annoyance. "If your idea of being sociable is to give me grandmotherly advice," she observed coldly, "I suggest that you remove yourself to another part of the hill. And, anyway, talk about Satan rebuking Sin! I should like to know who gave *you* a safe conduct through the trackless wastes."

Garve regarded her quizzically. "There are no safe conducts for English people in Palestine to-day," he said slowly. "It just happens that I'm paid to take risks, and I've grown used to them. If I stopped an Arab bullet, nobody would mind much. My few surviving relatives have all prophesied my early demise at one time or another, and they'd be so bucked at being right for once they'd forget to be sorry. The *Morning Call* would print a quarter column obituary, and no doubt I should be referred to as 'poor old Garve' in the office for a week or two. Then they'd appoint someone else to fill my job at a higher salary, and nobody would ever mention my name again."

Esther laughed softly, too amused to be annoyed any longer.

"Now, if *you* were bumped off," Garve continued, obviously enjoying himself, "you'd have half the British navy tearing across the Mediterranean to avenge you. They'd land a small army, blow up a few villages, arrest a couple of hundred Arabs who hadn't done anything, in the hope of getting the one who had, and altogether make the situation in Palestine about twice as bad as it is already. They'd call it 'pacification.' And all because you hadn't the sense to take reasonable care of yourself."

"Please!" Esther protested. "I know I'm headstrong, but I'm not a *bit* important. In any case, everything seems very quiet in Jerusalem at the moment."

"It depends where you are," said Garve grimly, "and how long you've been here. The train from Haifa to Jerusalem was bombed a fortnight ago as it was leaving Galgylia and eleven people were blown to pulp. The night before last a Jewish policeman was ambushed, shot, and mutilated on the Nablus road. It wasn't so quiet for him—not till he was dead, anyway."

"I didn't know," said Esther in a subdued voice. "The atmosphere of Jerusalem seemed so normal yesterday. People were going about their business laughing and chatting just as usual, as though there were no such thing as politics in the world. Why, I remember thinking that the innocent air of the place seemed almost too good to be true after all the fuss there's been in the papers."

"Exactly. That's why the *Morning Call* has sent me back. The quietness *is* too good to be true. The feeling is widespread among the police, the military, and the Jews, that something is going to happen soon—something big and very terrible—but nobody knows what or when."

"How thrilling," cried Esther, excited by his tone. "Tell me—that is, if I'm not being too curious—what *are* you doing in Jerusalem, besides looking at sunrises. Do you 'snoop'? Journalists on the films always seem to snoop."

"I don't like the word," said Garve. "It offends my sense of professional dignity—but I suppose that's just about what I do. Mostly at night. In the daytime I'm having all my work cut out keeping out of harm's way. You see, my paper is strongly anti-Arab, and during the troubles last year it was constantly urging the Government to send out more reinforcements and take what they called a 'firm line' with the terrorists. If my news stories didn't square with policy, the stories were spiked. Once or twice they were actually altered by sub–editors, who didn't realize that every word I sent was weighed like gold, and that a change of *nuance* might cost me my life. I kicked up hell's own row about that, but the damage was done, and the Arab leaders blamed me for everything the paper said about them. I had several narrow escapes, and my departure from Jerusalem was accompanied by a frenzy of curses in the Arab Press. Now that I've come back I anticipate the same thing starting all over again. As you observed so succinctly, it's thrilling."

"I didn't mean to sound girlish," said Esther, all contrition once more. "It must be perfectly beastly for you. Oh, I say, look!"

In silence they stood side by side watching the spectacle of the sky. Great shafts of light were striking up fanlike from the horizon as though the grim mountains of Transjordan were in blazing eruption. Dawn was coming now at a run, storming the heavens with burning spears. In a few moments, as though thrown by some gigantic juggler, the sun came hurtling into the sky. First the highest points of Jerusalem caught the yellow light, while the walls stood dark in sombre shadow, and then the warm flood came sweeping down the slope of the Kedron Valley and up the other side, till it lapped the feet of the watchers and passed over them.

As Esther emerged from the concealing gloom, Garve saw for the first time that the face which had so delighted him in profile was set in a mass of warm, chestnut curls, dazzling in the sun's rays.

"How incredibly lovely," cried the girl, gazing in ecstasy at the revealed city.

"Wonderful," breathed Garve, gazing at her hair.

She turned sharply at something in his tone, saw that he was looking at her, and smiled tolerantly as at a foolish boy.

"In the circumstances, I'll forgive you for being personal," she said.

"What circumstances?" asked Garve bluntly.

"Well, I've had my share of empty compliments, but this is the first time that a man of the world—and a hard-boiled journalist at that—has ever climbed a steep hill to see a sunrise and looked at me instead!"

Garve eyed her disapprovingly, for her flippant, not to say flirtatious, remark clashed with his mood.

"My exclamation was quite impersonal," he assured her. "The sun makes everything beautiful, and for a moment your hair looked like a halo." He pointed to the glittering domes of Jerusalem, glad to change the subject. "In case you've ever wondered," he said, "you can see now why they call this place 'Jerusalem the Golden.'"

Esther nodded. As her eyes took in the dry and stony panorama, she suddenly gave a little shiver.

"Cold still?" asked Garve. "Here, take my scarf."

"It's not that," said Esther. "You'd think that a city that was bathed in sunshine all day would look friendly, but it makes me feel afraid. It's so hard and glaring, and the shady bits look so black against the rest. It's all striped—like—like a tiger that may spring on you at any moment."

Garve looked at her curiously and with a new interest. "So it affects *you* like that, does it?" he said. "In that case I've blamed my Fleet Street upbringing unnecessarily. Sometimes in the white heat of the day I've had the impression that the Kedron Valley was grinning at me, and showing its teeth like a bleached skull. But then the *Morning Call* pays me to imagine things like that, and they look well on paper as a background for riots and sudden death."

"I bet 'menacing' is the word you use," said Esther teasingly.

"And, please, why is the valley such a mass of stones? It looks an awful rubbish heap."

"It's an old Jewish burial-ground," Garve told her. "The Arabs and the Jews both think that on the Day of Resurrection the Almighty will conduct the Last Judgment here. I believe that's why the Arabs had the Golden Gate blocked up—you see it over there on the left? It leads straight into their mosque, the Dome of the Rock, and they didn't want hordes of resurrected Jewish spirits marching in to take possession. So the story goes, anyway, but it's probably apocryphal."

"Never mind—it's quite a good one. What a terrifying place the valley would be to cross at night—alone."

"A bit spooky," Garve agreed. "In the moonlight the stones look just like old bones. But ghosts apart, the valley is probably safety itself compared with the old city—that's all the part inside the walls. It looks clean and bright from here, even if it *is* hard, but when you get inside it closes in on you. It's dark and smelly, and if you haven't a guide you find yourself wandering into terrifying hovels hewn out of rock and inhabited by cut-throats and religious fanatics of innumerable denominations. But it's a fascinating place all the same, and grips the imagination because of its age and associations, and incredible mixture of peoples."

"I'm dying to explore," said Esther. "I met a man last night at a party—Anthony Hayson, do you know him?—said he was an archaeologist. He told me I should hate all the religious associations because they've been so commercialized."

"Hayson?—yes, I've heard of him—fellow from Oxford, isn't he? He's right, of course. It's a nauseating spectacle to see the way half a dozen Churches squabble over the holy places and exploit them. If you were looking for Christian charity in the world's capitals, you'd be wise to come to Jerusalem last of all."

"It's a pity. A lot of people must be bitterly disappointed."

"Lord, yes. Many of them come for the wrong thing, anyway—they make the mistake of trying to strengthen their faith in the miracles by providing them with a background of local colour—and it doesn't work. It's much easier to believe that Christ ascended into heaven when you read it in the Bible than when you're rooted to the alleged spot by the well-known law of gravity. But there's plenty of Bible atmosphere if you know where to look for it. There's more up here, for instance, than in the city. After you've been inside the walls you begin to understand why Christ came up into the Mount of Olives to pray. The feeling of relief hasn't changed in two thousand years. I daresay some of those trees on the hillsides were standing in Christ's time, and you don't have to pay two piastres to look at them! He may easily have walked on the very stone we're standing on. The hills were the same, and those purple mountains over in Moab that look like the mountains of the moon—they haven't changed."

The girl's eyes were shining with excitement, but she said nothing.

"This country comes to life in the most unexpected way," Garve went on. "Last time I was in Palestine I went fishing on the Sea of Galilee. I couldn't have fed five thousand on what *I* caught, I don't mind telling you, but then I'm no angler. It was as smooth as a sheet of glass, and seemed so small you simply couldn't believe the Bible story about the tempest. But next morning when I walked down to the shore after breakfast there was a stiff wind blowing down the valley, and in some peculiar way it had taken the surface of that lake and whipped it up into great waves that smashed on the jetty with a noise like an artillery bombardment. A small boat couldn't have lived five minutes out in the open."

"And I suppose that visit counted as work!" said Esther enviously. "Does the *Morning Call* move you about much?"

"Quite a lot, especially lately. I was in Abyssinia until the rains came on—that was my first war job. Then they discovered I spoke Arabic—result of a youthful enthusiasm and an interest in the East—and they sent me out here to 'cover' the riots. When the place got too hot to hold me, and I was beginning to think I'd earned a holiday, they gave me six weeks in Madrid. Directly there was a lull there—nothing happening except a few people getting killed each day!—they moved me to Bilbao, and I was nearly wiped out at the bombing of Guernica. Now, here I am, back again in Palestine. Life is certainly not devoid of incident."

The sun was by now beginning to beat down uncomfortably on the open ground, and Esther was glad to accept Garve's suggestion that they should return to the shade of the city. They scrambled down quickly between the olives, climbed over a low wall of limestone, skirted a patch of scanty barley, and found themselves with a stone's throw of the brook Kedron. The warm air was alive with the whirr of grasshoppers, and once Esther was startled in her descent by a lizard which darted under a stone with a dusty flick of its tail.

"Now where?" asked Garve when they had reached the road. "I must see you home."

"If you're going to make it sound like a duty," said Esther, her red lips pouting, "I'll go by myself."

"Spoilt—badly spoilt," thought Garve to himself, but he grinned amiably and murmured something about combining duty with pleasure.

As they approached the Damascus Gate the environs of the city began to come to life. Arabs from the villages were riding upon the haunches of their asses, bringing great bundles of oranges and lemons, or bales of embroidery for the daily market. Mangy camels toiled slowly up the hill bearing the chattels of whole families. Fierce, dark-eyed Bedouin faces from Transjordan stared at Garve, and again at Esther, sometimes resentfully, sometimes just in cold curiosity. The gate itself was already the scene of stirring cosmopolitan life. There was much noise and gesticulation among the little knots of tarbooshed town Arabs who conversed as though they were arguing, and argued as though they were at war. Queues of Arab buses and taxis were drawn up by the gate, waiting in vain for European and hopefully for Arab custom. Beggars, rotten with disease, sprawled in the dust and whined for alms. Garve gently took Esther's arm, and, attracting as little attention as he could, pointed out the various types who made up Palestine's population.

Never in her life had Esther seen or imagined so strange and confusing a spectacle.

As they watched, fascinated, while a grey-bearded fellah haggled for a handful of dates as though he were buying a whole plantation, a man approached them who was smartly dressed in European clothes, but for his red tarboosh. His face was handsomely tanned, his carriage erect and proud, his features good. In perfect English he asked whether the lady and gentleman would like a guide.

Garve replied quickly and decisively in several sentences of fluent Arabic. His emphatic tone was just beginning to have an effect when Esther plucked his sleeve confidingly and said, "Let's go—there's plenty of time before breakfast," in a voice loud enough for the guide to hear.

Garve motioned the now eager man to a distance, and turned grimly on the girl. "Are you mad?" he demanded angrily. "I tell you these places are not safe. At this very moment we're being watched by a dozen pairs of hostile eyes. You think that because a man is sitting on the ground, quietly smoking a hookah, he's harmless. He may just as easily be an agent of one of the terrorist societies. They're everywhere —you can't trust a soul in Jerusalem."

Esther gave an exclamation of impatience. "I'm sure you're exaggerating. You're not writing a story for the *Morning Call* now, you know. I believe you're one of those awful people who like talking about danger in order to make themselves feel important."

"And *I'm* quite sure," retorted Garve, now thoroughly roused, 'that you are one of those dreadful women who feel affronted when they find that social status carries no absolute guarantee of safety in all circumstances."

"How dare you?" cried Esther, stamping her foot in a way which, in other circumstances, Garve would certainly have found attractive. "I believe you're *afraid* to come with me."

Garve grinned mockingly. "In my adolescent days, my dear Miss Willoughby, that taunt would probably have worked. I am old enough now, however, to realize that in addition to being an unusually charming young woman, you are also temperamental, impetuous, and exceedingly foolish—and why you didn't bring your nurse out with you I can't imagine."

Esther's eyes blazed. "I suppose you think you're awfully funny. Personally, I find you merely impertinent. Nobody asked for your advice *or* criticism. And if you won't come with me, I'll go by myself."

"Now—please!" said Garve, suddenly pleading. "I'm not exaggerating—it really *is* dangerous."

"Guide!" called Esther in peremptory tones. The man, who had been standing just out of earshot, advanced with alacrity.

"I want to see the city," said Esther. "For one hour."

"Yes, miss," said the man.

"What's your name?"

"Saud, miss."

"Saud? Are you an Arab?" Esther had always imagined that Arabs invariably had dark skins, and this man was hardly darker than Garve himself.

"Yes, miss." The guide's immobile features alone betrayed his race.

"Very well, Saud, let's go." She turned to Garve triumphantly. "Good-morning, Mr. Garve. Thank you for your company." She relented a little. "I really *have* enjoyed our talk, you know. Good-bye."

Garve nodded grimly. Had he been a policeman he would have taken her into protective custody. He felt angry at his inability to do anything effective, at his failure to influence her. As Esther and the guide passed through Damascus Gate there was a little stirring of the fellahin squatting in the dust, and, Garve believed, a certain melting away.

He shrugged his shoulders, put his dignity and his hand in his pocket, and, cheered a trifle by the feel of the automatic that never left him, followed Esther through the gate. At least, he thought, consoling himself, if someone threw a bomb at her it would be a good, exclusive story!

2. Ordeal by Bomb

Once Esther discovered that she had succeeded in getting her own way, she stopped and waited for Garve to join her. Unperturbed by the sulkiness of his expression, she placed a small, exquisitely manicured hand confidingly on his arm, as though she had known him for years, and gave him a dazzling smile.

"You're very nice," she said softly, and in the bright sunlight she looked alluringly beautiful.

"On the contrary," retorted Garve gruffly, "I'm a fool. Even though a crack on the head would undoubtedly do you a world of good, I ought not to let you expose yourself. However, since you've made up what you're no doubt pleased to call your mind, we won't start quarrelling again. Hi, Saud, where are we going?"

"In one hour," said Saud tonelessly, "we can see very little."

"Never mind that. Just take us round the streets—the main streets. He added something in Arabic which sounded like a sharp instruction, and the guide nodded gravely and went a pace or two ahead.

"Can I see the Wailing Wall?" asked Esther demurely.

"If you behave yourself," said Garve, trying hard to look stern in face of the dancing mischief in her eyes. "But I don't suppose there'll be anybody wailing at this time of day. The best performance is given on Friday afternoons."

Esther's eager fingers again lightly touched his sleeve. "What about that place where the top of the mountain comes out into the floor of the mosque? Antony Hayson told me about it."

Garve raised his eyebrows. "Hayson again? He seems to be a knowledgeable young man."

"He's very handsome," said Esther. "There are so few presentable men in Jerusalem now—except the police."

"Considering that you've been in the city quite twenty-four hours," said Garve, abandoning once again all pretence at politeness, "you have naturally had the opportunity to comb it pretty thoroughly! Does Hayson like spoilt young women?"

"You can judge for yourself when you meet him," retorted Esther. "Anyway, what about our mosque?"

"Closed to-day to all but Moslems," said Garve snappily. He was beginning to feel hot, and to wonder again why he had bothered to come with her. "And you can't get into anything except a bad temper at this unearthly hour of the morning."

Esther laughed gaily. "I *do* like you," she declared shamelessly. "You say the rudest things in the most amusing way, and I know I'm a pig. From now on I'll really be good. Tell me some more."

"Well," said Garve, relenting in spite of himself, "you must have a look at the Church of the Holy Sepulchre before you leave Jerusalem, but we couldn't begin to see it in an hour. Solomon's Quarries, under the city, are well worth a visit—but I remember now, your handsome friend, Hayson, is digging there, so he'll probably offer to escort you. Then there's Hezekiah's Tunnel —a filthy old aqueduct—but I can't recommend that, because I'm still trying to summon up enough courage to explore it myself. I think the streets will keep us occupied for to-day. The very names take you back a couple of thousand years."

He pointed to a blue plate nailed on to an ancient slab of masonry, and Esther read the words, "Via Dolorosa."

"You can think what you like about it," said Garve. "Some say it is and some say it isn't. Mind that camel!"

Esther swerved to avoid a nuzzling nose, and a spot of high colour in each cheek betrayed her excitement. As they proceeded cautiously into the heart of the city, the lanes became more and more congested. They were so narrow that in places three donkeys could not have stood abreast. They descended and climbed in a series of irregular steps, so that even by day it was necessary to walk with care. Where a plan of Jerusalem optimistically showed a street, complete with name, the wandering tourist often found nothing but a dark entry between high walls. Walls were everywhere—high walls, low walls, new clean walls, dank and dripping walls, sunlit walls, dark looming walls—all of rock as solid as the seven hills from which they have been hewn. Behind the walls, striking the imagination with terror, garrets and hovels and noisome cells crouched behind narrow unglazed windows. Some of the streets—the main arteries of this uncanny city—struck straight and true from gate to gate, but others turned and twisted as though the builders of Jerusalem had set themselves deliberately to build a maze. Half of them ended blankly and unexpectedly in a wall. One could study the map for an hour before entering this warren, and still be cursing in a cul-de-sac within five minutes.

Here and there a street ran almost entirely underground, with only an occasional round vent in the stone roof to let in light and air. Shafts of vivid sunlight pierced these holes and stabbed the gloom like searchlights. Where they struck the ground the roughly cobbled surface was revealed in all its filth. Thousands of shuffling feet had beaten the excrement of animals and the decayed remnants of green merchandise into a soft moist mat, which deadened sound. To the left and right, hollows had been carved out of the living rock to serve as shops. Inside, in incredible dimness, picturesque jewellers pored over their rings and silver filigree, greedy merchants fingered Damascus cloth, cobblers hammered with straining eyes. One street was monopolized by leather sellers; one dealt only in the tourist knick-knacks of the East; in one the way was cluttered up with heaps of oranges and lemons, and piles of uncovered fish, round which the flies buzzed unceasingly, and rings of caraway-covered bread.

Several times Esther paused in doubt as some choice piece of drapery was thrust under her nose by a highly coloured Arab, whose name, she thought, should certainly have been Ali Baba. Each time, Garve took her arm and propelled her gently but firmly outside temptation's reach, praying that she would show no further signs of temperament.

"Another day," he said. "We mustn't stop."

Once, as she squeezed her way between a nosing mule and a peasant bent double under a sack of grain, a bearded old Arab squatting in the dusk of his shop called curses after them. Esther turned sharply, startled by the menace in the words, which she did not understand, but again Garve moved her on, not letting her mind dwell on the incident.

"Jerusalem, as you see, has its own traffic problem," he said, gently pushing a donkey's head from her path, "but no motorists, thank heaven."

"It's a wonderful place," breathed Esther ecstatically. "I could spend hours and hours here. Look at that striking fellow with the rings on his hand. I think he was nodding to you. Do you know him?"

"He was nodding to our guide," said Garve quietly. "Saud had a word with him as he passed. A friendly salutation—I hope. If a row started here we'd be quite helpless."

"Panic-monger," murmured Esther. "But it's certainly the ideal spot for a rough-house. People of so many religions and nationalities must have riots pretty often."

"Not as often as you'd think. The city is divided up into religious areas—invisible boundaries keep Jew from Arab, and Christians from both. That's why a guide is so useful, even if, like Saud there, he does nothing except walk on in front. He knows where we may go and where we mustn't. Every sect has its forbidden places, and on your own you keep on meeting villainous-looking guards with raised hands and peremptory orders to return the way you came."

"I see. I *thought* Saud was taking his duties very lightly."

"I told him to go on ahead. He's just near enough to act as a protection from other guides. If we were unescorted we should be assailed on all sides by offers of assistance. They become unpleasantly persistent, particularly when tourists are defenceless and ignorant of the city—and they can be dangerous, even in normal times. But they're efficient when they want to be—they know their Holy Places as you know the multiplication table, though they treat them with no more respect than you would lavish on a slot machine at Brighton."

15

While Garve talked, his wary eyes were constantly turning from one side of the path to the other, catching and analyzing the glances of strangers, weighing the hostility of some against the apathy of others. Presently the way became less crowded, the street narrower, the light dimmer. There were no longer shops or shoppers, and an increasing silence closed the party in. Saud was still marching along in front, his bright red tarboosh perched at a rakish angle, taking no notice of his clients, except to indicate occasionally by a dignified gesture that they were to strike on in another direction along a path which, without him, they would hardly have noticed.

"Two more turns, one right, one left, and we'll be at the Wailing Wall," said Garve. "It once formed part of the old temple, but it's now the outside wall of the great Arab mosque—the one you wanted to see. There—you can just catch a glimpse of the dome across that courtyard. The orthodox Jews come and wail here for the departed glories of Israel. It's a weird, wretched spectacle—the sight of them makes one ashamed of the human race."

"Do they really weep?" asked Esther.

"They do that—salt tears that trickle down their cheeks. And they cry out like souls in torment. Sometimes you can see them kissing the stones and poking bits of prayers into the cracks while they chant an ancient ritual. You remember the rioting here in 1929? That was before my first visit, but, by all acounts, it was frightful. Since then there's been a police box posted just before you get to the wall, in case of another outbreak, and during the day there's always an officer on duty. He ought to be about somewhere. Look, you can just see the box now."

The wooden shelter stood in the shadows. Saud gave it a hurried glance as he passed, and, suddenly quickening his pace, disappeared round the corner. Garve frowned and was about to hurry along after him when something about the interior of the deserted box caught his eye. He stopped and looked more closely. When he glanced up his face was grave. He knew now why there was no sentry to be seen.

"The policeman seems to have deserted his post . . ." began Esther.

"Quiet!" Garve's tone was peremptory. "There's something wrong!

See this." Esther peered inside. The box was quite empty except for a light service overcoat hanging from a peg, a tattered Sunday newspaper, and a telephone. Garve was pointing to a foot of useless cable which hung from the instrument, and a gleam of copper where an Arab knife had severed the wire.

Garve's fingers tightened like a steel band on Esther's arm. "Stay inside the box," he said in an undertone. "Don't move or make a sound. I won't be a minute." Flattening his body against the wall, he glided swiftly to the corner and peered round. His gun was ready in his right hand, but there was nothing to shoot at. He gazed steadily at the unpleasant scene, took a long, deep breath, and, with tightened lips, began slowly to creep back.

A cold shiver ran down Esther's spine as she watched him, for she knew he had bad news, and feared to hear it.

"Is the policeman there?" she called in an anxious whisper.

"He is," said "Garve slowly, wiping from his forehead the drops of sweat which had suddenly gathered there. "Lying on his face against the wall with six inches of knife between his shoulder blades. He's as dead as Methuselah."

Even as Garve debated the chances of their own safety, and the best way to secure it, he could not help admiring the manner in which Esther took the blow. Only a faint pallor and the quickness of her breathing betrayed the effort she was making not to seem afraid.

"Isn't it possible to join this wire up again?" she asked tremulously.

Garve shook his head. "They've taken a piece away—cut it right out. They're very thorough and very well instructed. Well, we'll have to get out of here somehow. If we hug the wall there'll be less for them to shoot at. Keep close behind me."

They had not moved two yards, however, before the crash came. A small black missile hurtled over the wall behind them, dropped behind the sentry box, and exploded with a flash and a concussion that seemed to split the earth. Garve, hurled off his feet, hit the opposite side of the street with a thud which racked every bone and muscle in his body. For a second or two he lay winded and in agony, struggling with nausea and faintness, oppressed by the knowledge that he must get up and do something. By sheer effort of will he forced himself up—lifted himself up, up—with his fingers scraping in the niches of the wall. The air was thick with acrid smoke and heavy with dust. As it cleared he saw that Esther was resting on one knee, not far from him, her face buried in her arms, her shoulders heaving.

Garve was no coward, but now his courage almost failed him, for he saw that her hands were red with blood, and the thought of what her face might be appalled him. He had seen a child once, in Madrid, after a rebel air raid . . .! Tortured by every movement, he groped his way across the few feet that separated them, and, with his arm round her shoulders, drew her hands away.

"Thank God," he breathed, not knowing even that he said it. Blood was still streaming from a cut over her left eye, but it was neither deep nor dangerous. Dazed, she allowed him to tie his handkerchief round her head.

Automatically he retrieved his gun, which was lying at her feet, and slipped it into his pocket. "Are you hurt anywhere else?" he asked anxiously. "Take it easy, but try to stand up. Arms, legs feel all right? By God, we've been lucky."

"Are *you* all right?" asked Esther faintly.

"Just bruised and cut about a bit," said Garve, gazing dejectedly at the knuckles of his left hand, which must have scraped the wall as he was thrown against it.

"The sentry box seems to have suffered most," said Esther, pointing to a mass of splintered wreckage strewn over the street.

"It probably saved our lives," said Garve. "I should think the bomb was home-made—they mostly are in these individual attacks. If it hadn't been, we'd both be twanging harps by now."

"Ugh! Well, what do we do next?"

"Stay right here until the police come. That explosion must have been heard for miles, and directly they find they can't get through on the phone, they won't lose a minute."

"Do you think Saud threw the bomb?"

"Probably, but we've no evidence—it might have been anybody."

"Was it you they were trying to get—or me?"

"If I had been with any other woman I should have said me. As it is, I don't know. They were given a golden opportunity to bring off a double event, and they did not waste it."

They waited silently now. Each moment that passed seemed like an hour, but, as Garve had anticipated, the police arrived speedily. Esther, plucking excitedly at his sleeve, first drew his attention to the sound of running footsteps. His own eardrums had not yet recovered from the shock of the explosion. He was a little fearful that the runners might be Arabs, and not the police at all, but the clatter of heavy boots on stone was reassuring. In a few moments two young men in the uniform of the Palestine force rounded the corner at the double, service revolvers ready in their hands. Immeasurably relieved that the responsibility was no longer his alone, Garve sank down heavily against the wall to nurse his bruises and console himself with his briar.

"Glad to see you, Phillips," he said, nodding to the taller of the two men, whom he recognized from a previous encounter. "It's been pretty exciting here the last few minutes."

Phillips, a muscular young giant with a sandy moustache and a gallant manner, was already bending anxiously over Esther, who had joined Garve against the wall.

"Good heavens!" he ejaculated. "Miss Willoughby! What on earth are you doing here?" He was unrolling a length of bandage from his kit as he spoke, and with a few deft movements had slipped off Garve's blood-soaked handkerchief and made a workmanlike job of Esther's head. "Better?" he asked solicitously.

"Quite all right now, thanks," said Esther "Just a headache. I think Mr. Garve has had a bad knock, though."

"Not a thing wrong with me," insisted Garve, puffing stolidly with relaxed muscles.

"We'll see about that. Give him the once over, Featherstone."

The second officer made a superficial examination despite Garve's protests, and announced that, so far as he could judge, no bones were broken.

Phillips nodded. "Glad we were in time, old man," he said to Garve.

"For us, yes." Garve indicated the Wailing Wall with a movement of his thumb. "You'll find your man over there with a knife in his back. Looks like Simpson. He doesn't need help any more."

"Christ!" said the young policeman soberly. "The swine—the infernal swine. That's the fourth this week." His worried gaze returned to Esther. "We'd better get you out of this right away, Miss Willoughby. Can you walk, do you think?"

"We'd better not try and get through the city again," Garve interposed. "I suggest you send Featherstone back to Willoughby's house for a car as quickly as he can go. He can tell someone else to collect the corpse. We'll pick up the car near the French Consulate. We can slip out through Dung Gate and walk round outside the wall. It will only take us ten minutes . . ." He moved, and a twinge of pain shot through his shoulder. "Well, perhaps twenty minutes. If you come with us we'll have two guns, in case they feel like finishing the job."

Phillips, who had had many dealings with Garve, and knew him for a man of sense, nodded and passed on the instruction to Featherstone.

While Phillips made the necessary arrangements, Esther struggled with an awakening conscience. She noted the pallor of Garve's thin bronzed face, and felt suddenly very humble.

"Are you angry?" she asked softly.

"With myself," said Garve. "Very! I was a fool. I knew perfectly well that I ought to have stopped you."

"I was very stupid and selfish," said Esther contritely, and he saw with horror that her dark lashes were glistening with tears.

"Don't you worry," said Garve awkwardly. "Here, have a cigarette." Fumblingly, he struck a match for her and hurled the burnt stump petulantly away. It annoyed him that after all his experience in handling people and situations he should feel he had bungled this one so badly.

He scrambled so his feet. "Ready, Phillips? Give Miss Willoughby a hand, will you? I'll bring up the rear. And for the love of God take it easy or you'll lose me."

That short journey was one of the most trying that Garve had ever known. By now the sun was beating down unmercifully on the hard, dry ground, and waves of hot air made breathing uncomfortable and walking a penance. The smell of the brook Kedron was fouler than ever in the heat. As the little party passed slowly and painfully along the undulating path leading from Dung Gate, Garve saw that the whole southern-side of the wall was deserted, as though the Arab population had been warned to keep away.

Phillips, brisk and smart, alone appeared to be enjoying himself. He had taken Esther's weight upon his arm, and kept up an even flow of light conversation during the whole journey. Garve, worried and aching, turned over the events of the morning in his mind, trying to link them somehow with what he knew of the growing Arab conspiracy. In the end he gave it up, and contented himself with thinking out the opening paragraph of the "story" he would cable to London that afternoon.

As they neared the Consulate he saw with relief that a big black saloon was already waiting. Featherstone had clearly lost no time. Two men were hurrying down the steep uneven path to meet them, and one—the one, strangely, who gave the greatest impression of haste—had a limping gait. It was Francis Willoughby, called unexpectedly from his breakfast, and jolting and slipping among the stones as though he set no value at all on his neck.

Esther ran to meet him, grave-faced and repentant. "I'm sorry, father," she said, as his hands rested on her shoulders and he looked her anxiously up and down. "Please don't look so worried—I'm quite all right."

"It's more than you deserve," declared Willoughby, but his eyes were moist with thankfulness, and belied the brusqueness of his tone. "Who's this young man?"

"Phillip Garve—he's the Palestine correspondent of the *Morning Call*. Mr. Garve—my father."

Willoughby gave Garve a searching look from under spectacularly red eyebrows, and held out his hand.

"I wish we'd met in pleasanter circumstances, Mr. Garve. Anyway, let's get home and discuss the matter in comfort. I'm sure you can't have had breakfast yet."

Garve bowed his thanks. He had read a good deal of Willoughby's stuff and admired his prose style. "It will be a pleasure," he said. He turned to Willoughby's companion with an inquiring glance at Esther.

"Of course," she said sweetly, "I forgot you two haven't met. Mr. Antony Hayson—Mr. Philip Garve of the London *Morning Call*."

3. Garve Tells of a Discovery

The big car made short work of the return journey round the outside of the wall. Garve occupied the front seat next to Jackson, the secretary-escort, who was driving, while at the back Hayson and Willoughby sat one on each side of Esther, and ministered to her wants.

By moving his position slightly, Garve was able to pass the time profitably by studying Hayson's features in the driving-mirror. The man was undeniably handsome, as Esther had said. His face was strong and regular, with clear-cut lines, his skin tanned a deep walnut, as though he had been excavating for months in tropical sunshine, his hair black and curly. His eyes were very dark, and gave to his face an expression of unusual serenity.

As a possible rival—and though Garve could have kicked himself for being so susceptible to Esther's charms, that was how he already regarded this fellow—Hayson was undoubtedly formidable. His attractions had the advantage of being spectacular. When he smiled he displayed a set of strong white teeth which any film star might have envied, and he had the poise and quiet self-assurance of a man who has been soundly educated among the right people. That faintly discernible Oxford accent, Garve told himself jealously, would have provided all the introduction necessary in any social circle throughout the far-flung Empire.

He noticed, with a quick spasm of irritation, the proprietorial air which Hayson had adopted towards Esther. His arm lay along the back of the seat behind her, not close enough or obtrusively enough to be familiar, but near enough to seem protective.

Even allowing for Esther's impulsive nature, thought Garve, the man must be a quick worker to have achieved so much in a single day without giving offence.

In a few minutes the car drew up outside the Willoughby establishment. It was a compact house of some eight or ten rooms only, solidly built of Jerusalem stone, and overlooking the Damascus Gate. A large open balcony and a flat roof provided a view to the east stretching away to the top of Mount Scopus and the Mount of Olives. Below, at the bottom of a rough garden of olives and cactus and prickly pear, stretched the road that Esther had travelled alone earlier that day.

Willoughby continued to cast occasional anxious glances at his daughter while breakfast was being prepared, but the cut on her head seemed to be giving her no trouble, and her spirits were rapidly rising again. Garve noticed with some interest that two Arab servants were employed—young men whom Esther addressed as Abdul and Feisul. Apparently she had decided to dispense with a maid on this trip. The Arabs looked harmless enough, and no doubt Jackson had his eye on them, but, all the same, Garve made a mental note to advise Esther to lock her bedroom door at night.

Willoughby proved an admirable host, even at breakfast. His alert mind roved from one topic of conversation to another, and his humorous blue eyes beamed from under his rugged red brows at each of the party in turn. He was a man, Garve surmised, of sixty or thereabouts, but he presented a singularly active appearance, and would, in fact, have been something of an athlete still but for the war wound which had slightly shortened his right leg.

When there was a gap in the talk, Hayson filled it with just the right mixture of deference and independence. He seemed always to say exactly the right thing. Garve, still aching abominably, found such self-possession increasingly annoying, and took refuge in a most unsociable moroseness.

After breakfast they all adjourned to the balcony, where they found comfortable chairs in the shade of a welcome canopy.

"Now," said Willoughby, when they were settled, "perhaps I can have a full account of this morning's episode?"

"I'd better do the talking," said Esther. "It was entirely my fault. I was horribly obstinate—wasn't I, Mr. Garve?"

Garve grinned. "You make it very awkward for me. Chivalry forbids me to agree with you——"

"To a journalist," said Esther reprovingly, "truth should always come before chivalry." She proceeded to describe the circumstances of their adventure, while the gravity of Willoughby's expression deepened and his eyebrows gave an occasional angry twitch.

"Well, young woman," he said severely, when the recital was over, "you've had a fortunate escape. Far more fortunate than you deserve."

"You certainly succeeded in giving us all a frightful shock," said Hayson, quite as though he were one of the family. "I think we're all very indebted to Mr. Garve for sticking to you so closely."

"Up to the point when the bomb exploded," said Garve, with a smile, "it was a pleasure."

"I suppose you didn't catch a glimpse of your assailant?" asked Hayson. "I mean, if you could describe him . . ."

"He was the other side of the wall," Garve pointed out, a little coldly.

"Of course. These fellows so rarely come out into the open. I'm sure you did all you could."

Garve squirmed, and was about to make an angry reply, when Willoughby diplomatically intervened.

"At least, Mr. Garve, I'm glad to know that you weren't a willing partner with my daughter in this escapade. Between ourselves, you know, I'm not surprised she got her own way. She rules me completely, though it's a dreadful confession to make." He glanced fondly at his daughter, and Esther pretended to sigh.

"Please, I didn't mean to be wicked," she murmured, and everybody laughed.

Willoughby turned to Garve again. "Strangely enough," he said, with a twinkle in his eyes, "several people have spoken to me about you already. I gathered the impression that you knew more about Palestine than anyone in Jerusalem, that you had an astonishing capacity for extracting confidences from policemen, and that nearly all the big shots in the city were regular readers of the *Morning Call*, if only to keep *au fait* with what was happening over here."

Garve laughed. "I should like to think that I had such an important public," he said. "By the way, Mr. Willoughby, what brings you to Palestine at such a time as this? It isn't exactly a restful spot."

Willoughby agreed. "I felt I wanted stimulating," he said. "I don't know about you, but I find I can always write in a more lively vein when there's something exciting happening around me. That was one reason, anyway. A more important one, perhaps, was that I felt a sudden urge to revisit the scenes of my comparative youth. I served with Allenby, you know, and Jerusalem impressed me very deeply. It's a stirring city, even when it's peaceful. The problems of the country fascinate me, and, if I may say so, I welcome this opportunity of hearing about the situation from an acknowledged expert."

"Look here," said Hayson genially to Garve, rising from his chair, "I'm sure you and Willoughby would like to be left in peace for a little while. I can see the conversation is going to be political, and politics bore me to death. If Miss Willoughby would care to pop over to my place for an hour or so, she could help me unpack those bits of Roman pavement that I dug up at Pompeii. Or are you too tired?" he asked solicitously, turning his warm gaze on Esther.

"I'd like to come," she replied with enthusiasm. "I've a slight headache, but thinking about it won't make it any better."

"Right you are," said Willoughby. "But for heaven's sake don't go roaming again." As they left he called after them: "You can take Jackson with you if you like," and solemnly winked at Garve, who sat in silence till the sound of her gay laughter had faded.

"Fine young fellow, Hayson," said Willoughby when they had gone. Garve, who was himself barely thirty, felt like a grandfather. "Amazingly brilliant, too. Took a double first at Oxford, I understand, before he discovered his passion for archaeology. He's done some good work at Luxor, and I think at Memphis. Immense application—speaks Arabic like a native. He's got a nice little house behind ours—you can just see the end of his garden from here. I was rather afraid my daughter might be a bit lonely in Jerusalem, but Hayson, like a good fellow, has promised to show her round—so far as safety permits, of course."

Garve's spirits sank lower and lower as he listened to this eulogy. The recollection of chestnut hair in the sunrise and tears of penitence under the Wailing Wall, had made him feel almost maudlin. Perhaps, he told himself, he ought to blame the shock of the explosion for his weakness. After all, she was only a flighty young miss, hardly different from thousands he had met and forgotten. Hardly different! What blasphemy! With a stern effort of will he pulled himself together in time to realize that Willoughby was asking him a question.

He frowned and thoughtfully pressed tobacco into his pipe. "You want to know what I think of the chances of real trouble? Well, to be honest, I think they're considerable. A lot of people in Jerusalem don't agree with me, of course, but perhaps I have exceptional opportunities to get behind the scenes. Last week, for instance, I took a trip into Transjordan. My paper hadn't sent me any specific instructions, and I was rather at a loose end. One gets tired of reporting a succession of murders, however eminent the people who are killed. Finally, I decided to cross over and try and get an interview with the Sheikh Ali Kemal. Have you heard of him, by the way?"

"His name's familiar," said Willoughby, all attention, "but I can't quite place him."

"Well, he's been in the news several times. He's one of Transjordan's stormy petrels, and has already been in jail once or twice for anti-British activities. There have been rumours that he was trying to raise a revolt against the Emir, who, of course, has been a friend of Britain. Altogether, he seemed an eminently suitable man to interview."

"Surely he would be deterred by the fact that the Emir can always rely on our support," broke in Willoughby. "The revolt wouldn't last a week."

"That was my view at first, but there were one or two things that worried me. First of all, the position in Palestine. Whatever views one holds about the British policy of building a Jewish National Home, there's no doubt that the Arabs here will never accept it. They're solid as a rock against a continuance of Jewish immigration. If Transjordan revolted, Palestine would rise too. The second thing that troubled me was the difficulty of knowing what was happening. Our troops are always on the watch for a sudden outbreak, but it's virtually impossible for them to know beforehand when or where the Arabs are going to strike. As you are aware, Palestine is honeycombed with secret terrorist societies. Hitherto, they've always struck independently, without any proper plan. An assassination here, a train wreck there, an aqueduct blown up somewhere else—unco-ordinated acts of violence that had no lasting effect. Recently there have been signs of a change. The terrorist acts have continued, but far more rarely. In my opinion the only reason they haven't stopped altogether is simply because whoever is behind them didn't want us to suspect a change of policy. I haven't a lot of evidence so far, but in my view the Arabs have at last found a leader with the authority to organize them. I believe there's a big conspiracy on foot, and for the first time in Arab history a brain behind it which makes it dangerous."

"And you suspect Ali Kemal?"

Garve hesitated. "I don't know. Until I saw him I thought he might be the man. He's undoubtedly a natural leader—he has fine physique and presence, he knows what he wants, and his personality is striking. His own Bedouins obey him as naturally as they eat. But he's vain and a little boastful. A good leader doesn't boast to journalists until he's established himself."

"I always thought that an Oriental who didn't boast was a rarity. He said too much, did he?"

"He said enough to justify my suspicions that an outbreak was being planned. He took some drawing out, mind you, and it was a long time before I discovered his weakness. I drank his coffee and we fenced amiably for some time. I tried to make him talk about the Emir, but he wouldn't. He made no secret of his anti-British feeling, of course, but he didn't say anything that the police could have arrested him for if they'd heard it. As I rose to go, however, I told him there were rumours that he was plotting against the Emir, and warned him, in quite a friendly way, that Britain wouldn't stand for it and would smash him if he tried it. Somehow that got his goat—his vanity was greater than his caution, and he lost his temper. The things he said about Britain then would have blistered a greener landscape. He virtually threw down the gauntlet to me, as the only available representative of the country he hated. He just loathes us, and would do anything to drive us into the sea."

Willoughby nodded. "I don't doubt that—but the wish is one thing, fulfilment is another."

"True, but another factor enters in here. So far, the Arabs have never been in a position to challenge our supremacy, because they've never been adequately armed. To-day they're getting arms, and in large quantities. They've got dumps that we know nothing of—I'm sure of it. In the old pre-war days, arming a subject nation was no light undertaking. To-day, with the whole world an armed camp and factories in every country turning out munitions at a rate never before known in times of peace, arms are as easy to buy as oranges in Jaffa. Of course, they have to be smuggled in, but Transjordan was made for smugglers. I don't doubt the convoys take a slightly different route on each occasion and only move at night. These Arabs know the mountains, and we don't—we can spot them by day with aeroplanes but at night we're powerless."

"H'm!" Willoughby looked a shade sceptical. "Of course, you're almost certainly right that arms *are* trickling in to some extent—and you know far more about it than I do—but I should have thought the menace wasn't as serious as you suggest. Have you any direct evidence—any first-hand knowledge?"

"Unfortunately for my peace of mind, I have," said Garve. "I'll tell you a story that hasn't appeared yet in the *Morning Call*. Two days after I got back from seeing Kemal, I was told that a *cache* of weapons was to be made that night in a cave near Bethany. I don't mind telling you it cost my paper a small fortune to get that information, and the Arab who gave it to me risked his life. He told me where to watch. I didn't trust him an inch, but the chance was too good to miss. You know how the mountains spread southwards from the Jericho road and how little we know of them. I went to Bethany just after dusk in Arab dress. That was easy. In the dark I made my way to a point which overlooked the little gully along which my informant had said the consignment would come. Very carefully I chose a place of concealment well away from the spot he had recommended. As it happened, my precautions were unnecessary. Just before midnight, in the pitch dark, I heard the sound of hooves on the hard dry ground. Presently a string of mules passed by me—almost under my nose. Each had a heavy pack and each was led. There were ten of them altogether. I waited, perhaps for an hour, and the mules came back. Their packs had gone and the Arabs were riding them. I followed my talkative friend's directions, and in a deep cleft where the mountain had split I found the weapons!"

"Rifles?" asked Willoughby.

"Machine-guns! Brand new and of a modern type."

Willoughby was duly impressed. "That certainly alters the outlook. It would only need a small army, adequately supplied with machine-guns, to hold these mountains almost indefinitely."

"Exactly. You're beginning now to see the extent of the danger. Personally, I should sum up the position something like this. I know the Arabs have arms, but I don't know where. I know they are making plans, but I don't know what. I know they have leaders, but I don't know who. And I don't know when the explosion is coming."

Willoughby grinned. "Apart from that, I suppose, you're well informed!"

"Just so!" Garve puffed vigorously at his pipe. "As I see it, there's only one course of action which is going to save the situation. Somehow we've got to strike at the centre of the plot. We've got to discover the mind behind it. If Ali Kemal is this man, we've got to prove it to our satisfaction, and then put him somewhere where he'll do no harm."

"It sounds like a big proposition. By the way, did you describe that interesting interview in the columns of the *Morning Call?*"

"I haven't done, so far," said Garve. "I'd like to—it was an expensive trip, and after all I've got to show something for the enormous sums the *Morning Call* is spending, whether it knows it or not, in establishing contacts. Still, this seemed to be a case where I ought to hold back. If Ali Kemal is our man, as seems likely, we should only put him on his guard by drawing attention to him."

"I think you're right. What about the machine-gun find——"He broke off as a light footstep sounded in the house, but it was only Esther and Hayson returning.

"Who's talking about machine-guns?" asked Esther gaily. She was flushed and obviously in high spirits.

Willoughby placed a comfortable chair for her, and Hayson drew one up beside her.

"Garve here has been doing a little sleuthing," said Willoughby "He's been watching the Arabs gun-running."

"Really?" said Hayson, handing round cigarettes. "By Jove! that must have been exciting. May we know more?"

"I'm afraid," said Garve, "that the question of publication is *sub judice*. In the meantime, I know you folks won't talk about it." He glanced pointedly at Esther, who pouted.

"Anyone would think I babbled like a brook," she said. "I think it's a shame to whet our appetites and deprive us of the meal." She walked across to Garve, gave him a smile which would have melted the heart of a sphinx, and said in a wheedling tone, "Please, Mr. Garve, may I come with you on your next Nocturnal Adventure?"

"Not if it's looking for gun-runners," interposed Willoughby. "If you land yourself in any more tight places, young woman, I shall have you handcuffed to Jackson." A mischievous light stole into his eyes. "I dare say, though," he added, "if you ask Garve nicely, he will take you down to the Dead Sea for a moonlight bathe."

"Will you?" asked Esther eagerly.

"With pleasure," said Garve. "I'll be a bit stiff for swimming for the next day or two, but the water is said to be excellent for muscular complaints." He rapidly consulted his diary. "Full moon on Friday. Is it a date?"

"Lovely!" exclaimed Esther. "Come to dinner at 7.30, will you? We shall have plenty of time to drive down afterwards."

"I shall live for Friday," sighed Garve, with mock gallantry. His thoughts were already racing wildly ahead when the deep, rich voice of Hayson scattered them.

"The road to the Dead Sea is very dark, winding, and dangerous," he observed. "I hope you're familiar with it."

"Bogey, bogey," said Esther, and laughed in his handsome face. His white teeth showed in a smile that was almost a caress, but as Garve caught his eye the smile faded and was replaced by a glance of cold displeasure.

"Jealous, that's what he is," Garve told himself gleefully. "Horribly, horribly jealous! And if he's jealous he can't feel so certain about Esther as his possessive and confident air suggests."

The conversation took a less personal turn, and shortly afterwards Willoughby found an opportunity to take Garve aside again. "Sorry I was heard talking of machine-guns," he said, "but Esther is the soul of discretion, and I know she won't breathe a word. By the way, have you told the police of your find?"

Garve studied Willoughby's calm, rather rugged features. "Not yet," he said. "Why do you ask?"

"Only that I found your story somewhat unsettling. It's not really my business, but I thought maybe the police should know. If they set a watch each night over the *cache*, they might get a line on the gun-runners."

Garve nodded. "Maybe I've been too secretive. It's true I can't watch everything. The first opportunity I get I'll tell Baird at police headquarters."

"And just one other thing," said Willoughby. "If you want any unofficial help at any time, count me in. I'm not so active as I was, I'm afraid, but I still get about, and it won't do me any good to be writing all day and all night."

"I'll remember your offer," said Garve gratefully. "All the same,

England wouldn't thank me if I ran you into unnecessary danger. She's looking to you for at least six more masterpieces."

Willoughby laughed without conceit, and they joined Esther and Hayson again.

4. Hayson Proffers Advice

Immediately after lunch, Willoughby excused himself and went off with the faithful Jackson to keep an appointment. Garve hoped that Hayson would be impelled to return to his excavating, but the call of archeology was apparently no more insistent than the call of journalism when a charming girl needed company.

Garve, reclining in a deck chair and puffing contentedly at his old briar, rested with an easy conscience. He had been blown-up that day in the service of his paper, and the most unreasonable editor could hardly ask for more. If a train were wrecked or a bridge dynamited he knew that he had good friends at police headquarters who would seek him out and let him know at once. In any case, he could no longer work up any enthusiasm over minor outbreaks of violence. They meant nothing to London. They were hardly news any longer. Much better, he thought, to concentrate on digging out the really big story that he felt was on the point of breaking. If he could only get an "exclusive" on a major revolt, his second visit to Palestine would have proved worth while. And the more he thought of Ali Kemal, the more certain he became that he had hit upon the focal point of the plot. It might break, of course, at any moment, before he could get to the bottom of it, but his contacts were good, and, in the meantime, there was nothing he could do—he glanced at Esther—well, nothing to-day, anyway.

Rest and peace seemed to be having the same attraction for Hayson. With a deliberation which suggested that he was taking up his position for the remainder of the day, he placed a chair near Esther in that possessive manner which angered Garve so much, and proceeded to make himself thoroughly comfortable. To Garve he was gravely courteous, but when he spoke to Esther he always switched on a brilliant smile, which he clearly realized was fascinating. Garve himself was fascinated by it. To Esther, in romantic circumstances, he feared it might prove irresistible.

However, since the afternoon was apparently to be spent *à trois*, Garve resigned himself to the necessity of being friendly, and, with the true instinct of the newspaper man, set to work to make Hayson talk about himself. He had already scented a possible story. Archaeological discoveries often made first-class copy, and a man of Hayson's ability would hardly be "digging" in Jerusalem without good reason. Garve openly and smilingly confessed his curiosity with a disarming apology for not minding his own business.

"Oh, that's all right," said Hayson, with the tolerant air of a man who knows he is worth interviewing. "As a matter of fact, I'm used to pressmen. I even edited a rag myself at Oxford."

Garve badly wanted to laugh, but hastily coughed instead. Even Esther did not seem very impressed.

"At Luxor," said Hayson, "we were inundated with newspaper people. I was deputed to act as a kind of public relations officer, and I found them a very decent crowd of fellows. But they didn't know much about archaeology."

"I bet they didn't," said Garve with a grin.

"Tutankhamen would have turned in his sarcophagus," said Hayson gravely, "if he had known how they were messing up his dynasty. They got the dates wrong, and the names wrong, and even the history wrong."

"I don't believe Mr. Hayson is as fond of newspaper men as he pretends," declared Esther. She looked cool and comfortable, and was toying with one of Hayson's Turkish cigarettes, which she liked.

"I assure you I'm quite sincere," said Hayson. "I know that scientists don't usually favour the popular press, but the garbled kind of pseudo-scientific article which appears in papers like—like——"

"Like the *Morning Call*," prompted Garve, chuckling.

"Well, like the *Morning Call*," said Hayson solemnly— "that kind of article is often as much the fault of the scientist as of the journalist. Now, when I talk about my work, I try to make it intelligible. I avoid technical terms as much as possible, and I don't try to parade a lot of abstruse knowledge."

"I wish there were more like you," observed Garve. "Anyway, to avoid any possible misrepresentation, I promise you that if what you are working at here makes a story, I'll submit my 'copy' to you for technical correction before I release it."

Hayson gave a little gesture of self-depreciation. "There's not really much to tell yet, and you mustn't exaggerate the importance of it. I'm searching for the Ark of the Covenant."

Garve whistled softly. "It sounds like a headline to me."

"I thought it was stranded on Mount Ararat," said Esther.

"You're thinking of Noah's Ark," said Hayson, and as he turned to Garve he was just too late to intercept a wink. "The Ark of the Covenant was built by Moses—you'll find all about it in the Book of Exodus. It was made of shittim wood, overlaid with pure gold, and was carried on gold staves. It was to contain, if you remember, two tablets of stone 'written with the finger of God.' Moses broke the first two, but according to Exodus they were renewed. And when we find the ark—if we ever do—we may find the tablets too."

"They'd make a good picture," said Garve irreverently. "I remember now—the Ark was supposed to have been hidden in Jerusalem, wasn't it. Under the city. And that's why you're working in Solomon's Quarries?"

"Exactly. Have you ever been inside them?"

"Oh yes—a little way—but only as a tourist, I'm afraid."

"Please, please," Esther interrupted. "You're going much too fast for me. "I haven't been inside Solomon's Quarries. Do tell me more about them."

"Solomon's Quarries," said Hayson, beaming on Esther as on an ignorant child, "are a great chain of underground caverns which run beneath the old city. Nine hundred years before Christ the stone for Solomon's Temple was hewn out of them. For two hundred years their existence was lost sight of. Then, in the middle of the last century, a man was walking past the Damascus Gate when he suddenly missed his dog. He turned on his tracks and discovered the animal crawling out of a hole under the wall, which was all overgrown with vegetation. He shifted a lot of debris, and discovered that the hole was really the choked-up entrance to a vast cave. Nowadays the upper workings of the quarries are one of the sights that visitors always want to see."

"I should think so," said Esther. "It sounds most interesting. Please go on."

"Well, all sorts of wild rumours began to circulate—it was sufficiently dark and dangerous inside for anything to be possible. One of the suggestions was that in addition to the gold and silver vessels and the jewels of Solomon, the Ark of the Covenant itself was somewhere cunningly concealed beneath the site of the temple. The quarries became the mecca of treasure hunters, and a stimulating problem for serious investigators. They were all unsuccessful. Several people broke their necks by falling over frightful precipices, and one man was discovered accidentally in the last stages of starvation after being lost for over a fortnight. In the end the search was given up."

"H'm." Garve seemed disappointed. "It doesn't sound so hopeful, does it?" He looked curiously at Hayson. "What makes you think you may be more successful?"

"I hate to be beaten," said Hayson slowly, his eyes on Esther. "Indeed, I'm rarely beaten. The Ark of the Covenant has never been found. If it had been destroyed some record of its destruction would surely have survived. If it still exists, it *must* be in the quarries. In any case, I intend to explore the caverns so thoroughly that I shall be able to say definitely, one way or the other, whether it is there or not."

"Surely you'll need some help?"

"Later on, yes. At the moment I'm fully occupied with a discovery I've already made. Deep down in the lower workings I've found some remarkable signs carved on one of the walls. I have a feeling that they may have something to do with the ark. In any case, they have a real antiquarian interest, and I'm going to get them deciphered."

Hayson's dark face was flushed with enthusiasm, and Garve caught the infection. "I'd like to go down with you one day," he said. "Maybe I could get a flashlight of the carvings?"

"You might," said Hayson dubiously. "I don't know how well they'd come out. But I'll be glad to show you round if you've a good head for heights."

"For yawning chasms, you mean," said Esther. "Do remember you're talking to a newspaper man. I hope you'll include me in your subterranean expedition?"

Hayson leaned slightly towards her, and gave her a glance so bold and full of meaning that Garve shuddered at his audacity.

"I'll take you by yourself, Miss Willoughby. I really couldn't be responsible for two people at once."

"Have you been working in the quarries very long?" asked Garve.

"Nearly three months now. I'm afraid none of the big men—the really big men—take the enterprise very seriously. The scientific papers humour me because of Luxor, but they don't believe I'll succeed."

"Do you have any trouble with the Arabs?"

"Nothing to speak of. There's a man at the entrance who looks after tourists, and I sweeten him with a few piastres now and again. He's even helped to keep people away occasionally when I didn't want to be disturbed."

Garve nodded. "I only hope nothing happens to prevent the completion of your work."

Hayson looked interested. "Trouble with the Arabs, you mean? You don't really think there's any serious danger, do you?"

Garve shrugged his shoulders. "You've been in Jerusalem longer than I. Do you sense nothing in the air?"

Hayson smiled rather superciliously. "I'm afraid I only work on data," he said. "I'm not a politician—or a journalist. I try to take an intelligent interest when people start talking about 'The Situation,' but all these squabbles bore me."

"Do the train wrecks and the assassinations and the bombings bore you?" asked Garve with some heat.

"I'm shocked, of course," said Hayson calmly, "but I find it very difficult to believe that they mean serious trouble. These Arabs behave so childishly. Their secret societies are schoolboy stuff—with a trace of real horror, I admit, but infantile all the same. When I hear that a corpse has been found with a knife through it, and that a piece of paper has been attached to the handle with the word 'Revenge' inscribed on it in Arabic, and signed 'The Black Hand Gang,' or words to that effect, I refuse, as a scientist, to take the thing seriously. I'm sure that dangerous secret societies don't strike so melodramatically."

"And yet," observed Garve reflectively, "we know that they strike in a very deadly way. Dozens of Arabs, probably hundreds, have already paid with their lives for refusing to keep in step with the extremists. No one is safe, not even the leaders themselves. Death, as you know, is the immediate penalty for the slightest sign of weakness. Such intimidation may drive cautious men to rash deeds."

Hayson's face was clouded and his voice irritable. "I refuse to be troubled by their quarrels, anyway. My only concern is to be left in peace in the quarries. Very selfish, no doubt, but an important scientific discovery matters far more than a few lives."

"At least," said Garve unkindly, "you've a safe retreat down below if a revolt does break out suddenly. With a little food and plenty of patience you could live in the quarries for days. I suppose there's water?"

"Water? Yes, there's water!" His tone was so grim that Esther felt her spine creep. "I shouldn't like to be alone down there without a light. It's—well—eerie, to say the least of it." Garve had a sudden idea. "I suppose there's no possibility that the Arabs store their arms there?"

"I've never seen any traces, but it would be an incomparable hiding-place. The thought never occurred to me."

"We might keep our eyes skinned when we go down together," said Garve. "Tell me, isn't there supposed to be another entrance to the quarries somewhere?"

"I believe there is. I seem to have read somewhere that there's a way in from the temple area. Yes, of course—it was through that entrance that the Ark of the Covenant was supposed to have been carried. But I never heard of anyone who knew anything definite."

"Did you ever know anyone who'd been through Hezekiah's Tunnel?" asked Garve.

Hayson blew a smoke ring and watched it uncurl and vanish. "Hezekiah's Tunnel? No. I don't think I ever did. I'm a bit vague, but it isn't exactly a health resort, is it? I always understood it was an extremely messy and almost impassable underground water-course."

"That's right. Hezekiah cut it to provide the city with water when the Assyrians came down like a wolf on the fold. It's about the only place in Jerusalem I haven't scrutinized, and I'd like to see it."

"Aren't you carrying your passion for knowledge rather far?" asked Hayson. "Personally, I wouldn't go near the place. Why, you'll be wanting to take a dip in the brook Kedron next."

Garve grimaced horribly, for the stench of the brook was still in his nostrils. "Thanks, I draw the line there. Seriously, though, I can't see that exploring the tunnel is any more dangerous than prowling about in the quarries."

"Mr. Hayson," Esther reminded him, "is serving the interest of science. You are merely proposing to satisfy your vulgar curiosity."

"On the contrary, I spend all my time trying to satisfy the vulgar curiosity of the great British public, which adores anything subterranean. Seriously, do you think I could get a guide?"

"Surely," said Esther, still teasing, "a newspaper man doesn't have to have a personally conducted tour?"

"Sensible people don't take unnecessary risks," Garve reminded her, with an unsuccessful attempt at severity.

Esther made a wry face. "I should have those words set to music, Mr. Garve. They occur in your conversation like a refrain."

Garve refused to be put off. "There *must* be someone in Jerusalem who's been through the tunnel. Look here, Hayson, you've been in the city a good while. Have you really never heard anyone speak of it?"

"I tell you, Garve, it's a foolish project," said Hayson with more heat than the occasion seemed to warrant. "I wouldn't send my worst enemy through it."

His brooding eyes met Garve's, and each knew what the other was thinking. Garve flushed a little. "I wouldn't let that worry you," he said earnestly. "I should regard myself as under a real obligation to you if you could give me any assistance."

Hayson hesitated and pondered. "Well—Hezekiah's Tunnel? Yes, there *was* a man—but it's absurd, Garve—the place is little better than a sewer."

"Please," said Garve stubbornly.

"Well, don't say I haven't warned you. Esther will be my witness." ("Esther!" thought Garve. "Damn the fellow's nerve!") "I remember now—I did once run across an Arab who had been through the tunnel—or said he had. It was soon after I first came here, and I wanted a guide to show me round the Holy Sepulchre. I picked a man up at a little Arab café just inside the Jaffa Gate on the left as you enter the city. A villainous looking fellow he was, with only one eye and a face pitted by some horrible disease."

"He probably caught it going through the tunnel," said Esther cheerfully.

Hayson ignored the flippant interruption. "He told me if I ever wanted to go anywhere else he could always be found at the café in the early morning. He was a good guide, but his face frightened me, and I always avoided him afterwards."

"I believe I've seen him," said Garve, "though one cut-throat is very like another."

"He'll probably try to knife you in the tunnel," said Hayson gloomily. "Take my advice and keep away."

5. Enter Jameel

Before he returned to his hotel, Garve called at police headquarters to report his discovery of the arms dump. Baird, the young and able officer with whom Garve had already had many dealings, took full particulars and instructed two reliable men to go down to Bethany at dusk and keep watch all night.

Garve stayed for a brief chat, sent off a wire to London, together with a request for more money and a hint of good stories to come, and went home to nurse his bruises and recoup his vigour with a good night's sleep. He preferred living in an hotel, if only because there was always a commissionaire on duty to keep an eye open for possible intruders. Garve, who could no longer walk by daylight in the streets with any certainty of safety, was in no mind to come home late at night to a dark and lonely apartment, with an Arab possibly lying in wait behind a curtain to stab him in the back. His hotel was solid and European, and catered primarily for tourists.

A hot bath greatly relieved his aching limbs, and half a tumbler of whisky made a good night's rest a certainty. As soon as his head touched the pillow he sank dreamlessly to sleep, and knew nothing more until the chambermaid woke him at nine next morning with hot water and orange juice.

The sun was shining brilliantly and he whistled a cheerful tune as he dressed. He was just going down to breakfast when the telephone rang by his bedside.

"Hallo, hallo," said a voice impatiently as he lifted the receiver. "Is that Garve? This is Baird."

"Morning," said Garve. "Anything wrong?"

"I don't know. You weren't drunk the night before last, were you?"

"The night before last—let me see, that was when I found the machine-guns, wasn't it? No, not incapably. Has somebody said I was?"

"One of the men I sent down to Bethany last night has just been on the phone. He says they found your *cache*, but there aren't any arms there of any sort—plenty of hoof marks and that's all. Are you sure you didn't dream it?"

"I was wide awake and quite sober," said Garve. "What time did your men get there?"

"After midnight. They ran into an Arab fight three miles outside the city and had to bring two men back, one of them dead. When eventually they got to Bethany it was quite dark and they had some difficulty in following your directions. What do you make of it?"

Garve pondered. "Well, it seems incredible, but the Arabs must have moved the stuff. I suppose they discovered that we knew, though I can't imagine how. Do you think when they saw your men they put two and two together and gave the alarm?"

"It's possible, but unlikely. I suppose no-one saw you when you were prowling round the night they dumped the stuff?"

"I don't think so—I should never have got away alive. Damned funny altogether. I'll have a talk with you about it later ... I'm going to be fully occupied this morning."

"More sleuthing?"

"Something of the sort. By the way, is there any news of Ali Kemal?"

"Nothing to his discredit. He's sitting pretty in the desert and pretending to be a good boy—in the daytime. It's impossible to keep track of him at night. I wish we'd got him under lock and key."

"So do I. Never mind, perhaps he'll forget to pay his income-tax! So long."

Garve hung up and stood for a moment, puzzling over the new development. This wasn't the first leakage there'd been in recent months. Perhaps some of the police themselves weren't incorruptible. They were a mixed lot, some of them Arabs who no doubt had nationalist sympathies. Besides, the secret societies had lots of money, and they would pay highly for information. And money was more than usually persuasive in Palestine.

After breakfast, Garve walked quickly down to the Jaffa Gate. As always, the immediate neighbourhood of the gate was thronged with people, most of them selling things. Several guides nodded to him, but they had given up offering their services long ago. He stopped to have a brief talk with one of the policemen on duty, and then slipped into the little café on his left, which Hayson had mentioned the day before. A swarthy Arab was smoking a hookah near the door, and took no notice at all of Garve's entry. A guide whom Garve knew was sipping coffee by himself in a corner, and the proprietor, a fat and rather elderly Arab with gold earrings and jewelled fingers, sat half asleep against a small counter. The café was dark after the glaring sun, and pleasantly cool. Garve took a chair with his back to the wall and facing the door. He called for coffee, lighted his pipe, and prepared for a long wait.

The time passed pleasantly enough, for Jaffa Gate was always thronged with picturesque people. Garve amused himself trying to pick up little snatches of Arab conversation, but men talked in whispers in Jerusalem now, unless they were bargaining or squabbling, and he learned nothing but the price of oranges and lace. A whole hour passed. Customers came and went, but no-one appeared who remotely resembled the man whom Hayson had described. Garve began to feel that he was wasting a beautiful morning. He wondered if Hayson were in the quarries or making love to Esther in his bold fashion. Of course, the guide would not come—they never did when you needed them. Garve did not want to publish his interest in Hezekiah's Tunnel or he would have approached some of the other guides. He was just contemplating a stroll over to the Willoughbys' house to break the monotony of the morning when two more customers came in. They were both Arabs, and the one nearest to Garve was young and keen-eyed and was wearing European clothes. The other wore the long gown and white head-cloth of a countryman, and as soon as Garve saw his features his spirits rose.

The man was hideously disfigured, sightless in one eye, and heavily pockmarked down the whole of one side of his face. At once Garve became a different being. He had been a little bored, a little lackadaisical—now he was keyed-up and wary. He waited until the guide turned full face and quietly beckoned him over. The man came, salaamed, and waited.

"Sit down," said Garve quietly. "Tell me, what's your name?"

"Jameel," said the guide. He was short and powerful, with forearm muscles which swelled and rippled under the light brown skin. His face, till disease attacked it, might well have been handsome. His single eye gazed stolidly now, waiting.

"Jameel," said Garve, "have you ever been through Hezekiah's Tunnel?"

The eye glanced fearfully to left and right, as though anxious to see that no Arab was within earshot.

"Hezekiah's Tunnel, excellency? Yes, once I went through it."

"Would you like to do it again?"

"No, excellency. It is not a pleasant place. But if you would like to see the Holy Sepulchre, the Wailing Wall, the Dome of the Rock, the Via Dolorosa—I can show you all these. For thirty piastres—the whole day. I am the best guide in Jerusalem. I know all the history. I will show you where Jesus Christ placed His hand. I will show you His footprints. . . ."

Garve shook his head. "I've seen them all. I want one thing and one thing only. I will give you a hundred piastres to take me through the tunnel."

"It is just a wet hole in the ground," said Jameel. "It is easy to fall and get hurt. It is narrow and dangerous. I am the only guide in Jerusalem who has been through it." He spat in disgust. "And you offer me a hundred piastres."

"It will take you a long while to earn a hundred piastres showing tourists the Wailing Wall," said Garve. "How many clients have you had this week?"

"There are no tourists," said Jameel sulkily. "But the tunnel—no.

45

I would sooner starve in comfort. It is an evil place. And it would be necessary to pass through it at night."

"At night!" exclaimed Garve. "Why?"

"In the daytime, excellency, the women of Siloam wash their clothes in the Virgin's Fountain where the tunnel starts. If you stirred up the water then, there would be very serious trouble."

"Did *you* go through at night?"

"Yes—alone."

"How long does the journey take?"

"An hour, if all goes well. But it is a journey which might have no ending, as I have told you. The pools in the tunnel are deep."

Garve sat back and regarded the stolid staring eye. The more he saw of it, the less he liked it, and the less he liked the idea of the trip.

"I've never known a guide so indifferent about earning a hundred piastres," he said irritably.

"We should need special boots and lanterns," said Jameel. "And they would have to be carried to the tunnel and carried back."

"Lazy devil," thought Garve. Aloud he said, "Say a hundred and fifty piastres altogether, including thigh boots for the night and lanterns."

"I have a wife and eight children, excellency. If harm befalls me a hundred and fifty piastres will not keep them in food for long." The eye stared greedily.

"How much do you want?" demanded Garve.

Jameel did not waver. "A thousand piastres."

Garve smiled. He knew now that it was simply a question of time, and for the next half-hour he proceeded to play the game of haggling, which is governed by the same rules from Suez to Shanghai. Twice he rose as though to leave the shop; twice the Arab gathered his draperies around him as though about to make a dignified departure. But neither of them went.

It was nearly midday before the price was fixed at five hundred piastres—about five pounds. Jameel promised to be at the Pool of Siloam, whence the tunnel began its tortuous journey, precisely at midnight, and to bring boots and lanterns with him. He undertook to tell no-one of Garve's intention, though the promise was clearly worth nothing unless it suited his own convenience.

Garve turned as he was about to leave the table. "One other thing, Jameel. No tricks!"

"Tricks, excellency!"

"If anyone's dead body comes floating into the Pool of Siloam to-morrow, it will be yours. Understand? I'm no tourist!"

"And I'm no terrorist," said Jameel with dignity. "I'm a guide."

Garve nodded and departed.

He lunched at the German café near the post office, and then walked down to the Willoughby home. To his disgust he drew a complete blank. Willoughby, said Abdul, had gone with Jackson to Tel Aviv for the day; Miss Willoughby had left with Mr. Hayson half an hour ago for the quarries.

"Hell," said Garve. He wandered off disconsolately. It was just his luck, he thought savagely. In ten years he had never met a woman who appealed to him with any urgency, and now that he had found one whom he could not forget, there was a brilliant and handsome rival, with a most impressive turn of speed. And in a quarry, of all places! Helping her down steps, lifting her over wet places, guiding her among precipices! What opportunities the fellow would have!

Eaten with jealousy, Garve made his way to police headquarters, where he found Baird just coming off duty. He suggested a drink, and they retired to yet another café. Baird was still worried about the arms dump, and kept on sinking into a moody silence, until Garve could hardly restrain his nervous irritation.

"Sorry," said Baird at last. "I'm rotten company to-day. I don't feel that we've got any grip on the situation, and—well, I don't like it. I wish something would happen quickly."

"When it does it will be too late to stop it," said Garve. "Have there been any developments to-day, since you rang me?"

"Only that we've completely lost sight of Ali Kemal. He moved off during the night and he's somewhere in the mountains over in Moab. We sent out two planes before lunch, but they haven't been able to trace him. It looks bad to me?"

Garve pondered. "There can't be a rising without a signal," he said. "We knew that all up and down the country the Arabs are armed; we know that the mountains are littered with dumps which we can't find, but the revolt, when it comes, will have to be concerted to be successful. It's no use Ali Kemal sweeping across the Jordan with a thousand horsemen. We should get the news before the Arabs did, and have troops at the key points before the revolt could start. Someone will have to give the word 'Go' in a way that the whole country will hear at once."

"They could fix a date," said Band, "the same as other conspirators have done."

"They daren't. Somebody would give it away. Secrets like that have to be kept in the minds of a few leaders. No, they'll have to arrange a signal which everyone will recognize—when it comes. Something which will make it easier for the outbreak to succeed. I'm only groping, Baird, but in the back of my mind there are little confused ideas which, I feel, ought to make a pattern. I've got a feeling that I know the key to the riddle. Sorry, it sounds silly, doesn't it? Listen, you *must* find Ali Kemal!"

Baird gloomily chewed his nails. "It's easy to say, Garve. You know what those mountains are like. They're simply riddled with caves. Kemal knows every contour, every track. His men scatter and collect again almost before we can get a 'plane off the ground. At dusk they're up by the Syrian frontier, and by morning they're camped outside Petra or lost in the endless desert. We can't arrest them, because they're doing nothing unlawful. They carry no arms except a rifle each, and as long as they keep the other side of the Jordan they're permitted to do that. If we took Kemal up on suspicion we should have a row on our hands right away. We've got to wait until Kemal makes a mistake."

"Well, it's your job, not mine," said Garve thankfully, though he felt nearly as uneasy as though it were his own. They chatted a little longer and then Garve left for his hotel.

He dined early, snatched a couple of hours' sleep, and shortly before eleven prepared for the night's adventure. An old but very thick tweed suit and a sweater gave him all the protection he would need against the keen night air. Into his left-hand jacket pocket he slipped an electric torch and a small flask of whisky. Into his right he dropped his revolver, having first inspected the mechanism to see that it was functioning properly. He felt strangely elated, as he had often felt before on setting out to cover an exciting story. At half-past eleven he stuck a cloth cap on his head, left his key with the night porter, and set out at a brisk pace for the tunnel.

6. The Fight in the Tunnel

His footsteps rang out cheerfully on the hard ground, and a brilliant moon drove his shadow before him as he walked. He remembered with a sharp thrill of pleasure that in forty-eight hours he would be swimming with Esther by its full light. The idea of a midnight dip was perhaps less attractive to-night with the temperature well below shivering point, but then Jerusalem was in the mountains, and its nights were rarely warm. In the deep cutting of the Jordan Valley the weather would be sub-tropical.

All his senses were keyed to concert pitch to-night, and his tough, healthy body tingled with excitement as he left the road and started to descend a rough and stony path. The great wall of the city rose on his left in white majesty, while in front of him the rocky wilderness of the Kedron Valley shimmered in a silvery pool of light. He could just make out the dark shadows of Siloam's tiny village on the hillside opposite, but nothing moved in it, and no lamp burned. There was something unearthly and awesome about the peacefulness of the night in this valley of tombs and memories. He remembered what Esther had said about not liking to walk through it at night. He could understand her feeling that way about it. The temptation to fling a quick glance over one's shoulder was almost overpowering. Stones rattled down the slope like following footsteps. A backward glance would be reassuring, but panic started that way. Garve took a firm grip of himself and plodded on. He was, he told himself, too imaginative for this sort of job.

He was wondering how unpunctual the Arab would be, and was schooling himself to wait patiently, but to his surprise Jameel was already standing by the Pool of Siloam as he breasted the last steep slope. The man's disfigurement showed with more sinister effect in the moonlight, and again Garve had doubts of his own wisdom. The Arab greeted him in a reassuring manner, however, and the two oil lanterns he had brought burned with a steady purposeful flame which was very comforting.

Jameel yawned. He was less obsequious out here on the hillside than he had been in the café.

"The boots were heavy," he grumbled. "Allah permit they are the right size."

Garve drew the thick rubber leggings to his thighs and found them satisfactory. "Fine," he said briefly, taking a lantern. "All right, Cyclops, let's get it over."

Jameel hesitated. Garve had no idea what was passing in his mind, but it was almost as though the Arab were waiting for him to go first. But that was ridiculous, of course. The man was scared, perhaps, and not unnaturally.

In silence they approached the mouth of the tunnel, gashed darkly in the moonlit slope of the hill. As they drew nearer, Garve's ear caught the splash of running water, and something else—a low moaning which chilled his flesh.

"Stop!" he cried. "Is there someone in there, Jameel? What tricks are you playing?"

"It is all right, excellency. That is the sound the tunnel always makes. Have you never listened to a sea-shell on the shore?"

Garve nodded, ashamed of his fear. Holding his lantern high in his left hand, he plunged after the guide into the stream of brown and slimy water which ran from the tunnel's mouth.

In a moment they were underground, with Jameel a yard or so ahead. The passage started as a deep and narrow rift in the rock, with the roof out of reach of the yellow lantern light, and the walls pressing in until Garve's wide shoulders could barely pass. The lower portion of the wall was moist and clammy to the touch, and pale green fungus covered it like an evil growth. Higher up, however, there were patches of dry rock, whose roughly hewn surface bore the marks of axes sturdily applied nearly three thousand years before.

"How far does the tunnel stretch?" Garve called out, and his question reverberated like the shout of an army.

Jameel turned, his eye unblinking, a ghastly figure in the unreal light. "For a quarter of a mile or more, excellency. The middle part is the worst." He stood still in the swirling water, staring, with the yellow lantern level with his head, until Garve said irritably, "All right, carry on."

The guide's stare unnerved him. He thought grimly how Esther would tease him if she ever got to know he had been scared like this. He determined that his foolish exploit should *not* come to grief, or, if it did, that she should never know.

The tunnel turned and twisted so rapidly that it was impossible, even when the light would have permitted it, to see for more than a yard or two ahead. The floor of the stream, which at first had been pebbly, began to feel less secure. The slime of ages had collected on the stones, and, once or twice, the foothold felt precarious. The roof was lower, too, so that Garve, who was taller than the Arab, was obliged to stoop as he walked. He was oppressed by the shrouding darkness, and fearful for the safety of his lantern as he slipped and stumbled. He felt that he would willingly have given five pounds for the sight of a clear star overhead, and wished heartily that he had taken Hayson's advice and kept away. This was no place for human beings. The water smelt musty, the air was stale and cold as a corpse.

Suddenly Jameel swore horribly as he slipped in the slime. His lantern flickered dangerously as he clutched at the wall to save himself from falling, and for a moment Garve thought it would go out. He watched, fascinated, while the drooping light revived, and breathed again. Although the torch nestling in his pocket would be quite adequate for emergencies, the lanterns gave a more widely diffused light, and the loss of one of them would be a serious inconvenience.

Slowly, laboriously, they struggled on, but Garve began too soon to congratulate himself on their progress. They had hardly covered another twenty yards before the Arab once more lost his balance and plunged to his waist in a deep pothole. He scrambled out in panic. His white gown, an awkward dress for exploring, was clinging uncomfortably round his thigh boots. Perspiration glistened above his eye.

"I had forgotten that hole, excellency. There is another farther up—a deeper one, which I remember. But the tunnel widens there, and with care we can walk round the edge."

"I hope you're right," said Garve. "You're certainly earning your five hundred piastres."

"I need it, excellency. I have many children to provide for, and times are hard, now that the tourists no longer come to Jerusalem. I am a good guide."

Garve grunted non-committally. "Well, let's get through. I'm sick of this damned tunnel."

The passage was levelling out and becoming wider. Instead of running in a deep narrow channel, the water now streamed along the whole floor of the tunnel, hardly covering their ankles. They were beginning to make good progress over the best stretch they had yet encountered when Jameel, to Garve's annoyance, came to a halt again.

"Just ahead of us is the deep pool which I spoke of ..." he began. Suddenly his voice trailed off and the gaze of his one horrified eye passed over Garve's shoulder and seemed glued to something in that part of the tunnel they had just traversed.

"Look, look, excellency—oh, Allah, help us!" he cried, and there was such terror in his tone that Garve, his imagination all too vivid, looked back in sudden fear, half expecting to find some subterranean monstrosity about to attack him.

It was an old trick. Even as Garve turned he knew his danger. There was nothing behind him but the blackness of the tunnel. He knew his life was in the balance, and for an instant of time, an agonized split second, he expected to feel the knife drive between his shoulder blades. At that moment no effort of his own could have saved him from the savage thrust already on its way, but as he gathered up his muscles to wheel round he slipped in the mud, his feet shot from under him as though they had been hit by an express train, and he crashed heavily into the stream with the Arab on top of him.

Jameel's lamp was still burning where he had dropped it, and its sickly light threw grotesque shadows on the walls as Garve, twisting, heaving, and turning, fought with all his speed and strength to prevent the Arab striking again. Once he gripped Jameel's wiry wrist, forcing the knife arm away from him till he felt his own muscles cracking. Then, with a quick feint, he slid out of the way and the Arab struck clumsily, grazing Garve's shoulder. Garve struggled to rise, but his feet could get no purchase in the mud. He kicked out wildly, and as he kicked the Arab struck again. The descending knife met Garve's ascending foot with terrific force and sank quivering into the heavy rubber heel of Garve's boot. The Arab gave a thick cry and let go.

Now they were fighting on level terms and it was anybody's victory. Garve was a little heavier, but the Arab was tough as a leather thong and difficult to hold. His long brown fingers clawed for purchase; he fought with his hands and teeth and head, his feet, his knees. There were no rules, and the prize was life for one of them. One moment they were locked together in the slime, half smothered in water, cutting and scratching themselves on sharp projections of rock, rolling from wall to wall. The next, they were aiming crouching unscientific blows at head and body. Time and again the Arab's slippery limbs tore and twisted from Garve's desperate grasp. His sodden clinging gown was a protection as well as an encumbrance. Once a sharp blow in the pit of the stomach from Jameel's boot almost put Garve out. He clung to consciousness through a mist of pain, aiming wild weak blows at the staring eye, hoping to keep the Arab off until the nausea and the agony passed. Jameel's face was streaming with blood where a kick from Garve's boot had driven the ornamented knife handle into his cheek. Garve braced himself to deliver a blow which would count, but as he jerked upright his head met the low roof with a jolt which seemed to fill the tunnel with a blinding light. If the Arab had had a weapon then the struggle would have been over, but Jameel's blows, too, were growing feebler as his strength failed.

The pace was too hot to last. Garve was nearly done, and Jameel's breath was coming in great sobbing gasps. There was no possible ground for truce—Garve knew that if he lost the fight the Arab would certainly murder him; the Arab knew that even if he escaped death he would spend the rest of his life in jail.

Garve gathered himself for a final effort. Crouching, he advanced upon the Arab, and a second before the man could attack again he lashed out in a mighty swing which carried all the power left in him. Luck, not judgment, was behind the blow. Before Jameel could dodge away, Garve's fist caught him flush above the left temple. With a groan the Arab staggered backwards, slipped, and fell with a great splash. Garve's knees sagged, the darkness seemed to close in upon him, the light of the one remaining lamp became a flickering black spot before his eyes, and he knew nothing more.

He returned slowly, unwillingly, to consciousness. He had almost lost the will to live. He was huddled in the brown stream, his head against the clammy wall. The taste of blood was in his mouth, and he could feel the warm trickle of it on his face. His knuckles were raw again, and every particle of his body seemed to have its own special ache. The only sound in the tunnel was the gentle splashing of the stream.

Garve could hardly believe he was alive. He glanced at the luminous dial of his watch. It was two o'clock. His limbs were numbed with cold. The second lamp had gone out, swamped by the Arab's fall, and the tunnel was darker than the blackest night.

He fumbled in his soaking jacket pocket for the torch he had brought, and as he touched the button a beam of light, not powerful, but adequate, cut through the darkness. He laughed a little hysterically. Thank God it still worked! If it had been broken he doubted whether he would ever have emerged from this abominable tunnel. He could not make out what had happened to the Arab. Presumably the man had made good his escape, but in that case Garve could not understand how it was that he himself was still alive. Painfully he struggled to his feet, and even as he did so he could not help thinking, with a perverse flicker of humour, what a facility he seemed to have for getting himself knocked about.

The Arab's knife, he noticed, was still embedded in the heel of his boot. He worked it gently backwards and forwards in the rubber, and finally forced it out. It was a poor weapon, deadly enough, but of cheap workmanship, and he tossed it to one side.

He flashed his torch around, still very dazed. There was nothing to be seen but the two lanterns, one of them broken to pieces. For a time he could not decide in which direction he had been going, till he remembered that he had been walking all the while against the current. Shivering with cold, soaked to the skin, and very bruised, he started once again to struggle through the water.

As the light of his torch gleamed on the surface of the sluggish stream he gave a cry and stooped down. Just ahead of him was the deep pool that Jameel had spoken of, and, protruding from its edge, in cold and clammy horror, was a dark thigh boot. With shaking hands, Garve caught hold of the boot and pressed it with his fingers. He knew then that he would never be troubled by Jameel again. That last blow on his temple must have knocked him clean out. He had fallen back into the pool and drowned where he lay, without a sound.

Garve was no sentimentalist, and he had seen men die for far less cause before. Yet, in that fearful passage, with the brown water swirling at his feet and the darkness pressing down on him, he felt awed and shocked at the suddenness with which death had repaid the Arab's treachery.

His one desire now was to get out of this interminable tunnel. Cautiously he crept round the edge of the pool, and as he flashed his torch on the water he saw Jameel's corpse, weighed down by its clothing, lying with its head three feet below the surface. Once he had negotiated the pool, his course became easier again, and he made rapid progress.

Presently he reached a point where the stream bore sharply upwards to the right, and the tunnel widened into a small cavern with a rocky ledge on his left. Following the direction of the stream with his eye, and momentarily switching off his light, he saw, not many yards away, the bright twinkle of a star, and his spirits rose with a bound. He was almost through.

With the approaching end of his journey came reaction from the apprehension which had gripped him, and, wet though he was, he could not bring himself to hurry over the last few steps. His professional curiosity began to assert itself again. He was standing, after all, where few men had stood in the last few hundred years, and it was highly unlikely that he would ever walk through the tunnel again. He climbed on to the ledge, out of the stream, and proceeded to wring some of the water from his clothes. The exertion of the last stretch of tunnel had warmed him, and he was conscious of a pleasant sense of achievement, corpse or no corpse.

Sweeping the wall above the ledge with his torch, he examined with interest the markings on the living rock—the laborious work of men who had lived almost on the threshold of human history. He found himself wondering why it had been necessary to swing the tunnel so sharply to the right at this point, and whether the ledge on which he was standing was natural or artificial.

As he stared in admiration at the hewn surface of the wall, and, as was his habit, sought for words with which to describe it later, a sharp exclamation escaped him. Perhaps it was only his imagination, but he could have sworn that the wall looked somehow different at this point. For one thing, different tools had been used—the chiselled markings were a different shape, a different size. The rock was of a lighter colour than that in the tunnel below. He picked up a small chip from the ledge and saw that one side of it was dull and smooth with age, and the other rough and bright. Garve was a layman in such matters, but he was convinced that that particular chip had not lain in the passage for three thousand years. With rising interest, he directed the beam of his torch upwards. To the right, above the stream, the roof was low and clearly visible, but immediately above him the rays of light lost themselves in darkness. As he swung the torch about, he noticed with a thrill that the ledge gave on to another ledge, five feet or so above it, and that in between were several rocky projections which made the climb a simple matter.

Quickly he removed his soggy jacket and rolled it into a bundle, which he placed on the ledge. He could explore better without it.

His gun he transferred to his trousers pocket, though he placed little trust in its effectiveness after the wetting he had received. The whisky flask he placed by the side of his jacket, having first taken a long and welcome pull at its contents. Unimpeded by the jacket, he drew himself easily up to the second ledge and flashed his torch ahead.

He whistled softly. Before him a new tunnel opened out, higher, wider, and altogether more negotiable than the one that Hezekiah had made. The ground was dry, smooth, and hard. Garve advanced cautiously. The floor rose at a steady angle of twenty degrees, and he judged by its direction that he must be almost under the city wall. Men had walked here recently—his roving light revealed a cigarette wrapper on the ground, and where it was sandy there were footmarks and some curious lines which suggested that heavy objects had been dragged through the tunnel.

He had climbed for perhaps five minutes, when the torch ceased to make a ring against the walls of the tunnel, and once more threw a beam of light ahead which lost its power in an open space. He saw now that he had reached something altogether vaster than the tunnel—a great amphitheatre of rock whose roof and sides were invisible.

He hesitated. He was on fire with curiosity, but his torch, for which he had neglected to bring a refill, would give him effective service for only a very little longer, and in this mighty cavern he might easily lose himself. With infinite care he hugged the wall on his right, working round it and watching his step. He proceeded thus for ten or fifteen yards until he came to another passage, branching off again to the right.

Only then did he realize where he was. These underground workings must be Solomon's Quarries. The second entrance to them, which rumour said gave access to the quarries from the temple area above, in reality led down to Hezekiah's Tunnel. And it had been hewn out very recently, with what stupendous labour Garve could only imagine.

He cursed heartily at his lack of foresight in not bringing a spare battery with him. The failing current warned him that he had no time to waste, and he turned about reluctantly, still clinging to the wall. He knew that it would have been madness to go farther.

As his fingers passed lightly over the surface of the rock he detected an occasional smoothness which aroused his interest. Turning the light upon it, he saw that in the rock a kind of fresco had been hewn. There were crude figures of men and animals, with strange hieroglyphics underneath them. Where the figures had been carved, the surface of the rock had been polished until it shone.

"I suppose it's this sort of thing that Hayson wants to decipher," Garve thought. "I must ask him about it."

He would have liked to make a more careful examination—the curious carvings seemed to run all round the wall at intervals of a few feet—but the light was growing dim. In a very few minutes he was back at the ledge and climbing down into Hezekiah's Tunnel. It took him only a very short time to complete the last stretch of tunnel, and as he climbed the steps which led up to the Virgin's Fountain he drew a deep breath of pure air and relief. The fountain lay like a mirror under the still rising moon, and its beauty almost hurt the eyes. He glanced with loathing at the tunnel, but knew now that he would have to go back there. He was not a reporter for nothing.

He trudged back to the hotel with dog-tired steps. His brain was too fatigued to consider any of the problems that lay ahead. He collected his key from the night porter, making no effort to conceal the fact that his clothes were soaked with water and blood. For fifteen minutes he lay in a steaming bath, then gulped down a stiff whisky as hot as he could take it, and, for the second night in succession, sank into an exhausted sleep as soon as his head touched the pillow.

7. A Damsel in Distress

So they were being married after all! Hayson had lost, and Esther was about to become Mrs. Garve. The minister, with a pock-marked face and one eye, was reading the final words of the service, and Jackson the chauffeur was hurrying up the aisle so that he might be the first to congratulate the bride. Ali Kemal was trying to get his horse through the church door. Silly fellow! And the bells were ringing—ding-ding, ding-ding, ding-ding. Why did people have bells at their weddings? Bells were so persistent. Damn the bells—surely they would stop soon—ding-ding, ding-ding.

Garve stirred uneasily in his bed and opened his eyes. The telephone was ringing not a yard away. With a great yawn he reached for the receiver.

"Hallo," he said sleepily.

"Good gracious!" came Esther's low, rich voice over the wire, "you sound tired."

"On the contrary," said Garve, "I am no longer tired."

"What do you mean?" asked Esther.

"I've just this moment woken up. What's the time?"

"It's nearly one o'clock. You *are* a sloth!"

Garve consulted his watch. Yes, he had slept for nearly nine hours. On the table by his bed stood a glass of orange juice and jug of water which had long since ceased to steam. He had no recollection of the maid bringing it in.

"It was nice of you to ring," said Garve. "As a matter of fact I was just dreaming about you."

"No! What was I doing?"

"Well—er—I can't very well tell you over the phone. Wait until I see you."

"It sound interesting, but if it was too bad to talk about, it must have been some other girl! Tell me, how did you get on last night? I've been quite worried about you."

"Have you?" asked Garve cheerfully. "Why the anxiety?"

"Well, father has just been on to police headquarters about something or other, and they said you hadn't made your usual call this morning. I thought perhaps you'd got lost in the tunnel. What was it like?"

"A bit damp," said Garve cautiously. "And dark, you know—dark."

"You're very mysterious, and vague. I don't believe you went near the place. I expect you spent the night in some low Press haunt, and now you're trying to blame the tunnel for your hangover!"

Garve tenderly touched his swollen face and sighed. "That's right," he said. "And I've been fighting too. Take my advice and never argue with a 'drunk.' "

"Oh, you're absurd. You seem cheerful enough now, anyway."

"The sound of your voice——"began Garve.

"I know. I've heard that one. What about coming round for a talk some time to-day? Mr. Hayson will be here for dinner——"

"That's fine. I'll come to tea."

"Don't be silly. I was going to ask you to dinner as well, but Hayson said he had an idea you'd be unable to come."

"The devil he did! Nice of him to arrange my time-table for me."

Esther laughed softly. "I don't believe you like him."

"My dear girl," said Garve severely, "I know you think there are only two presentable men in Jerusalem, but that's no excuse for making your coquetry so very obvious."

"I hate you," said Esther.

"Hugh! I should hate *you* if I didn't know you were just pulling my leg. As it is . . ."

"Yes?" said Esther.

"As it is, I just dislike you."

Esther laughed. "I had a very interesting time in the quarries yesterday," she said slowly.

"I can imagine it. Poking about in the dark! Were Hayson's researches advanced at all?"

"I don't think so. But he showed me something he said were his hieroglyphics."

"Ah!—I was beginning to suspect that he'd invented them for publicity purposes. Did he make love to you?"

There was a long pause—so long that Garve said, "Hallo, hallo," thinking he had been cut off.

"I'm still here," said Esther.

"I see—silence is golden." His voice was suddenly dry. "Look here, p'r'aps I'd better not come round to-day after all."

"Don't be silly," said Esther. "I want to talk to you. Honestly. Something rather important. I—I need your advice."

"You're a queer kid," said Garve softly. "Always fooling, and then suddenly serious. All right—I'll come, I'll be along about four."

"Thanks. I must go now—lunch is ready. Au revoir."

"Bye," said Garve. He replaced the receiver gently, lit a cigarette, and lowered himself carefully into bed again.

Esther puzzled him. Sometimes she seemed to be just a flirtatious little butterfly, but he knew that she could be sensible and kindly when she wanted. And, after all, why should she be serious with him? He had treated her all along in a very off-hand way, reprimanding her one moment as though she were a child of ten and teasing her in a casual sort of way the next. She probably thought he was just a cynical newspaper man—as, in general, he was—who didn't mind amusing himself with any charming girl. If that was what she thought, she was undoubtedly treating him in the right sort of way, and displaying remarkable sense. The question was, how was she treating Hayson? Hayson took himself very seriously. He seemed to be lacking in humour, and, judging by the way he looked at her, he was very much in earnest. Perhaps she didn't flirt with him. Hayson would be a difficult—yes, even a dangerous—man to flirt with.

Garve drew thoughtfully at his cigarette and began to turn over in his mind the events of the previous night. He had never really believed that Jameel would attack him. The man must have been mad either with greed or hate to do it. The question was, which? He had already been promised five hundred piastres for his night's work, and he could hardly have been such a fool as to imagine that Garve was carrying even that much money with him on such an expedition. He must have known, too, the colossal risk he was running if he succeeded in the murder. With his evil one-eyed face he could never have hoped to escape arrest for long. Not if he were working alone, at any rate. Perhaps, after all, the attempted assassination had been political. No doubt, he knew Garve—everybody knew Garve—and had simply decided to seize an excellent opportunity to rid his countrymen of an inquisitive busybody. In that case he would rely on whatever secret society he belonged to to conceal him till the search was given up. However, he was dead, and no one would ever know now what his motives had been. Garve thought of him, lying all bloated and swollen in the pool, and then looked out of his window at the warm and brilliant sunshine. Life was very sweet—all the sweeter to-day, because the night before it had seemed so near its end.

All in a moment Garve felt very tired of Palestine. It was a dry, hard, cruel country, and no promised land. He felt tired of the interminable wrangling between Jew and Arab; impatient of the policy which brought Great Britain in as guardian of the peace, and tried to populate the country with an unpopular race. Surely there were vast empty places in the world which the Jews could have colonized without this ceaseless bloodshed. For months now he had lived only in the storm centres of the world, and he longed for peace and kindliness. He imagined himself with Esther in some green and restful English village—accessible to London, yet away from its hurly-burly. A little quiet reporting for a change —days off which were really free from care—English food, green vegetables, golf. . . .

"Hell, I'm getting old," he told himself. But all the same he decided to ask for his recall directly he had landed his big story. And that he knew must soon come now.

His thoughts switched back to Hezekiah's Tunnel. Far more than the motives of Jameel, the discovery of the newly built tunnel intrigued him. It had been a massive labour; it must have taken dozens of men weeks to construct, particularly if they had worked secretly. And for what? Garve could think of only one explanation which made sense. If the Arabs were using the dangerous and unknown depths of the quarries as a vast ammunition dump, the tunnel would be necessary. The upper entrance to the quarries was too public—police often patrolled the walls, hundreds of people used the highway which passed within a few yards of it. One slip and their secret would be known, their work all gone for nothing. Hezekiah's Tunnel, on the other hand, was never visited. On the contrary, it was avoided. On a dark night arms could be brought through the Kedron Valley on mules without the Arabs going anywhere near the city or running any risk at all. It would be simplicity itself to unload them at the Virgin's Fountain, carry them down the few yards to the ledge, and hoist them up into the new tunnel. The quarries, as Hayson had agreed, were an ideal *cache*, and would provide a constant stream of weapons when required in the very centre of the revolt.

Garve sighed. It was quite obvious that he would have to spend one or two nights at the Virgin's Fountain. No doubt the police would be only too glad to do the job, but that way out did not commend itself. He took a certain professional pride in the things he had discovered so far. He was conceited enough to believe that he was the best "snooper" in Palestine. If the police started blundering around, the Arabs might take fright and change their hiding-place. When Garve went poking about they merely thought of him as a prying journalist. In any case, it was his story—once the police got hold of it it would become official, and the whole world might know. And that would be the end of his scoop. Also, in the back of his mind was still the uncomfortable feeling that the Palestine police force, composed as it was of British, Jews, and Arabs, was not the safest repository for any secret.

Clearly the next thing to do was to explore the interior of the quarries thoroughly. He would have to tell Hayson of his discovery and enlist his aid. The fellow was objectionable enough as a rival, but he knew the quarries and their dangers better than any Englishman in Jerusalem, and he had an inquiring turn of mind. Two people could clamber about better than one; they could carry more equipment; they could help each other in case of difficulty. Hayson was not interested in newspapers to any extent; if anything were discovered he would be reasonably discreet. He looked a solid, reliable fellow—blast his eyes!—and, anyway, as long as he was with Garve he couldn't be with Esther.

Garve began to whistle cheerfully and proceeded to dress. He was making good progress in spite of his stiffness, when suddenly he caught sight of his face in the mirror and his whistling stopped abruptly.

"My God" he ejaculated, "I can't go visiting like that!"

Across his forehead stretched a dull red scar, one eye was nearly black and his upper lip was swollen. He looked nearly as villainous as Jameel himself had done, and ten times more battered than he felt.

"Oh, well, it can't be helped," he decided, shrugging his shoulders. He shaved with difficulty, washed the congealed blood off his forehead, bathed his eye and lip, and finished dressing.

Over lunch, which he took in the hotel, he tried to concoct a plausible explanation of his injuries. None that he could think of sounded dignified, least of all the one he had given jestingly to Esther. He didn't want her to think he ever got as drunk as all that. How could one get one's face bashed in with dignity? He had fallen downstairs! No, that sounded as though he had just learned to walk. He had walked into a lamp-post! That didn't sound very sober either. He had tried to rescue a damsel in distress! No, Esther wouldn't swallow that two days running. Whatever he said he would feel horribly like Don Quixote. Exploring old sewers was almost more ludicrous and certainly less romantic than tilting at windmills. He could not tell her the truth, because that would mean a lot of questions about Jameel, and there would be quite enough trouble about Jameel as it was. Oh, well, he would think of something.

Directly after lunch he made his way to police headquarters and found Baird reading a copy of the *Morning Call*, four days out of London by air.

"Morning," said Baird. "Just finding out what's been happening in our city lately. 'A succession of dastardly attacks on police officers.' You're getting quite heated, old man."

Garve snatched the paper, glanced at the story, and handed it back with a snort of disgust. "That's not mine—some sub-editor has been jazzing my stuff up again. Dastardly, my foot! What do they expect the Arabs to do—stop the police in the streets with bunches of flowers and doughnuts?"

Baird grinned. "Got out of bed the wrong side to-day, eh? Heavens, man, what have you been doing to your face? It's—it's——"

"Worse than usual," said Garve irritably. "I know. I fell on it."

Baird suddenly became serious. "More trouble last night?"

Garve nodded. "I went through Hezekiah's Tunnel with an Arab named Jameel. Bloke with one eye. He attacked me with a knife, and we socked each other. He's dead."

"Suppose you pad the story out a bit," suggested Baird.

Garve proceeded to give him a full account of the incident, but omitted all reference to the second tunnel. At the end Baird found himself grinning again.

"You always were rough," he said. "Anyway, Jameel's no loss. We know him—had our eye on him for some time. He had a bad habit of skulking about at night. All the same, there'll have to be an inquiry."

"I know," said Garve. "You'd better send a couple of fellows along to bring out the body. And tell them not to fall into the pool themselves. You can let me know when you want me. Is there any news?"

"Nothing. No more murders—only yours!—no more ammunition dumps that disappeared overnight—nothing."

Garve frowned. "Some of you people think I'm just playing the fool, don't you, Baird?"

"No, no, old man, I'm only joking. You know your job all right. The only thing is, you're bound to get bumped off pretty soon, and it seems a pity. I'm not the only one who'll think so either."

"What do you mean?"

"Young lady with the auburn hair——"

Garve swore rudely. "You read too many cheap novels, Baird. Any news of Kemal?"

"Not a word. He's gone to ground. Oh, by the way, there's a cable for you. Just come in."

Garve took the message. It was from his paper. "Understand trouble likely in Syria and Turkey if Palestine revolts. Keep in touch with Beyrout and Ankara."

"Fools," ejaculated Garve with unusual heat. "I suppose they think I stroll over into Turkey for my morning constitutional. Give me a telegraph form, there's a good fellow."

Baird handed him the slip and he wrote, "*Morning Call*, London. Please send bicycle. Garve."

Without a word he passed it back to Baird, who glanced at it and raised his eyebrows. "Tired of your job?" he asked, grinning.

"Sick of it. I'd like to keep poultry and be useful. Well, so long."

He stopped at a shaded kiosk for a glass of orangeade, sent off the wire, and then proceeded at a leisurely pace to the Willoughby house.

Esther was out on the balcony, and she rose to greet him with a smile which faded as soon as. she saw his face.

"So you *have* been fighting!"she exclaimed reprovingly.

"Boys will be boys," said Garve. "Mind if I smoke?"

"Not if it won't hurt your mouth. How did it happen?"

Garve puffed contentedly at his pipe. "I fell down a hole."

"One hole wouldn't have done all that," said Esther.

"Well, a succession of holes. Hezekiah's Tunnel is full of them." He stretched his legs contentedly in the sunshine and smiled at Esther. "It's nice to be here."

"You shall have some tea in a few minutes. It was good of you to come."

"The most selfish thing I ever did in my life," said Garve promptly.

"Anyway, what's on your mind? You're the queerest woman. You ring up and start flirting violently, and the next minute you sound as worried as though you'd lost a fortune."

Esther flushed and looked, Garve thought, delectable. "Flirting violently! It sounds horrid, but I suppose I do. I'll tell you why I wanted to talk to you. Mr. Hayson asked me to marry him last night."

Garve gazed at her curiously. "What do you expect me to do about it? Punch him on the nose?"

"Please. I'm trying to be serious."

"But my dear girl," said Garve abruptly, "what has it got to do with me? It's hardly fair to Hayson to talk him over with me, is it?"

"I must talk to someone," Esther exclaimed, and Garve could see that she was deeply disturbed. "I tried to tell father about it this morning, but he's so busy, poor dear, and there really wasn't time. You see—well, you seem so sensible. You know when I'm teasing and being all temperamental, and you treat me the right way. You laugh in the right places, and I seem to get on with you so easily. You're a friendly person. I do such silly things. I've always been like that —impetuous and harum-scarum. I'm always sorry afterwards. Do you honestly think I encouraged Hayson?"

Garve tried to look judicial. "I wouldn't say that you made flagrant advances—not up till yesterday anyway, when I lost track of you. It's true you gobbled up his obvious admiration, but I don't blame you—it must be very dull for you here. Blown up the first day and proposed to the second!" He grinned. "You've asked for frankness, you know. I think you're quite hopelessly spoilt, as I must have told you at least a dozen times. By the way, I gather from your tone that you didn't accept him."

"He wouldn't let me say yes or no," said Esther disconsolately. "If he'd been an ordinary person I should have been able to deal with the situation—you don't know what a blow it is to my pride to be asking your advice, and I'd far sooner have kept quiet about it. The trouble is"—she hesitated—"well, he frightens me."

"*Frightens* you!" said Garve, sitting up. "What do you mean?"

"He's so intense and strong—strong-willed. His eyes frighten me. He takes command of the situation so completely. He almost hypnotizes me. You must admit he's rather fascinating. He's used to having his own way. His vitality overwhelms me. I can't understand him at all—he's so different from anyone I've met before."

"It certainly sounds as though he's swept you off your feet a bit," said Garve, chewing nervously at his pipe-stem. He still felt very uncomfortable. "Suppose you give him a rest for a day or two and allow yourself to simmer down."

"That's just the trouble. He said he'd come to dinner and take me afterwards to see the city walls by moonlight. He didn't ask whether I wanted to go—he just arranged it."

For the first time Garve began to feel really worried. "You certainly have changed since you bullied me into taking you round the city yesterday," he observed. "Do you *want* to see the walls by moonlight?"

"I don't know," said Esther. "In a way I do—yes, desperately—but I tell you I'm frightened. Oh, don't you see——?"

"If I were your elder brother," said Garve severely, "I should advise you to plead a headache and go to bed early. You may be in love with the fellow or you may not, but canoodling in the moonlight isn't the best way to find out! That's my advice, anyway."

"He said that nothing would prevent him from coming," said Esther miserably, and something in her tone made Garve shiver.

"For heaven's sake, young woman, take a hold on yourself. Anybody would think he'd placed a spell on you."

"It was the quarries," said Esther faintly. "He took me right down into the earth. At first it was all great fun—he joked and helped me over the difficult places, and was very interesting. Then I suppose he got on my nerves. He kept on warning me about precipices, and made me listen to water trickling hundreds of feet below, and when we'd climbed down and down for hours I suddenly realized how completely I was lost and dependent on him. We sat down on a rock, and he made his torch throw ghostly shadows about, and—oh, I can't explain it—I felt myself going all weak, and then he asked me to marry him—it was such a strange place to choose—and he talked and talked until I was quite dazed. One moment I thought I hated him for taking me down there at all, and the next I felt I just wanted to stay there with him for ever."

"Take it easy," said Garve gently, as her voice rose excitedly. "I can see there's something very wrong somewhere. Maybe after all it's just as well you told me. I know what we'll do. I'll stay here and have some tea with you, and then I'll stroll over and tell Hayson you're indisposed, and keep him occupied for the rest of the evening."

"Do you think you can?"

Garve grinned. "I'm quite certain I can."

"All right, then," said Esther meekly. "Now, let's talk about something nice."

For the next hour Garve set himself to chatter foolishly. Most of the time he talked with one eye on Esther, noting with rising anxiety her flushed face and heavy shadowed eyes. As soon as dusk fell she became uneasy again, and suggested going indoors. She watched in silence while Garve fastened the big windows, and sighed with relief as the lights went on.

"I think I'll go upstairs and read for a little," she said. "I can always ring for the servants if I want anything."

Garve nodded, but wished horribly that he could stay and look after her himself.

"By the way," Esther added as he prepared to leave, "you didn't tell me about your dream, after all."

"Oh that!" said Garve. He looked into her eyes until her lids drooped over them. "I dreamt you were marrying *me*. Our subconscious minds play queer tricks, don't they? Good-bye—and don't worry."

"Good-bye—and thank you." Her pathetic little smile followed him down the drive, and as he turned into the highway she waved.

"Poor kid," said Garve to himself, feeling less like a hard-bitten reporter than ever in his life before.

8. Thrust and Parry

Garve's forehead was puckered with deep lines of thought as he covered the short distance which separated the Willoughby house from the square stone dwelling which Hayson rented. He felt ill at ease, and a little uncertain of his next move. He had nothing against Hayson—the man had upset Esther, it was true, but he was not the first suitor to have pressed his plea with more vigour than consideration. Esther was in a highly emotional frame of mind, and perhaps when she had had time to think the matter over she would regard Hayson in quite a different light. Anyway, it was really none of Garve's business, as he had said, and, little though he liked the man, he could not see that he had any substantial grounds for picking a quarrel with him.

Hayson, smart and self-possessed as usual, opened the door himself in reply to Garve's knock. As he looked out, and before Garve spoke, there was a moment of uneasy silence which lasted just a fraction longer than was strictly polite.

"Hope I'm not disturbing you," said Garve apologetically.

"Indeed, no," replied Hayson, staring. "Come in, my dear fellow; come in and make yourself comfortable."

"You seem surprised to see me," observed Garve.

"Surprised?—no, no, honoured, I assure you. I was just wondering what you had done to your face—that was why I stared so rudely. Here—you'll find this chair all right. Will you smoke?"

"If you don't mind," said Garve, "I prefer a pipe. He glanced appreciatively round the spacious room, which was furnished with an almost extravagant regard for comfort. "Cosy place you've got here."

71

Hayson's lips smiled, but his dark eyes had no laughter in them. It was all like the cautious opening to a deadly duel with rapiers.

"Snug, isn't it? I work such a lot in uncomfortable places that I feel entitled to a little luxury at home. The house is small enough, but ample for my needs. This, as you see, is the lounge, and the next room is my study. I'm afraid it's too untidy to show you—my collection of relics has grown so large lately. Some time you must see it—I've had a small laboratory fitted up and a dark room for my photographic work, of which I'm very proud. I like to think there is nothing like it in Jerusalem. But tell me —you have met with an accident?" "Oh, this?" Garve's hand crept to his face. "As a matter of fact," he said, "you weren't far wrong about Hezekiah's Tunnel. It's the devil of a place."

"Ah! You had a fall?"

"Several—but it wasn't that that did the damage. I wish I'd taken your advice now about that guide fellow. He was a regular cut-throat."

"Good heavens! Did he attack you?"

"He did. The blighter tried to pinch my money."

Hayson nodded. "Well, I won't be unkind and say, 'I told you so.' What happened?"

"I was lucky and managed to scare him off after we'd had a bit of a scrap. He got away—but the police will probably catch him. He's fairly conspicuous."

"I sincerely hope they do," said Hayson, his dark eyes not leaving Garve's face. "A scoundrel like that is a peril to the whole community."

Garve suddenly wanted to laugh at the stark unreality of their conversation. Here he was lying flagrantly about Jameel's fate, for reasons which he could hardly have analyzed himself, and Hayson was sympathizing with him over his unpleasant experience in tones which were far more polite than convincing. Actually, thought Garve, Hayson was probably feeling highly delighted over the whole episode.

Abruptly Garve changed the subject. "By the way," he said, "the real reason for my visit is that I have a message for you from Miss Willoughby."

"Indeed," said Hayson, suddenly very intent. It was almost as though he had been waiting for her name to be mentioned. "I am expecting to see her quite shortly."

"I'm afraid you won't," said Garve, and he could not keep a faint unpleasantness—a more than accidental abruptness—out of his tone. "She tells me she has a frightful headache, and asks me to present her apologies to you for not being able to see you to-night."

"I'm sure she could not have chosen a more excellent ambassador," said Hayson with biting courtesy. "I am so sorry to hear she's indisposed. If you'll excuse me, I'll go round at once and find out if there's anything I can do."

Garve puffed comfortably at his pipe. "Miss Willoughby specifically asked me to say that you were not to bother to call as she had gone to bed, and left instructions with the servants that she was not to be disturbed."

"You have a retentive memory," said Hayson. The antagonism between them was becoming more marked the more carefully they chose their words. It was touch and go, Garve felt, whether or not in a few minutes there would be an open, perhaps a violent, breach.

"I am always glad to convey a lady's message," he declared, watching Hayson's eyes. "I understood that, having invited yourself to dinner, you proposed to take her to look at the walls by moonlight. I am sorry that she has missed the experience—they are a never-to-be-forgotten sight. But strong moonlight is so bad for a headache, and I advised her that in the circumstances it would be better to postpone the outing. Don't you think I was right?"

"Undoubtedly," said Hayson, with a smiling mouth. "It was very thoughtful of you. Tomorrow, no doubt, her headache will be better, and the walls will still be standing."

Garve gently blew out a cloud of smoke and scattered it with his hand. "To-morrow I shall be taking Miss Willoughby for a dip in the Dead Sea. You will remember our making the appointment—you advised me that the road was not very safe. Perhaps the night after ...."

"Yes," said Hayson, and his face was a mask, "the night after."

Garve silently studied his features. Rarely had he seen so strikingly handsome a man. The lips, perhaps, were a little too sensual, but the lines of the face were almost beyond criticism. Beneath a fine forehead those dark eyes glowed and burned with almost unnerving power. It was Hayson's eyes which always drew one's attention in the end. His face was strong, pleasant, commanding. Garve was looking at his eyes now. They had a magnetic attraction. No wonder Esther had been distressed by their gaze—no wonder she had felt herself falling under their influence.

"By the way," asked Garve casually, "have you got any other plans for *to-night?*"

"Nothing special," said Hayson cautiously. He was always cautious ("scientific training," thought Garve). "I was keeping the evening open, of course. Anything on your mind?"

"I should like you to take me down the quarries," said Garve without beating about the bush.

"To-night? Good lord, no."

"Why not? Darkness makes no difference when it's dark all the time. Besides, there's a reason." Briefly Garve told Hayson of his discoveries in the quarries, and of his strong suspicions about a dump, still without giving any hint of Jameel's fate.

Hayson studied the glowing tip of his cigarette. His impassive face gave nothing of his thoughts away. Presently he said, "I know the chamber with the carvings round the wall. I never dreamed there was a passage out of it to the tunnel. As I told you yesterday, I've never seen any signs myself of a munition dump, and if there were one I think I should have seen it. I imagine you're wasting your time."

Garve grinned. "You certainly do try and put a fellow off. First the tunnel and then the quarries. I believe you regard the underground portions of Jerusalem as your special preserve."

"If you're suggesting that I'm trying to keep you away because I've something to hide ..." began Hayson slowly.

"I was joking," said Garve, surprised at the man's resentment.

"That's all right. At least you'll admit that my warnings about the tunnel were justified."

"Unquestionably," said Garve with a rueful hand on his face. "But I'm afraid warnings don't stop me. I'm one of those rash fellows who rarely listen to advice when I've made up my mind."

"You mean—you intend to search anyway—whether I come with you or not."

"Certainly," said Garve without meaning it at all.

"And you intend to go to-night?"

Garve thought of Esther left for Hayson to visit, but decided to risk the bluff. "I shall go to-night. If there is a dump the police ought to know without delay."

"Have you told the police of your suspicions?"

Garve shook his head. Not till afterwards did he realize his lack of caution. "I want the story first. When *they* know, the world will know too."

Hayson appeared to consider the matter, and suddenly shrugged his shoulders. "Well, if you're as set on it as all that I suppose I'll have to humour you. But please remember, if either of us comes to grief, that it was you who suggested the trip. If there *is* a dump, it may be guarded, and then we're for it. You realize that?"

"You take such care of me," Garve murmured. "I can't think why." Again it was dangerous ground, but the temptation was great.

Hayson either did not notice the implication or pretended not to.

"I shouldn't like to be held responsible for the death of so distinguished a member of the journalistic profession," he said lightly.

Garve grinned. "You certainly do look on the bright side." Suddenly his mood changed, and he became businesslike and serious. "Tell me, what equipment do we need, if any?"

"Old clothes and something to light the way. Nailed boots. We'd better take a length of rope too—just in case of difficulty. I'll get my things together and meet you outside the quarries—say in an hour. Have you your own torch?"

"Yes—a good one. Shall I bring some grub?"

"It isn't necessary—we shan't be in there more than an hour or two—but just as you like."

Garve departed at once, glad to be active again, and keen to be started. The glimpse of a light in Esther's room was reassuring. Just in case Hayson contemplated a quick visit, she would be well out of the way. The thought passed through Garve's mind that perhaps Hayson would try to give him the slip. Suppose he did not keep his appointment at the quarries at all, but went over to Esther's instead?

Garve considered the possiblity and rejected it. For some reason Hayson was clearly determined not to let him visit the quarries alone. Was it feasible, after all, that the man *had* something to conceal down there?—in spite of his indignant disclaimer? Was it possible that his story about the Ark of the Covenant and all the rest of it was just a blind? True he had shown Esther some hieroglyphics, but that was easy, for Esther would hardly know hieroglyphics from turnips—particularly in her present frame of mind. Garve proceeded on his way, confident that he would meet Hayson at the appointed place.

The preliminary preparations for expeditions of this sort were by now becoming a matter of ordinary routine to Garve. The tweeds he had worn in the tunnel had been dried by the hotel staff, and the bloodstains cleaned off without comment. He wore again the cloth cap which had saved his head so many times in the tunnel. He carefully cleaned and reloaded his gun, refilled his flask with whisky, and put a new battery in the most powerful of his collection of torches. Before he left he ordered and consumed a quick sandwich and put an additional packet in his pocket as a precaution. Finally he filled his pipe to his satisfaction, lighted it, and set off for the Quarries just as dusk was falling.

9. In Solomon's Quarries

The entrance to Solomon's Quarries is roughly midway between Damascus Gate and Herod's Gate, on the north side of Jerusalem. Hayson was already waiting when Garve arrived. He had a rucksack over his shoulder, from which the end of a coil of rope was peeping, and he carried a powerful torch, similar to Garve's. They plunged at once into the quarries. On the left as they entered was a small table, where, in the daytime, an ancient Arab sat and sold candles and masonic curios to tourists.

"He's been having a thin time lately," said Hayson. "I doubt if anybody has been near the place except myself during the last few weeks."

"Yourself and Esther," thought Garve, but said nothing. He asked aloud, "Why masonic curios?"

"Masons from all over the world forgather here. There's a theory that the builders of the temple were the first Freemasons, and they sometimes hold lodge meetings down here at night. But not lately."

"Does your Arab friend still come here when there are no tourists?"

"Oh yes. He knows he will always get a few piastres from me, and he's useful on the rare occasions when I want any help. Besides, there's always the possibility that some stranger might drop in, and it's a point of honour with the old man to warn every visitor against the frightful precipices inside."

"Very useful. And I suppose he checks them out, and, if they didn't come, he could raise the alarm."

"That's the theory, but it wouldn't be much use, because anyone who really got lost inside would very soon break his neck trying to get out."

"Still, it would be comforting to know that somebody knew one's whereabouts. Now if *we* were to lose ourselves to-night, nobody would know anything."

"Nobody," said Hayson grimly.

"All the more reason for being careful," thought Garve, and from that moment he remained alert in mind and body.

They quickly left the small patch of daylight which penetrated the mouth of the quarry, and descended sharply down a wide smooth passage, which presently broadened into a huge cavern. Their twin torches threw beams like searchlights on the walls near by, but, as in the lower cavern which Garve had already visited alone, the roof and distant walls were lost to sight.

"It's very beautiful," said Garve in wonder. "The stone looks so clean and white."

"It's a remarkable stone," Hayson declared as they stopped to examine it. "Up here it's soft to work as well as white. When it's exposed to the atmosphere, though, it gets hard very quickly. That's why it's so excellent for building. Down below, the rock is harder and different altogether."

"You can see it's an artificial excavation," said Garve, studying the markings.

"No doubt about that. Solomon's men had a Herculean task. I should say there's enough stone been taken out of this quarry to build the whole city of Jerusalem twice over."

Suddenly a dark patch high up on the wall dislodged itself and came fluttering through the torchlight past Garve's head into the darkness behind.

"Bats," said Hayson. "Thousands of them. You'll get used to them before you see daylight again."

Garve felt a little shiver run down his spine at Hayson's words. "Before you see daylight again!" It sounded almost like a threat. Was it possible, after all, that Hayson was hoping to leave his rival's body in the cave? If so, Garve had played his game to the last detail. Yet what could the man do? Push him down a precipice?

Garve would see that that did not happen. Hayson might have a gun, but Garve had one too, and was used to producing it quickly and unexpectedly when required. In physical strength and toughness, Garve knew himself to be Hayson's superior. A rough-house with him would not last so long as it had done with Jameel. In any case, he was almost certainly alarming himself for nothing, but it was curious that he had placed himself in almost exactly the same position on this night as on the night before with Jameel. Fortunately, Hayson, like Jameel, was the guide, and at all times would have to go first.

"There are seven passages leading out of this cavern in various directions," said Hayson. "They are all more or less on the same level, and all but one end in a cul-de-sac. At the end of them you can see in each case where the quarrying operations finished. Had they been continued they would have emerged on some hillside or other, but the quarrying stopped short each time. Naturally, this is the least interesting level of the whole quarry. It is the only part that visitors usually see—and it is the safest. Now, if you follow me closely we'll find the passage that isn't a dead end."

"Where was it that you found your hieroglyphics?" asked Garve.

"Eh? Oh, those! Right down at the bottom. Near the cave that you discovered yourself. There's another level before we get there, and a good deal of climbing about to do. You'll be stiff to-morrow."

"I'm stiff already," said Garve cheerfully. "I feel like a troglodyte after all the underground work I've been doing during the last few days."

"Underground work seems to describe your activities very accurately," said Hayson. "Come on."

Leading by a yard or so, he struck straight across the great chamber, Garve following closely. They plodded along for perhaps twenty yards, and then Hayson swung right at an angle of ninety degrees, and, a little farther on, right again. In a few minutes, Garve gave up trying to keep his bearings. Either this great cathedral of rock was vaster than anything he had dreamed of, or else Hayson was deliberately trying to mislead him.

"Wouldn't it have been quicker to walk round the wall till we came to the passage?" Garve suggested, thinking of his own explorations.

"You must take it that I know the best way," replied Hayson tersely.

As he spoke his torch revealed the mouth of the tunnel they were seeking. Its walls were cleanly hewn and straight, with here and there niches where the Phoenician workmen, so Hayson said, had placed their lamps. The going was easy compared with Hezekiah's Tunnel, and Garve was about to comment on the fact when the passage came to an abrupt end. Unlike the other tunnels which Hayson had referred to it was blocked, not by rock and rubble, but by a well-built stone wall.

"Hallo, have we taken the wrong turning?" asked Garve suspiciously, flashing his light at Hayson. "I thought you said this wouldn't be a cul-de-sac."

"It isn't," said Hayson coldly. "Please believe that I know what I'm doing."

"Sorry," said Garve. "What do we do—cry 'Open Sesame'?"

"This," said Hayson didactically, "is a sunken portion of the temple wall. If you flash your torch in the corner there to the right you'll see there's a slit about a foot wide running up to the tunnel roof."

Garve obeyed, and his torch discovered the dark crack. "Are you suggesting we get through there, Hayson?"

"It's the only way. I've often done it, and if anything you're a shade less bulky than I am. There is another alternative, if you prefer it—an eighty-foot drop from the cavern we've just left. If we'd walked round the walls as you suggested, we'd have fallen into it. The Phoenicians probably had a way down, but some part of the path must have crumbled away."

Garve regarded him curiously, shielding his torch so that the full glare did not fall on Hayson's face.

"Do you mean to tell me you've learned all these things in a month or two, exploring on your own?"

"I've had a little guidance, of course," said Hayson briefly. "Well, let's get through."

"After you," said Garve promptly. It wasn't a situation that he liked, and he began to realize that his faith in his own powers of self-protection had erred on the side of optimism. Whether he went first or last, he would be helpless as a child as he passed through that narrow aperture. The feeling that Hayson had brought him here to kill him returned in full force. If Hayson, having squeezed through, had placed himself in a position in the slightest degree threatening, Garve would have produced his gun then and there. But Hayson's own hands were well away from his pockets, and the one which did not hold the torch helped Garve.

"I can't pretend to explain all these curious holes and passages," said Hayson. They were stooping now in another narrower and more hastily hewn tunnel. "I expect they all served some ancient purpose."

"Or some modern one," amended Garve. "This particular bit looks to me to have been broken through fairly recently."

"Perhaps," said Hayson non-committally. "Now then—mind your step."

They descended so sharply that at times they had to find hand-hold as well as foot-hold on the uneven floor. "Keep well to the right," called Hayson. "There's nothing on your left now but space."

Garve groped for the wall at his right and pressed his back against it, then he swept his torch round in front of him. They were on a sort of rock ledge not more than three feet wide, and at their feet a black hole gaped.

Hayson suddenly gripped his arm and he jumped violently. "It's all right. I only wanted to make sure of you in case you were troubled with vertigo. Listen!"

Garve stood motionless as the rock itself and strained his ears. They were too deep down in the heart of this hollow mountain of stone for any sound from the outside world to reach them. Garve's ears had first to become attuned to the awful silence before he realized that, far below them, water was running.

He shivered. "How deep is the hole?"

"I don't know. Possibly no-one ever will know exactly." Hayson stooped and picked up a heavy piece of rock. Taking care not to lose his balance, he heaved it over clear of the edge.

It fell for perhaps two seconds. To Garve they seemed like sixty. Out of the depths came a dull "plop," and then silence again except for the steady trickle of the underground stream.

"I should say a hundred feet," announced Hayson. "Presently we shall come out into another chamber—I call it the central chamber for convenience, since it's in the middle level—and all along one side of it there's another drop like this. It isn't a place for weak nerves, is it?"

"Nor for solitary exploration," said Garve with emphasis. He knew that the remark cast not a little doubt on Hayson's veracity, since the man had certainly given the impression that his researches had been conducted in secret. Hayson could not have missed the implication, but he no longer seemed to care what Garve thought about him or his work. There was something sinister in his very indifference. His tone almost suggested that what Garve did or said or thought no longer mattered.

They had just started to move again along the ledge when the first accident happened. Hayson stumbled, as it was so easy to do on the rough ground, and dropped his torch as he clutched at the wall. It struck the ground awkwardly and clattered over the edge of the chasm.

"Damnation," ejaculated Hayson, staring in futile anger into the abyss. "That was unforgivably careless of me."

Garve's torch was still throwing a strong white beam ahead, and looked good for hours. "It's certainly devilish awkward," he said.

"I ought to have kept tight hold of it." Hayson seemed completely crestfallen. "It must have been a case of familiarity breeding contempt. I've been over this ledge so often that I didn't pay it sufficient respect."

Garve became a little irritated. "Never mind, man; it isn't a matter of life and death. Now, if you'd fallen over yourself . . ."

That seemed to set Hayson off again. "We'd better go back, Garve. We can't *feel* our way."

"Don't be silly," said Garve. "I'm not leaving till I've seen all there is to see. We've got one perfectly good torch throwing a beam like a lighthouse, and that's all that is necessary."

"Suppose anything goes wrong with it?" suggested Hayson nervously.

"Suppose the roof falls in!" Garve was beginning to suspect that the man was a craven at heart. Hayson was a very different person now from the iron-willed rival of an hour or so before.

"If you insist we'll go on," said Hayson; "but I'll have to have your torch. I can't lead without a light."

Garve handed his torch over. "Don't drop it, that's all. I can't think of anything I'd like to do less than recross this ledge in the dark."

Presently the tunnel turned sharply to the right, away from the precipice. Instead of descending steadily, it became a series of sharp drops, the greatest of which was more than eight feet deep, and required a good deal of care in negotiation. Another few minutes and a passage opened out into a second spacious cavern. Garve stood upright and drew a breath of relief. "The central chamber," said Hayson. "We're now in the heart of the quarry. Over to the right there is the great hole in the roof which leads up to the cavern in the top level. On the left is the second precipice I spoke of. To the right of that again is a tunnel leading into a smaller chamber, which I've always wanted to explore and have never yet had time for, and from there down to the third level which you discovered yourself."

"It's a hell of a place," said Garve sombrely. "I wonder if I could find my own way out—supposing you were taken ill."

"You'd do better to shoot yourself," said Hayson. "It's an easier death, I should say, than slow starvation or falling from a height."

"Depends if you shoot straight," said Garve. "I've known men to shoot themselves and live in agony for hours afterwards. By the way, we haven't seen any trace of my hypothetical ammunition dump yet."

"Not a sign. If the Arabs had wanted a really safe place they couldn't have found a better spot than somewhere in this chamber, but I've been round it pretty thoroughly."

"What about your hieroglyphics? I'm very intrigued by them, you know."

"We'll come to them," Hayson assured him. "Follow me."

He set off quickly over the rough ground, so quickly that Garve had difficulty in keeping up with him. He was just about to call to him to slow down when the second torch suddenly went out.

"What the hell are you doing?" cried Garve sharply. "Don't play the fool, Hayson."

"Something's gone wrong with it," came Hayson's voice, muffled and thick. In the pitch darkness not the trace of an object was visible anywhere.

"Well, keep still until I get to you. Don't mess about with it. Where are you, damn you?" Garve moved forward a pace or two, groping, but found nothing.

"Hayson!" he called again. He tried hard to keep the note of alarm out of his voice.

"I'm here," came Hayson's voice again, almost under his nose—so near that the sound of it made him jump. "Shouting doesn't help. It must be the bulb."

Garve stretched out a violent hand. "Let me look, you fool." His arm struck something and Hayson cursed.

"Careful," he cried. "Careful. My God, now you've done it. You've knocked the bulb out of my hand."

"Hell!" ejaculated Garve, and there was a moment's silence. Then he added more coolly, "Keep still and don't tread on it. If we feel around long enough we're bound to find it. Don't move, though. If we once lose the spot we're finished. I've got some matches."

He fumbled for the box and struck a light, while Hayson produced matches of his own and followed suit. The flickering flames were woefully inadequate. Garve had only time to catch a glimpse of Hayson's burning eyes and pass his light cautiously over a square foot or so of ground before the darkness closed over them again like a cloak.

"The floor slopes a bit here," said Hayson. "The bulb may have rolled away. Stay where you are to mark the spot and I'll look."

An outside observer might have laughed at the two crawling

figures striking match after futile match. Garve stared at the spot where the bulb had been dropped, scanning the circle of rock round him while the feeble flames lasted. Hayson went crawling away down the slope, his progress marked by the pathetic scrape of matches and the little bursts of puny light which were getting farther and farther away.

"It couldn't have rolled as far as that," called out Garve in exasperation. "The floor's too rough—it's probably right at my feet. Come back and help me."

Hayson had stopped striking matches. He was ten yards away, swallowed up in the blackness. He made no reply.

"Hayson," Garve called again. Out of the darkness came a sound suspiciously like a laugh —an hysterical laugh perhaps, or perhaps a vindictive, jubilant laugh.

"Where are you, Garve?" came Hayson's voice, and it seemed now very far away. "I can't find you. Strike a light."

Garve obeyed, and the match spluttered and died. "Another," came the voice, not perceptibly nearer. It was like a command.

Garve felt in the box. He had six matches left. Suddenly he knew—knew with absolute certainty and conviction—that Hayson was playing with him. He did not intend to come back—he simply wanted Garve to waste all his slender store of matches and then he would leave him. Acute danger always made Garve cool. He struck a match.

"This is my last," he called in a loud voice. "Can you see it?"

"Yes," replied Hayson; "but it's a long way away. Are you sure you haven't another? My God, if you haven't we're lost."

"The box is empty. Can't you come towards my voice."

"I'll try. Start counting aloud. I don't know how I got so far away."

Garve began slowly to count. "One, two, three, four ..." He counted up to ten. "Are you still there, Hayson?"

"There's an echo," came Hayson's voice, distant and despairing. "I can hear you in two places. But go on counting."

Garve counted again. "One, two three, four ... Are you there,

Hayson?" There was no reply. Straining his ears in the darkness he seemed to hear, far off, a faint movement.

"Hayson, are you there?" he shouted. Was it his imagination, or could he just discern far away through the velvet darkness a pale glow of light? In any case, it vanished almost at once.

"For the last time, Hayson, can you hear me?"

There was no reply. Hayson had gone, and Garve was alone in the cavern.

10. Lost!

So Hayson *had* intended to murder him. Garve felt a chilly spasm run through his body. Perhaps *had* murdered him. He had had a plan all the time, and had carried it through with consummate cleverness.

At last Garve realized how incautious he had been. Knowing that Hayson hated him, distrusting his intentions, he had deliberately made the path to murder smooth. And Hayson had taken the absolutely safe way. He had been acting all the time, of course. He had simply let Garve knot his own noose. He had watched while Garve ran his own head into it and pulled it tight.

Garve looked back over the events of the evening and could find no satisfaction in them anywhere. With mortification he saw how Hayson had played with him. It was Garve who had suggested going to the quarries. Hayson had tried to prevent him, knowing that the attempt at dissuasion would fail. His quick mind had seen all the possibilities. He knew how keen Garve was to find the ammunition dump. He knew that he would go on whatever the difficulties. His reason for coming had not, after all, been fear of discovery in some secret nefarious practice in the cave, but merely that he wished to make absolutely sure of Garve's death, and no better opportunity was likely to present itself. Of course, Garve could see it all now—now that it was too late. Hayson had stumbled deliberately in order that he might have an excuse to lose his torch. He had counted on Garve's enthusiasm to go on outweighing his caution. He had made *Garve* insist on going on, waited until Garve handed over his own torch willingly, almost eagerly. He had kept it until they had reached the most inaccessible and dangerous part of the workings. Then—oh yes, it had been so simple—he had probably just unscrewed the bulb. In the impenetrable darkness that followed, he had counted on Garve's giving him reason to drop it. If he *had* dropped it—but why should he have done? It had been such a scramble—it had all happened so quickly—Garve had not even had an opportunity to examine the torch. No doubt Hayson had kept the bulb all the time. By now he had probably put it back in the torch. That pale glow that Garve had seen—that might easily have been the reflection of the torch back in one of the tunnels. Hayson would be out of the quarries in half an hour. No doubt he would throw the bulb away.

Yes; he had certainly been clever. Not by word or action had he made it conclusively clear that he had intended to leave Garve in the cave. Garve would have had no case to take to a jury. Hayson

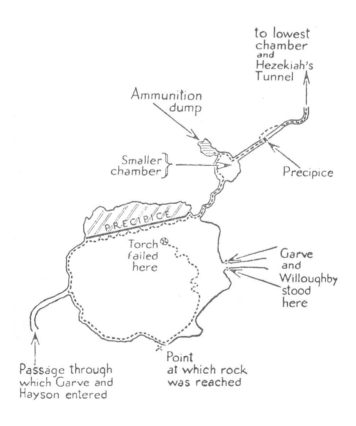

had shown every concern for his safety. Right up to the end he had pretended that he was getting lost himself. He would blame the tragedy on the darkness. Why had he taken such care not to show his hand? The answer gave Garve a tiny ray of hope. He had not been a hundred per cent sure that Garve would die. The odds were incredibly against his getting out, but there was always the odd chance. As it was, if he did get out, Hayson would have nothing to fear. If Garve accused him to his face of attempted murder, he would ridicule the charge and demand proof. And there was no proof. It was a cold, deliberate, damnable plot to get rid of a rival, but it had been carried through with every show of courtesy and consideration.

Garve thought of Esther and squirmed. Hayson would go back to her, would try to get her in his toils again—probably he would succeed. He had realized that Garve's influence was counteracting his own—that he could sway Esther by herself, but not Esther with Garve behind her. Garve had been the stumbling-block—Garve had to be got rid of. Esther would soon forget him—probably she would consent half willingly, half against her will, to marry Hayson, while his own flesh rotted in a cave that no-one ever visited. Nobody would look for him, nobody knew he was there. He had made that clear to Hayson—God, what a fool he had been!

Anyway, there was only one thing to be done now. Somehow he had to get out of the quarries. Life was very precious to him. It had always seemed worth while, but never more so than now, when his love for Esther was growing day by day. His confidence was undiminished, and he told himself with conviction that to escape was not beyond his powers.

He tried to consider his chance impartially. At least he would not die of thirst, for he had seen water dripping from the roof and running down the walls in a dozen places. There was no immediate danger of starvation, thanks to his foresight in bringing a packet of sandwiches. He remembered now that Hayson had advised not bothering about food. That alone should have given him pause.

He had five matches, and to those he might well owe his life. In this one matter Hayson had left something to chance, and Garve's normally alert faculties had functioned just in time. But what were five matches against such Stygian blackness as this? However, they were better than nothing. In addition he had a flask of whisky and a gun. The latter might still be useful, he thought grimly—just as Hayson had suggested. A bullet was certainly better than slow starvation, but the precipices would have to be risked.

Hayson had the rope, and as Garve's mind dwelt on the journey back, his spirits sank. Even supposing he could find the passage from which they had emerged into the central chamber, even supposing he did not follow by mistake some minor passage from it, he felt dubious about being able to negotiate safely in the darkness that eight-foot drop that they had descended with the help of the torch. There was probably some projection at the top that Hayson could sling the rope over on his return journey, but to scale it in the dark and unaided would be perilous. Garve shuddered to think what would follow a broken leg, or even a sprained ankle. It would be a bullet or nothing, then.

However, thinking about the consequences of failure did nothing to make success more likely, and Garve decided to eat a sandwich as the better way to encourage himself. He discovered a healthy appetite after the physical exertion of the descent, but resolutely restored the rest of the packet to his pocket against a greater hunger. He washed down the frugal repast with a mouthful of whisky—neat but heartening—and considered his first move.

He had completely lost his bearings, as was inevitable. What was it that Hayson had said about this central chamber? On one side it ended in a wall, with a great hole above reaching up to the top level, and probably quite unscalable. On the other side, it ended in a precipice dropping down to the bottom level. And somewhere to the right of that precipice was an opening leading to a smaller chamber—so Hayson had said—and ultimately to Hezekiah's Tunnel. Thank heaven he had listened to Hayson's words!

The question was, should he seek an exit upwards or downwards? It was important that he should have clearly in his mind what he was trying to do—whether to return the way he had come or to find Hezekiah's Tunnel. At the moment, if Hayson had spoken the truth, which was by no means certain, he had a rough idea of the layout of the quarries in relation to his position. Once he began to move he might easily become hopelessly fogged unless he kept a definite objective very clearly in mind.

He gave the matter some thought, and eventually decided that the evils that he did not know could not possibly be greater than those he had already experienced. He recalled that the way back involved not merely scaling a height in the darkness and negotiating a narrow ledge above a precipice, but also choosing between six or seven passages running out of a single chamber at the top. By the time he had tried half a dozen of them, he might well be too exhausted to go farther. It was a risk either way—the descent to the lowest level might easily be impassable without a rope and in the dark, but it was an unknown risk, and Garve was an incorrigible optimist.

Above all, it was essential to go slowly and not panic. This appalling darkness, weighing down on him like the lid of a coffin, made him feel already that he was buried alive, and could only escape by lifting that mountain of rock and hurling it away. He must keep his thoughts strictly to the immediate task.

Even then he hesitated. What was the immediate task? He was sitting in an unknown spot somewhere in the vastness of a cavern of unknown size and shape. He did not know in which direction lay the wall and in which the precipice. Whichever way he moved, he would clearly have to work on the assumption that he was heading for the precipice. If he could have built a fire he would have done so—then, if the worst came to the worst, he would have returned to it and started again; but the cavern floor was naked of anything combustible, and it seemed unwise at this stage to start burning his clothes. If only he had had a ball of twine, like Theseus after the Minotaur! He considered unravelling a portion of his clothing, but discarded the idea at once as brilliant but impracticable.

"Well, God help me," he murmured finally, and crawled slowly away. He knew the danger of moving in a circle, particularly if the chamber were vast enough, but there was nothing he could do about it. Inevitably he would travel at best along a zigzag path.

Garve had never moved more slowly, unless on those occasions in his early reporting days when he had been ordered from the scene of a crime by the police. Each time before he drew his body forward he swept his hand all round in front of him, covering an area of a square yard or more with each sweep. Then he crawled forward on his knees, taking care not to advance beyond the safe area, and repeated the operation. At each move he advanced perhaps two feet, and each advance occupied a full minute. After his arm had performed its encircling movement for the thirtieth time, he stopped to rest and wiped the sweat from his eyes. He had covered sixty feet, and the luminous hands of his watch stood at half-past eight.

The brief rest restored him physically, but not mentally, for he was scared of losing all sense of direction, and took care to face the way he was going as he rested. The slightest lack of concentration at this point, the smallest shifting of the body on its axis, might well mean curving back on his tracks. He sat motionless for five minutes by his watch and then started off again.

The temptation to stand up and run was very great. If he ran he was less likely to take a circular course, and there was a fifty-fifty chance that he would reach the wall in safety. Otherwise—he wondered morbidly what it would feel like to be running and suddenly find no ground under one's feet, and know that awful falling sensation. Did one think as one fell—did one say to oneself, "In a second my body is going to hit a mass of jagged rock and be smashed to pulp?" In any case, it would be all over quickly and there would be no more of this nightmare of darkness. He began to feel certain now that he was moving in a circle. Surely the cavern could not be so huge. Round and round and round, he thought —crawling like a silly insect till his knees wore out and his nerves and muscles failed him and he lost consciousness. What an awakening it would be from that unconscious sleep! To wake, dreaming of Esther's arms around him, and find that no sun had risen, no day broken. To wake to this suffocating opacity of blackness, all sense of direction lost. Good God, yes, it would be fatal to sleep. But already he felt sleepy—the regular rhythm of his sweeping hand—the "One—two"as his knees moved forward, the strain of expecting at each move to touch nothing but space, had all helped to make him drowsy.

"I must pull myself together," he thought. "I'm getting apathetic—soon I shan't care whether I live or die." He took a long swig of whisky and considered how relative all values were. A man left alive and solitary in a world struck suddenly dead would hardly wish for life. His sanity would go pretty soon. Garve was like that—"alone, and yet alive." Was he going to lose his reason? Would his brain crack—would he walk round this rocky tomb in the hours that lay ahead, muttering and mumbling insane nonsense? The whisky revived him a little, and warmed him. He tried to concentrate on something pleasant—something amusing—that ridiculous cable, for instance. Well, a bicycle would have been a lot of good in his present predicament! Pretty funny, that! He laughed, and his laugh terrified him. He took care not to laugh again.

If only it had been light—if only he had had just a little light, what a difference it would have made. He must look a pretty rum spectacle, crawling so laboriously and feeling his way in fear along a perfectly flat rock floor with a precipice far behind him. If it *was* behind him! Oh, for a light! He found himself framing wheedling phrases about that light. Just a tiny one!—just a glimmer for a fraction of a second—just a faint pallor to relieve him from the frightful sense of oppression and claustrophobia which was wearing down his resistance. He wondered whether it would be forgivable to strike a match. It was a serious matter, and he considered it seriously. The longing was intense, but the value of a match incalculable. He remembered a fable by Robert Louis Stevenson about three men who were discussing the striking of a last match, and drawing lurid pictures of the fire that might be started by it, and the terrible damage done—and then, when they had struck it, it had gone out. But what was that to do with his case, anyway? He had five matches, not one. If he struck one he would have four—God in heaven, how tired he was.

For the sixty-fourth time his hand swept the rock floor, and this time it struck something. With fumbling fingers, Garve searched the darkness and everywhere he encountered reassuring solidity. He had reached the wall of the chamber at last.

With the gesture of a man welcoming a long-lost son, he stood up and stretched his arms out to it. His breath came in little sobs as his fingers curled in among the crevices. He could almost have wept in reaction. It was several minutes before he realized that, after all, it had been the precipice rather than the wall that he really needed to find. It was near the precipice that he hoped to discover the mouth of the tunnel leading down to the lower workings. But now that he had found the wall he clung to it as though he would never leave it. Nothing would persuade him to plunge again into the uncharted interior of the cavern. The wall was his hope.

He was faced now with a new problem. If he followed it to his left, he would be bound to arrive sooner or later at the tunnel he was seeking, and before he reached the precipice. Unfortunately, there were probably other passages leading from the chamber as well as the one he wanted. He had only to follow one of them to become hopelessly lost. On the other hand, if he turned to his right and continued along the wall until he reached the precipice, he would have to work his way all along the edge of the abyss in order to find his tunnel.

On balance, the latter alternative seemed to offer greater physical danger, but also less chance of a mistake, and Garve turned to his right along the wall. He felt greatly cheered at having attained his first objective without mishap, and began to make better progress. His immediate problem was easier now, for the hand-hold provided by the rough rock wall made it possible for him to walk upright and feel his way with his feet. Each step had still to be taken with very great caution, for at any moment there might be nothing to step on, but the physical effort was very much less than when he had been crawling.

He had taken some twenty paces when his left hand, groping for the wall ahead, encountered nothing. He stopped and pondered. Somewhere along this wall should be the tunnel through which they had entered the central chamber. Perhaps this was it. First he groped his way cautiously round the corner of the rock and assured himself that it was really a turning and not just an irregularity. Then he dropped to his knees again and felt his way to the opposite corner. Yes, it was a passage all right, and he had safely negotiated it. As long as he could continue to make steady progress, however slow, he felt that the darkness would not worry him much more than it was doing. A major obstacle, turning his thoughts in again on his meagre hopes of life, might well drive him mad.

Now even greater caution was required, for the precipice could not be very far ahead of him, though at what distance he did not know. The only safe assumption was that the next step was the perilous one. With that thought in his mind, Garve covered a further twenty paces. Then, while his out-flung hand found the rock as usual, his outstretched foot groped in vain for something solid. He had reached the precipice. He listened, and, far, far below he could hear water splashing.

He drew back into safety and again considered his position. From the point he had reached, the edge of the precipice ran to his right until it met the cavern wall again. Near that point was the exit he was seeking. To get there he had to negotiate the whole length of the precipice. That crossing would be full of risks. If he clung to the very edge, with empty space on his immediate left the whole time, and the sound of that faraway stream coming almost from beneath him, he might be seized with vertigo and roll over the edge. It was hardly likely to be a straight line, the edge of this abyss, and there might be deep cracks running inwards to provide additional hazards. On the other hand, if he once left the precipice and attempted to take a parallel course inside the cavern he might well lose it altogether. In the end he decided that the safest course was to make a series of shallow loops, first away from the precipice and then back to it. In this way he would be moving most of the time on solid rock, and could always regain his bearings by keeping to the left till he reached the edge.

The plan involved some loss of time, but otherwise it worked admirably. He was crawling again now, using his hands as before to feel his way. His loops varied considerably, and once he went so far into the cavern without realizing it that it seemed as though he had lost the edge for good. In sudden fright he turned so sharply that on that particular loop he felt that he must actually have lost ground. It was so easy to make a mistake—the slightest variation in the position of the body so altered the angle of movement that the wriggle of a shoulder might double the length of the loop.

At the end of the tenth loop he returned, not to the precipice, but to a rock wall. Working his way along it to the left he came in a few feet to the edge. Somewhere on his right now, and not far away, if Hayson had spoken the truth, was the passage he wanted.

Garve wondered suddenly why Hayson had told him of this exit. It had been unsought information, and seemed to mar the perfection of Hayson's scheme. Garve could not believe that Hayson, who had thought every detail out with such care, would have been so casual in this respect. The only other conclusion was that Hayson had told him deliberately, either because the passage was not an exit at all, and would serve merely to fog him completely, or because it was a particularly dangerous passage. In any event, Garve had come too far now to retrace his steps without a trial of Hayson's tunnel.

At this point it seemed legitimate to use a match. Garve took from his pocket a few old fragments of paper, placed them carefully in a tiny heap and set a light to them. The yellow flame burned clearly if unsteadily, and Garve's pulse leaped with the flames as he saw by their light an opening in the rock wall not three paces to his right, with no pitfall in the way. He watched his bonfire until the last piece of grey ash had ceased to glow and the cavern had become, if anything, darker than before. Quickly, before he had forgotten the direction, he strode to the tunnel. It was so narrow that he could touch both sides at once with his outstretched arms, and down one wall a trickle of water ran. He collected a handful and slaked his thirst. The passage wound in what seemed to be a double S bend, and then both walls ended abruptly in space.

"The smaller chamber," thought Garve. "All right so far."

At once his nostrils became aware of a very faint and subtle scent. It was so faint that, had he been passing hastily through with a torch he might never have noticed it, but his sense of smell was keener through the inaction of his eyes.

The smaller chamber, Hayson had said. How much smaller, Garve had no idea, but he hoped sincerely that there was only one exit from it. In any case, only one course lay open to him—to work round the wall as before, until he came to an opening.

Still proceeding with great caution, he. circled to his left. The shape seemed very irregular, and at one point he negotiated a jutting corner which turned back at an acute angle on the other side. He was just beginning to get worried lest he had turned into a wide tunnel by mistake when his outstretched hand touched something which was not rock. It was rough, and not so cold as the rock. With a feverish excitement which he tried his best to control Garve struck another of his precious matches. Before it flickered out he had seen enough to set his thoughts racing. The chamber was piled high with wooden boxes—and it was the familiar smell of wood sawdust and shavings that he had noticed. Garve ran his fingers along the box nearest to him. It was long, narrow, and not very deep.

"Rifles," he decided. He was not surprised to find the dump—only elated. By every reason of logic it had to be here. Not for anything else would the Arabs have cut that passage from Hezekiah's Tunnel or left traces of their recent comings and goings.

As his hand moved almost affectionately over the box an idea came to him like the flash of inspiration. Hastily groping round on the floor, he found a long lump of rock and weighed it in his hand. Yes, it would do! Using it as a hammer, he struck three blows on the end of the wooden box, which reverberated like the echoes of an explosion through the chamber. The wood split, and he felt the round barrel of the rifle. A few minutes' work sufficed to drag the weapon from its box. As he had suspected, it was wrapped round and round in several layers of tissue paper, and all the metal parts were packed in grease.

"Just as well Hayson *hadn't* explored this chamber," thought Garve. He was actually humming a little tune as he worked in the darkness. In ten minutes he had fashioned himself a flare. A foot long, two inches thick, and soaked in grease, it would burn for a considerable time. Standing well away from the dump, Garve struck a match and carefully applied it to the torch. It caught almost at once, and burned with a strong, smoky yellow light. Garve stuck it in a niche and set to work to break open some more boxes without a moment's delay. In the flickering light he could see that he was really standing in the entrance of a separate chamber, which, from wall to wall, and floor to ceiling, was stacked with boxes. They were all shapes and sizes, and he was pretty sure that machine-guns, bombs, and perhaps even light artillery were concealed in the depths of this vast arsenal. There were enough weapons here to keep a civil war going for a month under Palestine conditions.

Garve finished a fourth flare to his satisfaction, and pushed two of them down the inside of each trouser leg. Then he lifted the first torch from the niche and made his way, in comparative comfort, into the outer chamber. It was, as Hayson had said, quite small, and there was only one exit on its farther side. Now that it was no longer necessary to grope every inch of the way, progress was rapid. Garve noted with satisfaction that the passage descended sharply, and was already beginning to congratulate himself on the miraculousness of his escape when he jerked to a halt on the very edge of a drop. The passage ended, not in a cul-de-sac, but in a chasm. His buoyant spirits sadly deflated, Garve peered over the edge. There was nothing at all to see, except that the drop was sheer. He pushed a rock over. It fell plumb to the bottom in about a second. Thirty feet of unclimbable rock separated him from freedom.

This moment was the bitterest of the whole awful escapade. To be within sight of liberty and yet so utterly incarcerated! He knew now why Hayson had told him of this tunnel. Hayson had imagined him without a light. But for the accident which had given him a torch, he might easily have stumbled over this chasm without suspecting it was there. Even though he had discovered it, he would have been utterly powerless in the dark to negotiate it.

But was he not powerless, even with a light? Garve considered the situation carefully. He knew with certainty that all those boxes and crates of ammunition had come this way. They could have been drawn up by rope without difficulty, but if, as he surmised, Arab terrorists were constantly using this part of the quarries it was hard to believe that they had relied on such an uncertain method of levitation, involving as it did the constant presence of a rope and pulley, and the assistance of several other people. From the top to the bottom of this quarry Garve had gained the impression that it was a well-used Arab thoroughfare, and he could not believe that it really ended so abruptly at this spot.

His torch was burning low, and he lighted a second from it, sticking the first in a niche. By the double light he proceeded to make a thorough examination of his surroundings. Any thought of a descent over the edge was clearly out of the question. On his right the rock wall rose smooth and uncompromising. On the left—ah!

On the left the torch revealed a ledge rising from the side of the tunnel, widening slightly above the chasm, and descending into the darkness on the other side. Garve was getting desperate, and longed above everything, and at whatever cost, to make an end of uncertainty. With the torch in his right hand he crawled up the ledge on his knees and over the peak, keeping his mind with an effort on the contours of the ledge rather than on the depths of the chasm.

The ledge continued to descend, two feet in width, and surprisingly smooth. It was really easy, this descent, once given the torch.

The ledge dropped to a tunnel again, a tunnel of the third level, and Garve stepped into it with the increasing certainty that he had put the worst behind him. He was right. A few paces on and he stood in the amphitheatre that he had entered on his previous visit from Hezekiah's Tunnel. His flare made everything simple. Working round to the left he kept his hand against the wall, crossed the mouth of the passage, regained the wall, and discovered the smooth carvings which had so intrigued him before. The rest was child's play. In a few minutes he was dropping down into Hezekiah's Tunnel and climbing through the slimy stream to the Virgin's Fountain. He was free!

Free! A great exultation surged through him. Free to tell Esther that he loved her, free to save her from Hayson, free to make Hayson pay for his black treachery! Now that Garve had no longer to think of his own safety, a fierce anger shook him. Hayson had intended that he should lie and rot in that stone jail; he had planned it with merciless care to the last detail. An oversight, not a miracle, had saved Garve. Without a light—and a light far more lasting and substantial than matches could provide—he could never have found that last ledge or made his way along it had he found it. For Hayson it had been almost a certainty—and he had lost by a thousand to one chance.

Garve looked at his watch and found that it was just short of midnight. The air was strong and bracing, and the stars had never seemed more beautiful. Even the frightful smell of the Kedron brook seemed homely.

Garve sat on a boulder above the fountain and finished his whisky and sandwiches. He felt astonishingly fit—he would start to worry about the nervous reaction when it came. Then, though the hour was late, he set off without delay to have it out with Hayson.

11. A Warning—and a Precaution

As Garve approached Hayson's house he saw that all its rooms were in complete darkness, while the Willoughbys' home next door was still a blaze of light. It looked very much as though Hayson had returned straight to the Willoughbys. Garve decided to find out.

As he walked noisily up the short drive the door opened and Esther herself looked anxiously out:

"Philip," she cried, and there was such overwhelming relief in her voice that Garve felt repaid for all that he had endured that night. "Philip, you're safe! Oh, thank heaven. *Do* come in. Everyone will be so relieved."

"Quite like the prodigal's return," said Garve, not at all sure of his ground. "It's a bit late for a social call, but I thought I might as well drop in."

"Might as well drop in!" cried Esther indignantly. "I like your casualness, after giving us all the fright of our lives. Why, we were expecting to have to sit up all night for news. You'd better come and give an account of yourself."

Garve followed her into the lounge with an apologetic glance at his muddy trouser bottoms and boots. Willoughby was there, and the faithful Jackson, and Baird from police headquarters. Directly they saw him they all jumped up with various expressions of thankfulness. Willoughby shook him by the hand paternally, Baird poured out a stiff whisky for him, and Jackson regarded him with the sort of benevolent censure which is usually meted out to an erring child. Questions poured in on him from all sides, but he brushed them aside.

"Where's Hayson?" he demanded abruptly.

"No need to worry about him, my boy," said Willoughby soothingly. "He's quite safe. His knowledge of the quarries made it comparatively easy for him to get out. He's taken a search party back to look for you. Baird has lent him a couple of police officers."

"A search party!" Suddenly Garve threw his head back and laughed immoderately.

"Easy there, easy," said Baird, placing a friendly hand on his shoulder. "Here, have another drink. You're all used up." Obviously he thought that Garve was hysterical. "I expect you're famished. What about a sandwich?"

"Thanks," said, Garve. "Forgive me for seeming a bit—confused." He wolfed a couple of sandwiches. "I suppose I hadn't quite expected this sort of reception. Please tell me everything."

"Tell *you* everything," exclaimed Esther. "Why, we're expecting you to tell us. All that's happened at our end is that Hayson came rushing in soon after nine o'clock in a terrible state of mind and said that you were lost in the quarries, and could he have some assistance."

"Was that all he said?"

"He was too upset to talk much. He said that you had insisted on going on with only one torch, and that when that failed he had become separated from you looking for the bulb. He was frightfully concerned about you. He said it was a hundred to one that if you'd wandered away from the exact spot where he left you, nobody would ever be able to find you, and that you'd probably fall down a precipice. He gave us the impression that the chance of your getting out alive was pretty remote. We've been worrying ourselves sick."

"Too bad," said Garve sympathetically. "Did he—er—blame me for the accident?"

"He thought you'd been unnecessarily rash—and when we heard his story, so did we. I should say it's you who need a nurse—not I. Every time you go out you get into some sort of trouble. It would almost have served you right if he'd left you in the quarries."

Garve started to laugh again helplessly. The irony of the situation was *too* rich. Of course, he might have expected this. It rounded off and perfected Hayson's plan. Indeed, it was an essential part of it. If Hayson had simply come back and said nothing, and *then* Garve had turned up, the task of explanation would have been extremely awkward. Hayson had had to cover himself against the odd chance, and he was doing it with supreme artistry. When eventually the search party returned to report failure, they would be full of admiration for Hayson's tireless persistence. They would describe, with corroborative detail, how Hayson had insisted on exploring the most dangerous places himself, how he had led the way continuously, how he had become more and more depressed as their shouts drew no response. Garve could imagine just how it would happen. At no time would Hayson be running any risk—he knew the quarries so well, and he would take the policemen round and round and up and down, well away from the only place that mattered, until they were utterly confused and exhausted. Next day, no doubt, he would have insisted on going down again, until obliged to report in the end that there was no trace of his friend, who had undoubtedly perished over one of the many precipices. And every one would think he had behaved splendidly, and Esther would be touched by his devotion. Or alternatively, if, as was actually to happen, he returned and learned that Garve was alive and well, he would express his joy, and in everyone's eyes Garve would be under an obligation to him.

For the moment Garve realized that he was beaten. All along the line Hayson had been too clever for him. If he denounced the man now, nobody would believe him. They would demand evidence, and he could produce none. They would think he was the subject of delusions, and his reputation in Jerusalem would be ruined. Already, they obviously felt that he had treated Hayson inconsiderately, and that he had been insufficiently impressed by the speedy and selfless way in which the search party had been organized.

He slowly filled his pipe. "I guess I owe you all an apology for scaring you," he said awkwardly. "I seem to have caused a lot of trouble."

"All's well that ends well," said Baird tritely. "What we want to know now is how you got out."

"It was just a question of patience," said Garve. "I fumbled my way along in the dark and was lucky." Briefly he gave them a summary of his adventures, omitting much detail. He yawned. "I'll tell you more about it to-morrow."

"I'll keep you to that promise, if nobody else does," said Baird. "And while you're here, I've got a bone to pick with you."

Garve sighed. "Well, what have I done now?"

"That body in Hezekiah's Tunnel!"

Garve sat up sharply. "I told you to keep that to yourself, Baird. Have you no sense, man?"

"I would have done," retorted Baird, "if it had been there."

"Oh lord!" said Garve, sinking back, "don't tell me that's been spirited away too."

"There wasn't a trace of it. My men went through that tunnel with a fine-tooth comb. They had a devil of a time. They even dragged the pools. They found nothing at all—not a trace of a body, not a lamp, not a knife—nothing."

"So what?" said Garve. "Are you accusing me of faking the whole story?"

"No, I'm not," said Baird, though his words carried no conviction. "I admit I'm puzzled and disturbed. Mind you, if I didn't know you as well as I do, I would say that you'd gone potty, and were letting your journalistic imagination run away with you. First you report an ammunition dump, and when we look for it, it's gone. Then you say a man has been killed in a place that no sane man—no one but a reporter—would ever visit, and *that's* gone. I suppose it's just coincidence, but there's something very fishy about the whole business, and I can't pretend to understand it."

Garve gazed round the assembled company. Bewilderment was on every face, and Esther was staring moodily at the floor.

"Well, folks," said Garve, rising, "there are plenty of things that I'm puzzled about myself, and the body's one of them. Somebody must have fetched it out, but I can't imagine who. For the rest, there are a lot of things that I can't explain to you at the moment, and, if I did, you wouldn't believe me. I feel like a bad boy who's just had a kick in the pants, and the sooner I get home to bed the better."

"I think you're right, Garve," agreed Willoughby, rising. "You mustn't misunderstand us—personally I'm utterly and completely at sea about a number of things, but I'm not criticizing, and I don't think Baird is. We're all a bit overwrought with this adventure to-night. If you'll forgive my saying so, you've behaved—well, a bit queerly about it. Hayson's a good fellow, and you don't seem very grateful. After all, at this moment he's taking big risks for you. However, that's your affair. We're glad you're safe, and I suggest you get a good night's sleep. I think we'll turn in too. Hayson said he probably wouldn't be back till morning."

"I bet he won't," said Garve, fuming inwardly. In exasperation he turned to the policeman. "Look here, Baird, I'm pretty tired, but I'll make you an offer. Get a couple of torches from headquarters and I'll take you right now to the biggest ammunition dump you've ever set eyes on inside Palestine. What do you say?"

Baird patted his shoulder. "Get to bed, old man. You've overdone it. Get to bed, and tell me all about it in the morning."

Garve shrugged. "Please yourself. If it blows up before to-morrow don't blame me. Well, goodnight all."

Esther accompanied him to the door and looked hard into his face, which was drawn with lines of tiredness. For the first time she seemed to realize there was more on his mind than he cared to disclose.

"There's something you're keeping back, Philip, isn't there? Your strange behaviour—it's so unlike you. Why were you so puzzled that we were expecting you? Why were you so unpleasant about Hayson? Oh! I wish I could understand."

Her glance was so full of sympathy and concern that Garve wished he could take her in his arms and comfort her. "Please don't worry," he said gently. "There's nothing wrong with me—either mentally or physically. Curious things are happening in Jerusalem, and I'm in the thick of them. I don't understand the puzzle any more than you do yet, but I'm convinced the solution isn't very far off. Listen—you've not forgotten that you're coming swimming with me, have you?"

"Of course not," said Esther softly. She looked very cool and sweet in the moonlight. "I've been thinking of it all evening—it seemed that it was an appointment you might never be able to keep."

"You're a darling," said Garve breathlessly. "Forgive me, but you *are*. I think if it hadn't been for you I should never have escaped from that quarry to-day. You were my objective, my lodestar, you . . ."

"Perhaps you *had* better go home," observed Esther demurely, "else you may say something you'll be sorry about afterwards. And—thank you for keeping Hayson occupied. I *did* go to bed as you told me, but I had to get up again when I heard you were missing. I feel much better, though." She gave him a sweet smile, with nothing of coquetry in it, and his heart beat high with happiness.

"I'll be round for dinner, if I don't see you before. Good-night, Esther."

"Good-night," she murmured, and gave his big hand a friendly squeeze. "Sleep well."

Garve breakfasted in his room the following morning. He was just filling an after-breakfast pipe and recalling with a warm glow of satisfaction the picture of Esther in the moonlight when there was a knock on his door and a servant entered.

"A Mr. Hayson to see you, sir."

"Indeed," said Garve. "Show him up."

His face was a mask as Hayson's quiet steps sounded in the corridor. What devilry was the man up to now? He took his revolver from his pocket and began toying with it conspicuously as a shadow fell across the threshold.

"Come in, Hayson, and shut the door," called Garve.

Hayson came in. His sombre eyes were heavy with fatigue and his shoulders drooped. "I've just got back from the quarries," he began. "I learned at police headquarters that you were safe——"

"And came round at once to find out what I'd been saying about

106

you!" Garve's finger crooked menacingly round the trigger of his gun. "Upon my soul, Hayson, you have the most colossal effrontery."

"I don't understand you," said Hayson; "and for heaven's sake stop fooling with that revolver."

"Now listen to me," said Garve impatiently. "I don't doubt that it suits your game to come round here to-day. People would think it funny if you didn't, and it would be so much better, wouldn't it, if your account of our adventure could be made to square with mine. But I want you to realize that I know you did your best to kill me last night. We both understand why, so there's no need to talk about that. You were devilishly clever about it, and you covered all your tracks. You'll have no difficulty in making people believe that it was all an accident. I'm levelling no public accusations against you, but in private I may as well tell you right now that I regard you as a murderer and a criminal. If you came here with the idea of talking me round and persuading me of your innocence, you can save your breath. Your glib tongue will never influence me again. As far as I'm concerned, you're just a common cut-throat who ought to be hanging this moment from a gallows. Now is that plain?"

"If your courtesy were as great as your clarity," said Hayson, who had been listening to this speech with astonishing impassivity, "we should have less cause to quarrel."

"Courtesy!" said Garve contemptuously. "Good God, man, stop this play-acting. I can't believe you were ever such a fool as to expect a friendly reception from me to-day. I would as soon show courtesy to a snake. Have you any idea what it feels like to be left alone in a great labyrinth of a cave? Have you any idea of the night of exquisite mental torture to which you deliberately condemned me? Do you know how the imagination works in the darkness, what it feels like to contemplate slow starvation, what agony the mind suffers when it is balancing on the edge of insanity? Perhaps you do know—perhaps the realization of what was in store for me increased your satisfaction?"

Hayson sighed. "Of course, if you insist on taking this absurd and melodramatic attitude, I can do nothing. He spoke still with a studied mildness. "I can only repeat that there is no vestige of truth in your accusation."

Garve gave an exclamation of disgust. "You're wasting your time, man. Don't tell *me* you lost your way. You must have legged it for all you were worth to reach the Willoughby house soon after nine. You simply gave me the slip and bolted."

"Very well, have it your own way." said Hayson, "but remember, I deny it absolutely. For your own sake, I trust you won't repeat the ridiculous lie to any third person—or I warn you, there'll be trouble."

"Ah," said Garve, "so that's why you came here. You don't want me to let 'any third person' know what a swine you are? Well, I'm making no promises. You can rest assured, however, that anything I can do to make your life more difficult I shall do with the greatest pleasure. When I think how completely you're getting away with this it makes me writhe. If I'd had any sense I should have shot you like a dog in the quarry."

Hayson's smile was deadly. "You seem to overlook the fact that, if I had intended to kill you before, your attitude now would greatly increase my determination not to fail a second time. It is fortunate for you that I have a clear conscience and am not afraid that you could ever substantiate your ridiculous charge."

"I prefer not to rely on your conscience," said Garve. "If your last remark was intended as a threat, it leaves me cold. You won't catch me napping again."

Hayson yawned ostentatiously. "I find your self-confidence wearisome. All the same, if it isn't troubling you too much, I *should* like to know how you succeeded in getting out."

Garve smiled. "I expect you would. Yes, on second thoughts, I'm certain you would. Well, you know the phrase the politicians use, 'I explored every avenue and left no stone unturned.'"

"It must have taken you a long time," said Hayson thoughtfully. "Oh, incidentally, you might care to know that I found no sign of your ammunition dump on my return journey. I'm afraid that was just another of your delusions. As a matter of fact, I told the Willoughbys when I got back last night that I was a little worried about the way you had behaved in the cave. About your mental condition, I mean. This constant search for non-existent things is a bad sign, Garve—I'm not sure you haven't been overdoing it in Jerusalem."

"Go on," said Garve curiously; "what do you suggest?"

"Well, it's not my business, of course, but it seems to me that you've made some bad blunders since you've been here. You nearly got Miss Willoughby killed, for instance. Then you thought you were being very clever finding that first ammunition dump, but the Arabs had the last laugh. In Hezekiah's Tunnel you were beaten up, and in the quarries you escaped by a miracle. The fruit of all your feverish activity is precisely nothing. If there *is* an Arab plot in Jerusalem, which I doubt, you're as far from exposing it as ever. If you left Jerusalem you would hardly be leaving the scene of your trimphs, would you? And once you were away you would no longer be troubled with a delusion that I was trying to kill you. Nor would you be leading Miss Willoughby into danger. For instance—again it's not my concern—but you propose to-night to take Miss Willoughby on a little excursion. You know, Garve, I shouldn't if I were you. That road to the Dead Sea is excessively dangerous, as I've told you already. You remember, of course, the man who 'went down from Jerusalem to Jericho—and fell among thieves'? It's a dreadful reflection on our civilization, but there are still thieves on that road. Take my advice, and in your own interests leave Jerusalem to-night, and don't come back."

Garve stared for a moment at Hayson's smouldering eyes, and then laughed in his face. "It just won't work, Hayson. You've no influence over me. No doubt you would be delighted if I cleared out and left you in possession of an unchallenged field. You'll be disappointed to learn that *nothing* could persuade me to leave at this juncture. And now, do you mind taking yourself off? I'm sure we both understand each other perfectly." He rose and waved his gun towards the door. "Good-bye."

"Good-bye," said Hayson jauntily. "Oh, by the way, I'll have your torch sent round to you. You may need it."

"Thanks," said Garve. "You might send the bulb which you took out as well." With which Parthian shot he nodded abruptly and quietly shut the door on Hayson's back.

A little later he walked down to police headquarters in a very thoughtful frame of mind. Baird gave him a cheery "Good-morning" and a grin.

"Feeling better?" he asked. "By jove, you certainly were rocking on your feet last night."

"I'm grand," said Garve, "and cleared for action! Any news? Any cables? Any money?"

"Nothing, old man. Your paper has forgotten you, and the Arabs are quiet. It looks as though the trouble is going to blow over for the time being."

"I bet the Jews don't think so," said Garve. "Their Defence Force has never been more active, and their farm colonies are simply bristling with arms. They're standing-to for a first-class civil war. By the way, do you want to see that arms dump?"

Baird's blue eyes opened wide. "Why, man, you weren't serious, were you?"

"Of course I was serious."

Baird still looked sceptical. "You're quite sure you're not pulling my leg? I don't want to march all over Jerusalem in the heat of the day for another 'disappearance.'"

"I can understand your attitude, Baird, but this is different. It was too big a dump to move. I'll swear on oath that you'll have the surprise of your life. Come on, it's your duty to investigate."

Baird shrugged. "Well, it's your last chance. What do we need?"

"Two good torches, thigh boots, and a couple of policemen for escort."

Baird looked at him sharply. "Getting the wind up, eh? Think things are going to happen?"

"I'm damn sure something terrific's going to happen almost at once, but it's only a hunch, and I've no evidence. Let's get going."

The sun blazed on the stones and dust of the track as the little party wound its way down to the Virgin's Fountain. Garve was beginning to feel at home in this particular stretch of country, and as they approached the fountain his quick eye noted a solitary Arab figure slipping away down the hill with tremendous agility.

"See!" He touched Baird's arm lightly and pointed. "There's a watch on the tunnel. That means that the Arabs know I was in there last night, and guess I've discovered the dump."

"How *should* they know?" asked Baird.

"Maybe they were watching and saw us go in. I imagine the finding of this dump will make them speed up their plans, too. They know we can't blow it up, because it would blow up half the city, but they'll expect us to start moving it."

"You almost convince me that it exists," said Baird with a grin. "Anyway, here's the tunnel."

Garve led the way quite at ease now, while the two policemen followed less happily, and with constant exclamations and smothered curses. They negotiated the climb from the tunnel without difficulty, boldly crossed the chamber of the figured walls, and soon reached the point at which the narrow ledge had to be negotiated which took them up to the next level and the dump.

"Do I have to crawl up that?" asked Baird, aghast.

"I'm afraid so. It's not so bad as it looks. I crawled down it last night with a home-made torch."

They left the two other men at the bottom and reached the second level without mishap. Garve advanced with confidence, for the police torches illuminated their whole surroundings with a brilliant light, and in a few moments they stood in the antechamber before the pile of boxes.

"There you are," said Garve with the triumphant air of a showman who has just brought off a difficult trick.

Baird whistled softly and began poking about. "Rifes," he said, "rifles and machine-guns. Ammunition. Shells. Looks as though there are some field-gun parts up there."

He climbed excitedly over the towering heap of boxes, examining and exclaiming. From the depths of the antechamber he suddenly gave a startled shout.

"What's up?" asked Garve.

"There's all the devilry of war up here," called Baird. "Flame throwers, man—three of them—and a whole lot of gas containers. It's stupendous."

"I know," said Garve complacently as Baird climbed down again with excitement blazing in his eyes.

Baird slapped him so heartily on the shoulder that Garve winced. "I take back all that I ever said and thought about you," he declared sweepingly.

"It was forgivable," said Garve with a broad grin.

The two policemen were left to watch the tunnel mouth pending the arrival of reinforcements, while Baird and Garve returned to police headquarters. Baird could hardly hide his jubilation.

"It looks as though you were right about an impending revolt, Garve. They wouldn't have accumulated all this stuff without a special objective. Let's hope we've crippled the plan by finding it."

"I wouldn't be sure about that," Garve urged him. "You know as well as I do that they've got heaps of other dumps—smaller, no doubt, but dangerous enough. I hear there are more troops on the way from England. When do they arrive?"

"In three days' time—at Haifa."

"Then if the Arabs have any sense they'll spring their mine in the next forty-eight hours. Our finding the dump will push their plans forward, anyway, because they'll know we shall start to move the stuff. I should say if we can get safely past the day after to-morrow the plot will fail."

"The day after to-morrow," said Baird, "is Mahomet's birthday. There'll be celebrations all over the country."

"They may be able to celebrate the liberation of Palestine," said Garve grimly. "They're just on their toes to drive us and the Jews into the sea, and, frankly, I can't blame them. I'd feel that way if I were an Arab."

"You'd soon see the inside of the concentration camp at Auja el Hafir," said Baird with a grin.

Garve snorted. "You policemen are sometimes devilish unimaginative—though, I suppose, you're satisfied as long as you carry out instructions. Personally, I think it's sheer lunacy to try and stamp out nationalism by putting agitators behind barbed wire.

If we did it in England there'd be shouts of 'Hitlerism' right away, but Palestine is a long way from London, and I suppose it doesn't count." He hesitated. "By the way, I imagine you'll get some credit for to-day's discovery."

"I shouldn't be surprised," said Baird, a shade embarrassed. "I know it's your find——"

"You misunderstand me," broke in Garve quickly. "You're more than welcome, and I'll give you all the publicity I can when I write my stuff. I was merely wondering if you'd give me a little extra assistance in return."

"You bet I will," said Baird cordially. "What do you want—loan of a fiver, a shut-down on the other pressmen, or a free ticket for the police concert?"

"I'm taking a young woman for a trip to the Dead Sea to-night," said Garve.

Baird grinned. "Naughty, naughty! Well, any assistance I can render? I can't say I've ever chaperoned a newspaper man before, but——'

"Don't be an ass. I want an armoured car."

Baird stopped suddenly and stared. "You're pulling my leg again!"

"No, I'm serious. That car you used at Beersheba with the machine-guns fore and aft. Can you spare it?"

"Say, what's the idea. Are you going to start a riot at Jericho?"

"I won't, but someone else might. It's just a precaution. If it's not wanted, you won't have exceeded your duty, and if it is, you'll come in for another pat on the back. What do you say?"

"I reckon you know something," said Baird slowly. "It's carrying police protection rather far, but the car's got wireless, and if it's needed back here I can always recall it. You couldn't, I suppose, cancel the trip?" He gave Garve an ironic glance.

"'Fraid not," said Garve. "The fate of something far more important than Palestine may hang on it."

Baird chuckled. "I wish you luck. She's a charming girl. Well, what's the plan?"

"I'll be leaving Damascus Gate sharp at nine. I suggest your car picks up my trail where we turn into the Jericho road, and follows us at a distance of not more than a quarter of a mile. I shan't speed. You might tell your men to park themselves at a tactful distance when we get to the Dead Sea. We'll be leaving about midnight, and I'll give three loud honks just before we set off. O.K.?"

"I'll see to it," said Baird.

"You're a sport." They stopped outside headquarters. "By the way, that police concert—what's it for?"

"Raising funds for police widows and orphans," said Baird.

Garve nodded. "if you get an anonymous gift of twenty pounds, don't ask where it came from."

"Not me," said Baird wickedly. "I know where it'll come from."

"Oh?" said Garve.

"Office of the *Morning Call*, London, charged to 'Special inquiries.' I reckon you're going to pop the most expensive question any newspaper man ever asked!"

He ducked to avoid Garve's fist, grinned broadly, and vanished into the police station.

12. Dead Sea Interlude

Almost on the tick of nine Garve's powerful Ford drew away from Damascus Gate. It was a car which he rarely bothered to use when he was pottering about Jerusalem, but found invaluable when big "stories" broke in other parts of Palestine. He had once got ninety out of it, but the opportunity for real speeding did not often occur on Palestine roads, except in the plains. Esther sat beside him, looking demure and good. They had just finished a very pleasant *tête-à-tête* dinner, admirably prepared and served by the Willoughbys' Arab cook, and both she and Garve were cheerful to the point of exhilaration. If a shadow occasionally crossed Garve's face as his thoughts swung back to more serious matters, it was too fleeting for Esther to notice. Both of them were bent on enjoying themselves and achieving the object of their trip, as the abbreviated swim suit and more abbreviated slips in the back of the car testified. Esther had already tasted some of the keen delights of anticipation, for during their leisurely dinner Garve had whetted her appetite with a description of the route.

"It's a pity in a way that you won't see it in the daytime," he said as the car moved off. "You'll miss the colours—but it's almost equally beautiful by moonlight."

"It could hardly be more beautiful than it is now. I've never seen any country look so *washed* by the moon before." Esther gave a little ecstatic shiver—or was she cold? Garve's left hand drew her wrap a shade more closely round her shoulders, and returned without lingering to the driving-wheel.

"I'm not really cold," said Esther, "only tremendously excited. I apologize for being so schoolgirlish. I think it's because we've been waiting for this ride for so many nights, and I'm keyed up."

"That's fine," said Garve encouragingly. "By God, I feel the same—I'd like to stamp on the old accelerator in sheer high spirits and go shooting down to Jordan in a streak of speed. But it wouldn't do. See, this is where we turn left into the Jericho road."

His gaze, however, was to the right. A hundred yards or so away the sidelights of a stationary car were visible. Garve pressed his electric horn three times, and as he swung left, the stationary car moved off and slowly gathered speed.

"First stop, Dead Sea," he observed happily. "You know, I love this road. I've heard people say it terrifies them, and I've heard them describe the Jordan Valley as obscene and macabre, but I get a colossal kick out of it—probably because it's such a freak of nature. I don't suppose there's another place in the world where a mountain 2,300 feet high and a rift in the earth 1,300 feet deep can be found so nearly side by side."

Headlights suddenly flashed through the back window panel on to the windscreen, and Garve pulled down the blind.

"It looks as though we're going to have company," said Esther.

"It may be a police patrol," Garve told her, anxious that her evening should not be marred by any uneasiness. "In a normal year there would be a whole procession of cars with tourists running down for a midnight bathe. Now even the Arab bus has been cancelled. That's an experience, if you like—being driven down here in a bus. They hardly ever have an accident, but they habitually tear round corners as though the road were straight. They know every bend, though there must be thousands of them."

The car was gliding along at a steady thirty, and presently one or two lights glimmered away on the right.

"Bethany," said Garve. "It was near here that I found the ammunition dump which disappeared so mysteriously."

The road descended steadily in an interminable succession of loops and bends, a winding pass through the barren mountains of Judea. Continually the powerful headlights revealed ahead a great wail of parched rock, and it seemed that the road must end there, but always at the last moment it dipped and swung back to the right or to the left with startling unexpectedness. The great moon, now rising ahead of them, bathed the whole landscape in an unearthly silver light, so that even by night its dreadful sterility and tortured contours became clear.

"It's a brigands' playground," Garve declared. "These twisted hills are eaten out with caves which only the Arabs know. It's the real Biblical wilderness. See how the mountain slopes are littered with chips and boulders—just like the Kedron Valley, only worse."

"I'll listen to no harsh names about it," said Esther softly. "It's terrible enough, but it's so beautiful. I don't think it could look nearly so marvellous with the sun on it."

"Perhaps not—except when dusk is about to fall and all the hillsides turn a glorious mauve and the boulders throw long shadows. In daytime in the summer, of course, it's too infernally hot to bear. The vegetation, the reptiles, the insects—everything's tropical. The rock gets too hot to touch, and the air is acrid and stifling."

"I can feel it getting warmer now," said Esther, opening wide the window at her side. "There was quite a nip in the air in Jerusalem, but it's velvety here ... I say. What's that?"

Garve stamped on his brake and narrowly missed a small black shape which darted across the road in the path of the car. "Only a mountain goat. Heaven knows what they find to live on. I suppose there *are* tiny patches of tough grass, but I can't recall ever having seen one with the naked eye." He swung the wheel sharply to the right as the road wound away from a ravine between overhanging cliffs. At the top of a slight incline a solitary building stood out against the skyline and a light twinkled in its window.

"The Inn of the Good Samaritan," Garve explained. "I hope my running commentary doesn't bore you. It's the last outpost of civilization till we reach the Dead Sea, unless you count a police box. Are you quite comfortable?"

"Perfectly," said Esther, smiling. Her finely moulded face was joyous with excitement, and Garve could not refrain from turning continually to look at her as the car's ceaseless windings brought the moonbeams to and fro across her.

Now the road seemed to plunge more determinedly into the depths. The way became steeper, the straight stretches briefer, the bends more serpentine. Garve's foot maintained a steady pressure on the brake, while his keen eyes watched for any sign of movement ahead, and took comfort from the faint illumination on the blind behind them.

Esther clung a little dizzily to the side of the car. "Does the road wind downhill *all* the way?" she asked, smiling. "It seems incredible that we haven't reached the bottom. *Is* there a bottom? I feel as though I'm descending into some awful inferno."

Garve chuckled. "I assure you it's a heavenly hell when you reach the water. Remember, we're dropping over four thousand feet. Look—there's a sign you've never seen on a road before!"

As the little white post was picked out by the headlights she read the two words, "SEA LEVEL." She clutched Garve's arm involuntarily. "Do you mind—I won't interfere with the driving. It's such a curious feeling. Below sea-level! Just think—the Mediterranean is washing on the shores of Palestine above our heads. And *still* we go down."

The wind of the car's own movement blew warmly in through the open window. Esther threw her wrap and coat into the back seat and sat comfortably in a neat white blouse with sleeves which left her arms exposed.

"It was nice of you to advise me what to wear," she said primly.

Garve stole an appreciative glance at her and grinned. "So many people overdress," he said.

"Look—we're leaving the mountains."

Esther gazed in silent awe at the landscape which now opened out in front of them. They were dropping into a great plain, drenched in moonlight, and almost at their feet a silver streak of water lay like a drawn sword.

"The Jordan," said Garve tersely. "It looks near, but it's still several miles away. On the right, you'll see the Dead Sea as a tiny lake when we turn the next bend. Across the valley, fifteen miles away, you can just make out the Mountains of Moab. You know—the ones which looked like a lunar landscape from the

Mount of Olives—was it six months ago? Beyond them there's nothing but desert."

For a mile or two the car ran smoothly along the dead flat plain, and then swung right at a junction. To the left a signpost pointed to Jericho.

"Nothing much to see there but ruins and a dark village," said Garve, "though in the daytime it's rather a beautiful oasis in this rocky waste." He pointed ahead. "See the squat building and the wire fence—that's at the head of the Dead Sea—they're commercializing the chemicals from the water. Over to the right here is our destination. Believe it or not, but there's a rather pleasant Lido, where with luck we can get a drink."

The car drew slowly to a halt outside the brightly illuminated restaurant. As it came to rest and Garve switched off his headlights, the rear blind suddenly went dark too. Garve hummed softly to himself—everything was going according to plan.

He walked round the car and opened the door for Esther. Her fingers touched his arm lightly as she climbed out and faced him, hatless and coatless in the warm sub-tropical night. As she tossed the chestnut curls from her face, they shone like a halo, just as they had done on the Mount of Olives. She was very serene and self-possessed, unconscious of his fast-beating pulse.

"Stiff?" he asked, as she stretched herself with an "Ah" of satisfaction.

"A little—but it was worth it. You drive very well, you know—with some people I should have been terrified on that wriggling road. And you hardly bumped me at all."

"It's a good car," said Garve modestly, though, like all drivers, he loved to be praised for his skill.

Esther sniffed. "What's the curious smell?"

"Sulphur. You get used to it, and I believe it's quite healthy. Shall we see if we can raise a drink?"

They walked through the café on to a veranda illuminated with shaded lanterns and furnished with half a dozen round tables and wicker chairs. The Dead Sea lay just ahead of them in limpid motionless glory.

Esther seemed to have lost a little of her composure, and her breath came quickly between slightly parted lips.

"Is it real?" she asked in a voice hardly above a whisper. "Oh, Philip, what an exquisite place. How—how *incredibly* romantic." She stood immobile, basking in the night's loveliness, confident that Garve would say nothing to spoil it. He knew her mood, and watched silently by her side, content. Whatever happened, nobody could ever take from him that peace and beauty that he was sharing with her. It linked them in understanding as no words could do. In the end it was she who stirred first.

"How quiet it is. Is there no life down here at all?"

"Precious little. The water is too salt for fish to live in, and because there are no fish there are no birds. The sea is well named."

"If death were always so beautiful, no-one would ever fear it," said Esther softly.

They turned as the door of the restaurant opened and a young Arab approached them with a greeting. He showed no surprise that they were there, and waited with a friendly smile while they discussed their requirements.

"I'll have a dry Martini," said Esther. She looked curiously at the waiter. "Are you always open to stray visitors?" she asked. "Even this year?"

The Arab smiled and bowed. He was a young man of few words.

"Two dry Martinis," said Garve. "And we're taking a dip afterwards—we'll use your dressing-rooms. That will be all right, won't it?"

Again the Arab nodded and smiled. He departed silently to execute the order.

"They're used to odd people dropping in," said Garve. "Even when there are no tourists the police often come here at night for a swim and a drink when they're off duty. At the height of a normal season, of course, there's music and dancing and a crowd—but it's better like this—don't you agree?"

"Perfection would look tawdry by comparison," said Esther. "You see how I strain my speech to let you know how happy I am."

"I'm glad," said Garve simply. "I hope with all my heart that it will be a memorable night for both of us." Words crowded in on his tongue—hot passionate words—all those words of love and admiration which through difficult days and nights now he had stored away in his mind. Not yet! not yet! he told himself. Impatience would spoil everything. Romantic sentimentalist he might be, but he wanted this night to be a flawless one.

Speech seemed an offence against nature in such surroundings, yet there was so much that Garve wanted to say and to ask. He knew so little of Esther, and she of him. He only knew that what he had seen of her he loved. Her swiftly changing moods attracted him, though he required no counsellor to tell him there was danger in them too. Who cared?—at least there was life and movement in her, and he had always hated cow-like women. He loved her vitality, her small imperiousness, and the way she suddenly melted and relied upon him. She was wholly feminine, and never tried to conceal her womanliness. Queer that he should have lived so long and loved so little. Queer that he had never before met a woman who seemed just right. He felt proud to be with her—proud that she could sit so contentedly alone with him and want nothing but his company. He noticed for the hundredth time the proud tilt of her nose, the faintly provocative chin, the passionate mouth which turned inwards and upwards so alluringly at the corners, and sent his heart thumping and galloping about every time he looked at her. Perhaps he was making a fool of himself over her —losing his head over her. Again, who cared? He had often thought it stupid enough to fall in love, but then most men fell in love with such worthless women! Esther was a woman one could give one's soul for, and count it no loss. If one could live with any woman for ever, one could live with Esther. She would make the only possible wife. She would arrest his growing cynicism. With her, how could he ever grow middle-aged—let alone old? She knew how to find and make joy in life, she was adventurous in mind and body. She had spirit and independence.

Of course, he reflected, he was thinking only of his own requirements. How annoyed Esther would be if she could guess what was passing in his mind—if she could realize that he was so calmly weighing up her suitability. Or would she? Was not that the attitude of most males? He tried to put himself in her place. What had *he* to offer *her*? Nothing much in the way of looks, certainly, for he was no Apollo. He had a broad and infectious grin, which always seemed to draw a response from her, though no doubt it made him look fairly inane. He was lean and strong and active enough for any woman—probably too active for most. He could not imagine himself fitting into any quiet domestic scheme of things. His humour was a little mordant, but Esther would mellow it. Life as the wife of a journalist was an uncertain and hazardous adventure for any woman, but no doubt in interest and excitement there were reasonable compensations. And, in any case, marriages didn't generally happen by arrangement—he loved Esther, and if he could make her love him, then, by God! they would marry and chance the consequences.

He caught Esther's glance, quizzical and tender over the top of the glass, in which the moon glistened like a diamond. Hastily he recollected himself.

"I apologize," he said ruefully. "I was being frightfully rude."

"I like watching you when you're thinking," she said, "but I should like it even more if I knew *what* you were thinking."

"May I tell you?"

"I'm all ears."

"Well——" Garve stumbled and could not bring himself to say it. He reflected with a little sinking of the heart that at a time like this a man must always seem a bit stupid in a woman's eyes. He knew that Esther knew that he wanted to ask her to marry him. She was so cool and self-possessed again—friendly enough, yes, even encouraging, and yet ... He cursed silently. No doubt heaps of men had proposed to her. It would be almost a ritual with her now—and he had never proposed to anyone. In the jargon of his trade he felt that he was falling down badly on this assignment. Hundreds of times in almost every conceivable situation he had conducted delicate interviews with triumphant success. Hardly ever had he been at a loss for the right word, the right gesture. That was his job, and he was proud of his craftsmanship. Yet tonight . . .

"What about our swim?" he asked abruptly. "Do you feel like it?"

"I'm in your hands."

"I'll get the towels," said Garve, but to himself he thought, "I wish you were in my arms." He excused himself, and ran back to the car, boyishly eager not to miss a moment of her company.

He was back almost before she had risen from the table, and they walked side by side along the path of planks that led to the empty dressing-rooms. The moon provided all the light that was necessary.

Garve pushed open one of the little wooden doors. "There you are," he said, "complete with shower, which you'll find a boon after the dip, to get the salt away. See you by the water in three minutes."

He walked away, humming softly, but Esther called him back. "Do you mind if I have my swim suit?" she asked, wickedly demure.

"Oh—sorry," he said, and hastily handed the garment over.

"I know it seems a pity," said Esther, smiling, and the wooden door was gently closed upon him.

"You're a little devil," Garve called over the top of the door, but he only evoked a gay laugh in response.

He marched with resounding footsteps along the bare wooden passage to the far end, nearest the sea, and began to undress in another of the tiny cubicles. He felt proud of his well-developed body as it shone naked in the brilliant moonbeams which struck through cracks in the wood. On such a night, in such a climate, it seemed a crime to cover it up. He was thankful that he had only to put on slips—that it was unnecessary for him to do as Esther must do, and imprison rippling muscles and silky skin in dead wool.

He found her waiting for him, sitting on the wooden step which led down to the salt-stained shingle and the sea. The warm night air was almost motionless, and, when it faintly stirred, its touch was a caress.

He sat down beside her on the step and let his left arm fall lightly round her bare shoulder. Her slight movement was towards him rather than away, and as she turned his other arm slipped round her too. Passion gripped him, and suddenly he bent and pressed his lips to her mouth. For a moment she lay quietly there while he kissed her, and then her own white arms crept round his neck with a little sigh and she kissed him with an ardour equal to his own. Motionless they clung together in the moonlight, their almost unclothed bodies strained together, their hearts beating sledge-hammer blows.

Esther stirred and took her lips away, but her head remained on Garve's shoulder, and his strong, tender arms still gathered her to him. Her eyes shone with vivid happiness.

"I've been wanting you to do that all the evening," she whispered. "Oh, so badly."

"I wish you'd told me," said Garve foolishly, "because it would have been no trouble to do it before."

Esther's mouth turned up at the corners in one of her own specially mischievous smiles. "You needn't sound as though you're being obliging, anyway. I know I've been a dreadfully forward hussy, but you really did seem to need a surprising amount of encouragement."

"Only because it was you," said Garve, who was still struggling back from heaven.

"You mean if it had been anyone else you would have done it without difficulty and without encouragement."

"You know I don't mean anything of the sort. The mere thought of kissing any woman but you revolts me. I've been fumbling about so stupidly all evening, because—well, because I—I love you, my darling—because I love you so much that I've become quite unusually humble and lost all my self-possession. Esther, sweetheart, tell me you're not just flirting with me. Can I believe what your lips tell me? I'm deadly serious, Esther—I've fallen so completely and indescribably in love with you. I want to marry you and have you as my wife for ever. I'm just a lunatic about you. I think everything about you is marvellous, even your temper! Every little bit of you is unutterably precious to me—from your marvellous hair to your adorably pink toenails. Esther darling, you're not laughing at me?"

"No, no," she cried, and passionately sought his lips again, while on her lashes tears glistened like jewels in the moonlight. "I think I've loved you," she said, rubbing her cheek against his chin, "ever since you were so abominably rude to me the first day we met."

"You deserved it; but although I knew you were spoiled I couldn't dislike you. Sweet darling, tell me again that you love me."

She told him while he covered her mouth and eyes and delicate ears with kisses and caresses.

"And you *will* marry me?"

Esther laughed. "Do you want a promise to-night? I can tell you I love you with an easy mind, but marriage is a horribly complicated thing, and I don't want to be serious yet. Will you make do with my love—just for a little while?"

"Make do!—oh, my sweet, what a phrase to use. If I live to be ninety I shall never hope to know such happiness as this again. I have read of love, and written of it, and made fun of it, but I never dreamed what a revolution it could bring about in one's whole being."

They lay silent for a moment in each other's arms, till Garve said, "I could willingly stay here with you till dawn and after."

Esther smiled. "I know, but we mustn't—I promised father I wouldn't hang about all night. Shall we swim?"

"In a moment," said Garve. "First kiss me once again."

Her lips moved softly, moistly, under his, and her small hand lay flat on his bare chest. His right hand tenderly caressed her body, and as it found the shapely contour of her firm, round breast, she gave a little shiver and clung closer.

"Oh, Philip Garve, I love you so," she breathed in an ecstasy of happiness, and he knew then that he could do anything with her. But not to-night—not for the world would he give her cause for the faintest tinge of regret.

He dragged himself away from her and ran quickly down to the sea, so that she should not notice how much he desired her. He waded in, the water lapping warmly at his waist, and turned to watch her. She stood on the tideless verge, where the pebbles glistened with salt crystals, and he saw for the first time the perfection of her figure. Truly, nature had been gracious to her, for her head alone would have given her distinction, with its bunch of red-brown curls, its proud carriage, its sweet features—and there she was, with a body as well that any woman would envy or any man covet—firmly proportioned with its slim waist and wide hips, and poised with the dignity and grace of a young goddess.

She looked a little dubiously at the viscous water, smooth as silk and strongly sulphurous. Gingerly she dipped her foot in it and watched the powdery layer of salt spread over it as it dried.

"Come on in," Garve called. "It's marvellous." He came to meet her, and took her back with him.

"You must be careful," he said. "It's almost impossible to swim in it, and if you get a spot in your eye it will make you shout. The best way is to treat it simply as a bed, and lie on it."

"What fun!" cried Esther exultantly. She lay back on the water and gazed up at the moon. Her head rested on the salt-laden liquid as on a cushion; her body was half out of the water, her feet would not sink. Garve, floating beside her, took her hand.

"You could go to sleep like this," he said, "and take no harm."

"I'm going to try to swim," said Esther, with a flicker of her old stubbornness. She turned over with an effort and a splash, the heavy beads of brine falling from her naked shoulders like quicksilver. She struggled and began to laugh. To keep one's legs in the water was like trying to hold down a balloon. She splashed helplessly and ineffectively on the surface for some minutes, and then got a little in her mouth and choked.

Garve drifted over, paddling gently, and patted her back. "I like to see you tasting a new experience," he said with a grin.

"It's beastly," said Esther, still spluttering. "Like sulphuric acid."

"I know," said Garve, sympathizing in a useless sort of way. "The hills round here are full of salt, and they're gradually being washed down into the sea." He floated idly away and back again. "Feeling better?"

"Not noticeably. Let's go ashore and have another drink."

"That suits me," said Garve. They waded out and ran for their towels. It was so warm that they decided to have their drinks before they dressed.

Garve went off with a towel round his shoulders, and returned quickly with two glasses of amber liquid on a tray. Esther swallowed a mouthful and gave a long sigh.

"That's better." She leaned against the wooden doorpost and stared up at the moon.

"Tired?" asked Garve.

"Not a bit; but I think the moon's gone to my head a little. Have I said a lot of *very* foolish things to-night?"

"Nothing you need regret. Nobody's taken a shorthand note of them, and they'll never be called in evidence against you—if you want to change your mind."

Esther sat down beside him on the wooden step and began to stroke the back of his hand. "You're such a dear, aren't you—so kind and calm and philosophical. I shan't change my mind, Philip—I know that I love you, and I just couldn't do without you now." She pointed suddenly to the water. "The moon's sinking—look, it's made a silver bridge across the sea. Where do you think it leads to?"

"If the stories are true," said Garve unromantically, "it leads to Sodom and Gomorrah, which are supposed to be buried at the bottom. The water is frightfully deep; I once talked to an R.A.F. man who swore he'd seen the ruins plainly from ten thousand feet."

"It would be fun to walk on it, anyway," said Esther. "It looks so solid—do you think it would bear my weight if I ran across it quickly enough."

Garve's fingers gently ruffled her hair. "You're not much of a burden, my dear, but you'd need the agility of a fire walker."

Esther continued to regard the water speculatively. "Do you know what I'd like to do, Philip? Something quite dreadful."

"Put a little in a bottle and take it home," said Garve promptly.

Esther laughed. "Nothing so proper." She wiggled her bare toes. "I should like to have a last swim with nothing on."

"You're not drunk, are you?" asked Garve anxiously.

"Sober as a high court judge," Esther assured him. "Wouldn't it be lovely, though? I've always longed to swim naked in moonlit water, but somehow the opportunity has never occured."

"Little sensualist!" said Garve. "But I share your longing. Clothes in water are really a very fatuous concession to modesty. "What do you propose to do about it? I'm willing to do anything gentlemanly to assist within reason."

"Would it be an awful effort to shut your eyes? It sounds very silly, I know, but I don't think I'm brazen enough——"

"It would be an effort," said Garve solemnly. "If I had my old school tie I'd bandage my eyes with it. I'll tell you what. I'll turn round while I count twenty, like this—one—two—three—four . . . By that time you should be in the water. But I warn you I shall look at twenty!"

"I'll bet you will," said Esther wickedly. There was a demon of naughty laughter in her eyes. "Mind you don't fracture a vertebra turning your head. What happens after that?"

"Then *you* close your eyes while *you* count twenty-five," said Garve, "and I'll join you in the water."

"Why do I have to count twenty-five? You've less to take off."

"You're more impetuous and you'll count faster."

"You flatter yourself, sir. Anyway, I shan't peep. Are you ready? Then count."

She dropped a kiss lightly on the point of his chin and ran gaily down to the water. Garve controlled his head but failed to curb his imagination. In a second her swim suit lay on the stones, and she was wading out along the silver bridge, her slim white body a diminishing divinity.

Across the water she heard Garve's voice counting with a little curl of laughter. "Eighteen, nineteen, twenty. I'm coming."

"Wait," cried Esther in sudden panic. She was bobbing about in the heavy water like a cork. "Please, Philip, don't come. Please, Philip, I'd forgotten this water was so buoyant. It's quite impossible to get into it."

"A bargain's a bargain," Garve teased her.

"You're to go away at once. I shall hate you for ever if you don't. Do you hear?"

Garve chuckled. "At last you've found a place where you can't stamp your foot. Now, listen, young woman. I think you're treating me abominably, but I'm willing to negotiate a fair and honourable settlement. I'll go away—at a price."

"What price?" asked Esther.

"Forty kisses—to be given before midnight."

"You make them last so long," Esther protested. "And it's eleven now. There wouldn't be time. Won't you make it twenty?"

"All right, Lady Godiva." Garve moved off cheerfully. "I'm going to dress—though there's thousands as wouldn't."

He walked, whistling, back to his cubicle, and turned on the shower.

13. The Ambush

It was much darker when Esther again joined Garve. The moon was sinking behind the high hills, and though the stars were slowly coming into their own, they provided only a faint illumination. With the passing of the moon some of the romantic zest went out of the night, and sombre thoughts began to creep back into Garve's mind. As he struck a match for Esther's cigarette and noted once again the firm beauty of her features by its light, a sudden fear for her safety in the days to come shot through him like a pang of physical pain.

She rallied him. "Too tired to claim your forfeit, Mr. Sobersides? I always like to pay my debts, you know."

His arm stole gently round her and he kissed her with infinite tenderness, as though she were his child. "When you're away I start to think," he said. "I wish you were on a boat for England."

"I should love it—if you were there too."

Garve sighed. "When this job's finished, I will be—with luck. We'll be homeward bound together; but who knows what will happen before then? If I thought I could persuade your father to send you back at once——"

"You couldn't, and, anyway, I'm not a parcel to be sent home carriage paid. You know, I wouldn't go. If, as you're so certain, there's danger for us all, I'll be happier sharing it with you. But you may still be wrong. Tell me, Philip, now that we've started being serious, what happened in the quarries last night?"

"Hayson tried to kill me because he's in love with you himself," said Garve. "He arranged everything so that I should get lost."

Briefly he told her some of the things which hitherto he had told no-one, and she listened in rapt and silent horror.

"Murder!"she breathed, as though she could still hardly believe it. "Cold-blooded murder. And yet—he's like that—he has it in him—I've felt all the time that there was something ruthless and cruel about him."

"Go on believing that," Garve beseeched her. "Don't ever put yourself in the position where he can be alone with you. It won't be for long—I swear we shall all be out of this—or dead—before many days are past. But until we are, be careful, sweetheart."

Esther gave a little shiver. "He frightens me as no one ever has done. He's so intense. Oh, Philip, to think that I once admired him!"

"I have had moments," said Garve, "when I could not help admiring him myself. He has personality—terrific personality—and there is something admirable in that alone—yes, even when it has a criminal twist. I still can't understand him—I find it easy enough to believe that he could do murder, but somehow, not murder from mere jealousy. Have you ever noticed the shape of his head? It's the head of an idealist, not a criminal. But phrenology is an uncertain science, and he's obviously got the wrong stuff under his bumps."

Garve glanced at his watch and scrambled to his feet. "The time has come, the walrus said' . . . It's ten to twelve, and we must go." He kissed her again. "Thank you for the most heavenly night of my life."

Esther clung to him. "You kissed me as though —as though you were saying good-bye. Oh, Philip, take care of yourself too. You run such risks—and your life is worth so much more to me than to your old newspaper. There's always Jackson to look after me and father, but there's no-one to look after you."

Garve grinned. "There's a providence that watches over newspaper men," he said. "Come on—we're getting morbid."

He paid the bill as they passed through the café, and left a liberal tip for the still smiling waiter. "Arabs can be very charming," he said, "when they like." He stopped with his fingers on the door of the car and gave Esther a quaint glance. "When I helped you out," he said, "you were an inaccessible prize—hardly more than a stranger. What a lot can happen in a few hours!" He caught himself up abruptly. "My God, what a platitude! Never mind. I suppose that's what love does to a man."

As he let in the clutch he added, "If things begin to happen now, at least we shall have the consolation of knowing that we snatched an evening of happiness before the deluge." Even. Garve did not realize at what a speed things *were* going to happen during the next few hours.

The car slid away and Garve pressed the horn three times. They had not covered half a mile before headlights once again sprang out of the darkness behind them, and pursued them tenaciously as they gathered speed along the plain.

"Don't worry about that car behind," Garve said, since there seemed no longer any good reason for hiding its identity. "It's the police. This road has still a bad reputation at night, and Baird kindly provided us with an escort."

Esther nodded, and snuggled down beside him. "You think of everything," she said. "I don't know what it is about you which inspires such confidence, but really, you know, I don't think I could ever get really worried in your company."

"It's charming of you to say so, but I assure you that a single well-directed bullet would put an end to your illusion of security."

"You're always thinking about bullets," Esther protested. She looked up into his face from her half reclining position and saw that the muscles of his jaw were tightly drawn, his mouth set, his brown eyes fixed in unwavering intentness on the road ahead. He was alert, ready, watching the outermost tip of his headlight beam, studying every inch of the illuminated road. As they left the plain and began the long corkscrew climb up into the mountains of Judea, the task of keeping a proper look-out became more difficult. Each section of road ended swiftly in a blind corner, and the danger was that anyone preparing an ambush would be able to see the approaching car long before the car's headlights could pick out any unusual features of the road.

Garve was sufficiently familiar with the road to know where, if at all, the blow was likely to fall, at least within a mile or two. Obviously Hayson would not himself be lying in wait for the car. Unless his warning had been just an empty bluff, he would have to employ someone to do the job for him—probably a small band of Arab cutthroats. That was an easy enough task in Palestine, where cut-throats abounded. They would have to remember, however, when choosing the site for their hold-up, that parts of the road were ideal for highway robbery and murder, provided all went well, but death-traps if any hitch arose. Between these towering cliffs, for instance, which rose so steeply above the series of S bends the car was now traversing, a body of assailants might find it very difficult to escape. If they were mounted, as was practically certain, they would have to race along the road a considerable distance in one direction or another before they reached a place where they could leave it. If, during that time, they met a police patrol, they would inevitably be stopped or fired on. No, the popular place for an ambush—proved time and again by past experience—was somewhere where the hillside rose not too abruptly from the road on at least one side. Then, after the job was done, it was possible for the assailants to ride their agile horses up the mountain-side, where, in a few seconds, they would be completely and finally lost sight of.

Occasionally Garve's eyes left the road ahead for the fraction of a second, to make sure by a glance in his driving-mirror that the police car was hanging on his tail. Most of the time it was less than fifty yards behind; occasionally the distance increased to a hundred on a particularly winding bit of road, which Garve happened to know better than the police driver. But always it was in comforting proximity.

As the miles slowly slipped by, Esther began to show signs of sleepiness, and her head sank lower and deeper into Garve's shoulder. He was glad to let her doze—she would worry less, and there was probably nothing to worry about anyway. If there were, she would wake up soon enough.

The car soon passed the "SEA LEVEL" post and ran on, purring comfortably up into the ever-deepening folds of the hills. Nowhere was there any light or any sign of life, human or animal. The road was winding now through the remotest fastnesses of Judea, and Garve watched with redoubled care, for here was the beginning of the danger zone. His headlights sent a regrettably warning beam ahead, but without the moon he could not dispense with them. He peered to right and left as well as in front, as his speed fell to a mere fifteen miles an hour. Bethany now lay not very far ahead, and he was just beginning to congratulate himself that his caution had been unnecessary when it all happened.

The road was skirting the edge of a deep and precipitous valley, which fell away dizzily on the right. On the left the hillside rose more gently, while just ahead the road turned to the left, so that the headlights shone out over the valley and revealed nothing.

As the car slowly negotiated the corner and the lights swung back to the road, Garve's nerves suddenly went tense. Right across it, from hillside to valley, was a low but impassable stone wall. At such moments Garve never hesitated. Almost at the instant of time when his eye saw the wall, even before a dozen dark figures had jumped down into the road, he had brought the car to a slithering standstill, crashed his gear into reverse, and accelerated back towards the corner, his hooter screaming, Arabs on foot and mounted pursuing him. In those hectic seconds, when the outcome of the incident was still uncertain, Garve could still notice that, though the Arabs had rifles, they were only holding them in readiness to fire, not firing them. Of course—Esther was not to be killed!

With a quick flick of the wheel he ditched the car on the left bank of the road. The headlights of the police car were dazzling in the driving-mirror. A mounted Arab, dashing up with knife raised to strike, reined in his horse with sudden fear as he saw the second car. The feet of horses thundered on the road—great heavens, there must be fifty men at least. They were bearing down on the car—they reined and shouted. The police were on them—into them, by God. A man screamed, there was a volley of shots, the police car stopped with a rending of rubber on stone and a great jolt as it hit something. A dark face bore down on Garve, who fired at six feet. He saw a red hole appear in the man's forehead as the body pitched over the wheel of the car. A machine-gun opened staccato fire—then another. Pandemonium reigned—noise of the police guns, Arab rifles, shouts and menaces, cries of wounded, and the horrible wailing of a wounded horse. Garve's left hand crushed Esther down, down against the cushions. There was nothing for him to do but wait with his revolver ready. The hillside sheltered him from the left—and it was clear that the police car had the situation well in hand. Garve watched the vicious bursts of flame as they spat from the machine-gun at the back. Suddenly the firing ceased. The police car's searchlight swept the hillside in vain—the raiders had gone. Along the road lay four bodies, sprawling and motionless. A horse cried and kicked in agony, till Garve jumped out in desperation and shot it through the head. The driver of the police car joined him, his face smeared with grime and oil.

"Girl all right?" he asked tersely.

Garve nodded, and at that moment Esther walked over from the car. Garve took her arm, peering anxiously into her face.

"I'm perfectly all right," Esther assured him. "I can't believe it's happened, that's all. I think I was fast asleep—and then I woke up in Bedlam. Are these men dead?"

The driver nodded. "There may be some more on the hillside, but we shan't know till daylight."

The two machine-gunners climbed down, nodding sheepishly to Esther, saluting Garve, surveying their handiwork.

"Have you wirelessed Baird for an ambulance?" asked the driver.

"Yeah. He's sending it; but he says there's some trouble at Tel Aviv, and he can't come himself."

"Must be pretty big to keep him away from this. Well, we'd better get that obstruction shifted. It's a good old dodge—blocking up the road. They've done it pretty thoroughly too." The driver turned to Garve. "Near shave, sir. I reckon we were lucky to come through like that without a scratch."

"Damned near thing," said Garve. "I was afraid you'd ram me in the back—I was going a hell of a pace in reverse."

"It was that that saved you—if you'd stayed put they'd have swiped you before I could have cleared the corner. But I missed your tail by inches, and nearly swerved over the edge doing it. Jove, you should have seen them scatter. I bet they had the shock of their lives. If we hadn't been here I reckon nothing on this earth could have saved you."

"You're right," said Garve grimly. "They took no chances—it looked like a cavalry division charging down the road. They've left five behind, not four. I had to shoot one over by the car."

"Do we have to wait until the ambulance comes?" asked Esther, drawing her wrap closely round her against the chill mountain air.

" 'Fraid so," said Garve. "It's unlikely they'll make another attempt, but we'll all go home together and take no chances."

"In that case I'm going to help demolish the wall," said Esther. She slipped daintily round an Arab corpse and proceeded to lug the smaller stone from the hastily built barrier, while the two policemen, who were already working there, grinned and encouraged her.

Garve sat on the running-board of the Ford and filled his pipe. He felt the elation which always comes from swift and successful action. He had little or no compunction about the dead Arabs, who had planned a cold-blooded assassination with overwhelming numbers. Apparently Esther, too, was wasting no sympathy upon them, and Garve marvelled again at her pluck and spirit. He guessed that the vigour with which she was at present moving stones was something of a cover for her feelings, but the noise and excitement, not to mention the blood, had been shocking enough for any woman, and none of the three policemen made any attempt to hide his admiration.

"She comes of good stock," said the driver to Garve, jerking his head towards the diminishing heap of stones. "Brave and tough like her father. He was with Allenby, and fought over every inch of this ground."

"I know," said Garve; "but how are you so sure he was tough?"

"I was with him," the policeman told him. "Served under him, and loved him."

Garve nodded. "He's got guts all right, or he wouldn't have come out here now. Queer thing—the Arabs were on our side then, and we promised them protection and a home in Palestine. Now we're helping to drive them out."

"Ah," said the policeman, "and that wasn't the only promised land that never came to anything."

He was just beginning to expatiate on the duplicity of politicians in not providing homes for heroes, when the light of a car came into view a mile away up the hill.

"That'll be the ambulance," said the driver. "And none too soon—it's devilish cold up here."

By now the last of the stones had been removed, and Esther joined Garve at the car, rubbing the dust from her hands.

"That's better," she said, smiling. "I really felt quite shaky at first."

"We shan't be long now. Come and sit in the car while they load up. It won't be a pretty sight."

He gave her a cigarette, and while the ambulance men helped the others, he moved the Ford away from the hillside.

The police driver came over to them. "Right you are, sir—we'll clear up the rest to-morrow. You can step on the gas—they want the ambulance urgently at Tel Aviv. Awful mess there—Arabs laid a mine under a whole block of flats and hundreds are dead."

"Sounds like a story I'll have to cover," said Garve to Esther as they shot away.

"You mean you'll have to go there?"

"If it's as big as they say. It's too late to get anything on the wire to-night, but they'll want it in London early to-morrow."

"Can I come with you?" Esther asked eagerly.

"I shouldn't, sweetheart. You've missed your beauty sleep already, and you've no idea how incredibly beastly these big explosions can be."

Esther subsided. "I suppose I *should* be rather in the way," she admitted. "But I can't bear to lose you to-night. I shan't sleep a wink anyway. What a night, Philip! The first part so peaceful, so sweet, that it seemed as though there couldn't be any evil in the whole world, and then violence and murder and frantic hurry everywhere. I say, this car does go, doesn't it?"

"It does," said Garve grimly, hugging his near side as he took a left-hand bend at forty. "It'll have to to-night. At last things are warming-up—there'll be martial law to-morrow, if I'm not mistaken—same as last year."

Jerusalem was completely silent as they ran swiftly through the outskirts. Baird's car was standing outside police headquarters, and as Garve ran up the steps he met Baird hurrying out.

He stopped and gripped Garve's hand, and the light of battle was in his eyes. "All safe?" he asked, saluting Esther. "Man, you must have second sight. The murderous devils!"

"Never mind them," Garve interposed. "What's the strength of the Tel Aviv business?"

"A whole block of dwellings demolished. Bodies being dragged out by the score. Jews in a ferment, and grave risk of riots. Military taking control. Is that a story?"

"I'll say it is," said Garve. "Are you going right away?"

"Yes—I'm leaving Fairfax in charge—he'll give you any help you want here. So long—see you later."

"I'll be on your tail," Garve told him. He watched Baird's car as it shot away. The next thing was to get Esther home without delay. Garve was now just a pure newspaper man with a single purpose. His eyes shone with a fierce determined light. For days he had sent nothing important to his paper—and this was big enough to take the front page of any London daily.

Esther saw his excitement and called him to the car urgently. "There's no need to bother about me, Philip. It's only ten minutes' walk home, and I know you're dying to get away."

"Rubbish," said Garve. "It won't take me a second." He clambered in and the Ford roared away on third gear. Almost before he could change up they were passing Damascus Gate, and had drawn up outside the Willoughby house.

"You'll be all right now," said Garve, kissing her. "I'm a rotten lover—but to-morrow I'll make up for it. Try and sleep, darling. Goodnight."

"Good-night," she said softly. "I love you very dearly." She watched his tail-light till it disappeared, and then turned into the drive. She was hardly through the gate, however, before two dark forms slipped from behind a mass of cactus and seized her. She would have screamed, but a bundle of rags was pressed over her mouth, half stifling her. She was lifted easily by the head and feet and carried at a run into Hayson's drive. In less than a minute, during which time hardly a sound had passed, she was handed in through Hayson's front door, which closed upon her. The two Arabs slipped away into the darkness. The light in the Willoughbys' hall went on burning; it seemed that the rest of Jerusalem slept.

Garve, congratulating himself that at least Esther was safe for the night, turned the bonnet of his car towards the coast.

14. Garve Thinks it Out

He drew a deep breath of something very like relief as the Ford sped quickly through the outskirts of Jerusalem. For the past few days he had been simply marking time, from the newspaper point of view—collecting background but precious little news. To-night he felt that he was back on the job again. His watch told him that it was nearly half-past one, but time was nothing for him now till the story was cleared up. He felt as fresh as a sea breeze, as keen as an Arab knife. The racing engine found response in his racing thoughts—long ago he had discovered that his brain worked with speed and clarity on a long night drive. It seemed to tune-in to the throbbing power of the car. It had to be constantly alert for fast driving, and problems which had seemed difficult lying in bed were often solved with ease between the flashing kilometre posts.

For the first few miles the road claimed the greater part of his attention. All round Jerusalem rose the mountains of Judea, and it took an iron nerve and a confident touch on the wheel to negotiate them at speed. Garve was dropping to the flat fertile country which stretched from the mountains to the sea, and the car swayed violently from right to left and left to right as he skidded the back wheels round the constantly recurring hairpin bends with a short jab at the brake and a swing over. Always he was completely master of the car, skidding it to an inch, smashing down on the accelerator as it came into the straight again. It was savage work; constantly the body groaned as the sharply turned wheel racked it with unfamiliar strains and stresses, and showers of pebbles shot from the tyres as they sought for a grip on the corners. He hardly knew why he was driving so fast, except that on big stories he hurried from long habit. Sometimes it meant that one could get the story on the wire and actually catch an earlier edition than a rival; more often by arriving early, one picked up some interesting item of news, some specially human angle, which the late arrivals would miss. Like a crime, a news story was more easily dealt with when the scent was hot.

Garve considered, from various aspects, the story he was racing to cover. There would probably be plenty of scope for vivid writing, particularly if the blown-up block were well alight, as seemed likely. It would be a messy business prowling round among such bodies as had been recovered, but on a story bodies were curiously impersonal things. To a reporter the main thing was how many there were of them and their identity—how they had suffered and died could be sketched-in later with a few deftly chosen words. Garve knew he would have no difficulty in getting all the information that was available. He considered the story in relation to the *Morning Call's* front page. If the explosion were as big as he supposed, his account of it might be worth a column, provided of course no big news story broke at home at the same time. After all, it came under the category of an "Arab outrage," and was therefore news.

Presently he saw with relief that he was leaving the mountains and entering the long, flat coastal plain. The road ran straighter now and faster between hedges of prickly pear and carefully tended orange and lemon groves.

His thoughts swung back to his last few days in Jerusalem. Days and nights—they had been mixed up together in awful confusion. He had really found out a great deal, yet nothing concrete. He sorted out dates in his mind. Yes, Mahomet's birthday was to-morrow. That left the whole of to-day—as it was nearly 2 A.M. he could certainly talk of "to-day"—and one night. If the Arabs were going to carry out their "coup" they would have to take advantage of the next period of darkness. He would have to be back in Jerusalem for that—just in case it happened. If they had only known, they would have been wiser to have started the revolt at this very moment. The explosion in Tel Aviv was attracting all the attention of the police and military. The prospect of riots there would keep the authorities busy. It was a heaven-sent opportunity—if they had only known.

Suddenly Garve's pulse gave a leap and the car swerved dangerously. If they had only known! Was it possible that they *did* know? What other purpose could they have in staging this piece of violence at Tel Aviv? Martial law was bound to follow it, and their liberty of movement would be enormously curtailed. Indeed, if the Tel Aviv explosion was not intended as a blind, a smoke-screen, it was simply an appalling piece of clumsiness on the Arabs' part. Or was it the work of independent terrorists? Perhaps —but lately the Arabs had certainly given the impression of a new discipline and corporate purpose. And this explosion right in the middle of Jewish territory must have taken a lot of planning by a considerable number of conspirators.

The longer Garve considered the matter the greater his uneasiness grew. He had been so keen on this story that he had lost sight of the bigger problem. Perhaps at this very moment the Arabs were rising in Jerusalem, breaking into the arms dump, slaughtering the Jews, building defences against counter-attack.

The city had been so quiet when he left it—surely, with a general revolt due in an hour or two, there would have been indications—restiveness. No civil population could be as disciplined as that. Or, perhaps, the civil population did not know—perhaps they were still waiting for a signal they could recognize. In that case, who was in charge?—who was the leader?—where was Kemal?

Looking back when it was all over, Garve could never understand how he could have been so blind, when the answer should have been so patent to him. Primarily, inevitably, he blamed himself, but he always regarded his succession of tiring days and nights, his personal fears for Esther, and the small opportunity he had had for hard thinking, as contributory causes.

Thoughts of Esther had closed his eyes to the truth—the obvious, only possible, explanation—for days, but it was thinking of Esther which brought him to it in the end. If there was any substance in his sudden fear that he was leaving the biggest story of all behind him, Esther was in the very gravest danger. He stopped the car by the roadside, lighted his pipe, and considered the situation all over again.

That hold-up on the Dead Sea road, for instance—what were its implications? That Hayson had tried to kill him once again. Why? To secure Esther for himself. He had instructed his cutthroats not to shoot her—that had been clear. Suppose the attempt had succeeded, though. Garve's body would have been lying, no doubt, at the bottom of the hillside, finally and irrevocably disposed of. But what of Esther! Would the Arabs have left her there to make her own way home? Or would they have taken her with them? And if so, where to?

There seemed insuperable difficulties from Hayson's point of view. He must have realized that Garve would have told her the truth about the quarries and about his threat of an ambush. Hayson would never have dared to let her go back alone, for she would inevitably have told her father everything—and the weight of evidence was growing. Hayson would know that she would denounce him—that his own hopes of securing her as his wife would be ruined. What, then, was the point of it all?

The ambush only made sense, indeed, if the idea was to kidnap Esther and take her by force to Hayson in some place where he could have his will of her. But surely, even in Palestine, Hayson could not hope to get away with an outrage like that. Not if conditions remained normal —not unless the whole of Palestine went up in a flame of civil war and utter disorder. But that was just what *was* going to happen. Good God, perhaps he had *known*. Perhaps he had been in with the conspirators. Perhaps he was one of them—one of the leaders—the leader. The Leader Hayson! *Hayson!* It was *Hayson*! Not Kemal, but *Hayson*! Thus gropingly, belatedly, Garve came to the truth, and as each little bit of the jig-saw of his knowledge fitted in, he exclaimed aloud at his own obtuseness.

He had thought the man his personal enemy—that was where he had erred. When Hayson had tried to murder him, he had put the attempt down to jealousy. In all his relations with Hayson the future of Esther had been uppermost in his mind. From that personal aspect he had never been able to detach his feelings. From the first he had accepted Hayson as an adversary without having to seek a cause for his enmity. All the suspicion of his curious movements which normally he might have entertained had been canalized into personal suspicion. Now, perhaps too late, he could see why Hayson had been so anxious to kill him. As a journalist he had known too much. His inquisitive investigations had been a constant menace to the plot that was hatching. He had to be got rid of, and in a way which would throw no suspicion on Hayson, until the plot was ripe.

Quickly Garve ran over the events of the past few days in his mind. There was that curious business of the first arms dump. Garve realized now how slow he had been not to associate its precipitate removal with Hayson. He recalled the circumstances in which he had announced the find. He had been discussing it with Willoughby while Hayson and Esther were out, and Esther had asked, "What's all this about machine-guns?" Only Hayson could have passed on the information so quickly to the Arabs. Yet Garve had suspected a police leakage. Hayson had seemed too much a member of the family; Willoughby had spoken well of him; Garve's only suspicions had been that he had designs on Esther. That partly explained—heaven knew it did not excuse—his blindness.

It was astonishing how the fellow had wormed his way into the Willoughby confidence—and yet, perhaps, not *so* astonishing, for his self-confidence was immense, and he rang true enough until you knew him by his actions. No doubt his past record as an archaeologist would bear full examination. The simple fact was that all along the line Hayson had been too clever for them. That affair of Hezekiah's Tunnel, for instance—Garve had gone out of his way to get Hayson's assistance, and Hayson had tried so hard—so it had seemed—to dissuade him from the enterprise. Naturally, for he must have known that if Garve explored the tunnel he might stumble upon the newly cut passage to the quarries, and begin to suspect Arab activity there. When he had found that Garve was insistent, he had recommended one of his own terrorists as a guide. Garve had fallen completely into the trap. Where Hayson had erred was in underrating the tenacity with which, in a crisis, Garve would cling to life. The fight in the tunnel had gone the wrong way, and instead of Jameel coming out to report his task executed, Garve had emerged to report a struggle. Yes, it all fitted in. Hayson would wait, expecting Jameel to come and account for his failure, and presently would send an Arab search party through the tunnel, and they would remove Jameel's body. Again Garve cursed himself for his crass blindness. Hayson was the only man, except Baird, who knew even that there had been a fight in the tunnel. But his attitude after the event had been so disarming—his, "Well, after all, I told you not to go" tone, so irritating and yet so natural to an innocent man who had done all he could, first to dissuade and then to help. All the same, Garve remembered now that Hayson had seemed surprised to see him after the episode in the tunnel. No wonder.

Quite apart from the damning way in which the two disappearances and Hayson's special knowledge of the circumstances were connected, his very movements in Jerusalem had been suspicious enough. Everyone had accepted his own story of archaeological investigation in the quarries, and that he had antiquarian knowledge Garve did not doubt. All the same, he had produced no evidence of his activities in any concrete or convincing form. He had talked a lot about new hieroglyphics, but he had been very careful not to show them to Garve when they were in the quarries together. On the other hand, if he were the leader of a vast conspiracy, the quarries were the ideal meeting-place, particularly now they had two entrances. And—why, of course, it was as clear as daylight—a man with Hayson's detailed knowledge of the quarries could not have failed to be aware of the existence of that great ammunition dump. He had simply lied about it—he must have known. And if he had known, and said nothing to the authorities, that was adequate and conclusive proof of his guilt.

Now that the mask of antiquarian virtue was torn away, Hayson's every act convicted him. He might, as an individual with a personal spite against Garve, have bribed Jameel to kill him—that was conceivable—but it was not conceivable that in any private capacity he could have sent fifty mounted Arabs to hold up a single man.

That action, which by all the rules should have ended in Garve's death, implied a relationship with the Arabs of an intimate and authoritative nature. And what was it that Francis Willoughby had said?—"He speaks Arabic like a native." No proof, perhaps, for Garve spoke it excellently himself, but it fitted in with all the rest and Garve was satisfied. The truth was incredible, but it was still the truth.

What, then, did all this mean? It meant that Hayson, a British citizen, was leading and planning a vast revolt against the rule of his own country. If his plot succeeded, it would result in the deaths of thousands of his fellow-countrymen and in a deadly blow to British prestige throughout the East. The conspiracy on his part was an act of treachery. What was he getting out of the affair? Money, perhaps—he might be just a mercenary, bought by the Arabs for his qualities of leadership. Somehow that seemed unlikely. He did not give the appearance of a mercenary, even with the mask off. There was a light in his eyes which spoke of fanaticism rather than cupidity. He might have a grievance against Britain—some personal affront might have made him unbalanced, and turned him to a spectacular revenge. But even if he had a grievance, that did not explain why the Arabs should trust him, and follow him with the implicit faith and almost perfect discipline which had been features of their conspiracy. The Arab leaders were no fools—a man like Ali Kemal would want more than verbal guarantees of good faith before he would place his arms and his people at the disposal of a stranger—and a renegade Britisher at that. But then—was Hayson a Britisher? Who was he, after all? Who were his people? Garve cast his mind back to try and recall what Willoughby had told him about Hayson. Nothing of substance, really, and what he knew had no doubt come from Hayson. The man had been to Oxford and had done well, but that was no guarantee of patriotism. Garve recalled the features that he had come to hate so much. There was nothing particularly English about them—in fact, it would not be at all surprising to know that Hayson had southern blood in him. That would explain his confident, possessive, too swift approach to Esther. That would explain his fierce jealousy of Garve. It all fitted in. It was quite possible that he owed allegiance to, and was an agent of, some other country than Britain.

Strangely mixed with a growing fear in his mind, and a realization that now at last action, urgent and swift, was called for, Garve felt a sense of relief that the puzzle was almost elucidated. But now that he knew the facts, he knew the desperate nature of the situation too. Clearly that last arranged ambush had been Hayson's final throw before the revolt broke. It had been designed to make absolutely certain that Garve would not be in a position to explode the mine himself before zero hour. It would put him safely and finally out of the way. Worse, it was designed to put Esther entirely at Hayson's mercy. It had failed in its first objective—had it failed in its second?

Garve crashed his foot on the self-starter button and swung the car round in the silent road. Why, fool that he was, the danger was as great as ever for Esther. Hayson would have been informed long ago that the hold-up had failed. His spies, who must be everywhere, would probably have seen the procession of police from the city. They would chuckle at the exodus and make haste to complete and carry out their plans at once. And Hayson's plan, Garve was absolutely certain, involved Esther. Wherever he went, if his plot succeeded, he would undoubtedly see that she went too. Her father might easily be killed—Willoughby trusted Hayson, would be influenced by him. Garve hoped, as his throttle opened wide, that perhaps Esther had told her father something of the ambush and of Hayson before she retired—something to put him on the alert.

Once or twice doubts assailed him as he raced back to Jerusalem. Perhaps, after all, he had let his imagination take control too strongly—perhaps he had constructed a fabric of sheer speculation with no solidity in fact. In that case, he would find it difficult to explain to his paper why he had abandoned the biggest story that Palestine had known since the trouble started. Difficult—but not impossible—and, anyway, the story was no longer the first consideration. Esther had proved Hayson's chief weakness as a conspirator; she was proving, Garve thought, his own undoing as a reporter!

He had no plan in his mind, short of getting to Jerusalem and finding Esther. The first thing was to satisfy himself that she was safe, and to leave her in safe hands, as he should have done before. The next thing was to find Hayson, the very keystone of the revolt, the man upon whose brain and authority depended success or failure, and by violence or cunning get him under lock and key. Garve hoped that he would still be early enough to reach Hayson before the signal of revolt was given. If the signal, whatever it was, could be arrested at the source, the revolt might never happen. Without leadership, without co-ordination, rebellions nearly always fizzled out.

The Ford was back in the mountains again, cutting corners, skidding and sliding, shrieking protest from its tyres, and roaring exultation from its engine. Garve had never driven more ruthlessly, but the road might be expected to be clear at this hour, and seconds counted. Already in the eastern sky there was the faintest glow of the dawn to come. The new suburbs echoed to his exhaust and dropped back into their sleep. No city in the world had ever looked less like a rebellion, and all Garve's doubts returned. Perhaps at this minute Hayson was sleeping peacefully in his house, dreaming, at the worst, of ancient hieroglyphics. But perhaps ...

15. Esther Refuses an Offer

The kidnapping of Esther had been completed by Hayson himself. It was his own hands which grasped her slim body as it was passed in the dark over his threshold. Judging by the silence of the house, indeed, he seemed to have the place to himself. Still keeping the cloth over her mouth, he carried her into his lounge and deposited her on a cushioned divan.

Very cautiously he raised the gag. "I'm sure you're not going to be so foolish as to scream," he said softly. "It wouldn't have any effect except to give us both a headache, and this is a really filthy piece of rag."

Esther sat quietly staring at him with a white face. She was still too jarred by the sudden and unexpected assault, too uncertain of what was to come, to find speech easily. Hayson seemed cool enough. He offered her a cigarette, which she declined with a shake of the head.

Hayson stood over her. "I'm afraid I owe you a very big apology," he said smoothly. "I shall always regret that it was necessary to subject you to this violence, but"—he shrugged his shoulders—"it was the only way."

Esther struggled for words, her cheeks flushed now with two hectic spots of anger. "You've behaved outrageously," she cried, her breasts heaving with the emotion which still strangled her speech. "You must be insane—you—you murderer."

"Whom have I murdered?" he asked quickly.

"You tried to kill Garve to-night."

"Ah, *tried*. Do you know, for a moment you quite raised my hopes—I thought that after all I had been misinformed about his escape. I'm afraid I have only myself to blame for his survival. I was unwise enough to warn him in a moment of anger that he might encounter difficulty. I regretted it at once, and contemplated abandoning my arrangements, but time was getting very short, and I could not know that his precautions would run to an armoured car. I begin to think he has a charmed life. However, this little affair at Tel Aviv seems to have disposed of him just as effectively. He reminds me of a little boy running after a fire-engine. So enthusiastic."

Esther made no attempt to hide her horror. As his meticulously chosen words fell on her ears she shrank away from him in loathing.

Hayson changed his tone. "You think I'm mad, don't you, Esther? That's not surprising, but you're wrong. I'm as sane as you are, and when I've told you all I've got to tell you, you'll understand." He glanced at his watch. "I can spare precisely one hour—not a second more. A great deal has to be done before the morning, and everything is timed. I think I'd better do most of the talking to start with, but I want you to listen very carefully—because it concerns your father."

"I'm listening," said Esther; "but I warn you, you're going to pay heavily for your amusement if ever I get free. I suppose you realize that my father might come over here at any moment—and Jackson too."

Hayson gave a complacent laugh. "I admire your spirit, my dear—it is one of the most adorable things about you; but I assure you everything is arranged. There will be no more mistakes."

"We shall see," said Esther. "Well, go ahead with what you want to say—though I'm not in the least interested."

"You will be; but we're wasting time. First of all, then, let me correct one of your major misapprehensions. Garve has no doubt told you, and you firmly believe, that I have tried to kill him because of you—because I was jealous of him. It hurts me that you should believe that. I suppose in a way it is a sort of compliment to a woman to want to kill a rival, but most women prefer their compliments more delicately turned these days. I'll admit freely that I was jealous of him, but I wouldn't have killed him for that.

The simple fact is, Esther, that I am at war, and Garve is on the other side."

"At war?"

"Literally—and I want you to grant me belligerent rights. You see, I am not an Englishman. I hate and abominate the English for their arrogance and stupidity. My mother was Welsh. She came to Jerusalem before the war as secretary to an English diplomat. She married my father in Jerusalem. My father was—an Arab."

"An Arab! But ..."

"I know all that you are going to say. You English are all alike. No doubt to you, in your insular ignorance, an Arab is just another sort of native. That, at least, is how you have treated us. My father was light-skinned, very handsome, and exceptionally cultured and intelligent. He was wealthy enough to travel when he was young, to study in Europe. Perhaps I differ from him only in two respects—my skin is even lighter than his, and *he* admired the English. He thought the English could be trusted. He served with Lawrence against the Turks during the war, believing that England would liberate his countrymen as she promised. He was killed in action, fighting side by side with British troops. His name, by the way, was Hussein. When I went to England to study, soon after the war, and took my mother with me, it seemed simpler to call myself Hayson and pretend to be English. Even then I felt that one day I should be of service to my countrymen, and dimly I could see that I might be more useful if my origin remained a secret. That was made all the easier because I was born in England. Tell me, am I boring you?"

"No," said Esther, who was staring up, fascinated, at his brilliant eyes. "Go on."

"I did well at Oxford. I was interested in antiquities and attracted the attention of some influential people. Sometimes I met Arab nationalist leaders in London, and my father's name was a password to their confidence, because they had known his sincerity and loved him. I told them that in due course they could count on me. Then my mother died, and I found myself free to pursue my plans, with almost unlimited money at my disposal. I travelled extensively in

Europe and Asia. Ostensibly, I was 'digging up the past' —and making a very good job of it—but actually I was making valuable diplomatic contacts, and interesting people who mattered in the cause of Arab nationalism. I was also getting into touch with the agents of armament firms and investigating the best ways of smuggling arms into this country. As our friend Garve has undoubtedly realized, arms have been pouring across the frontiers for years. I have been making secret preparations for a revolt ever since my first visit to Palestine. I have been trusted to organize and lead the revolt. And now—we are ready to strike."

"Why are you telling me all this?" Esther broke in.

"I'm sorry. I must ask you to be patient—there's more to tell yet. I'm trying to make it clear to you, in the first place, that I'm not just the common assassin you thought me, nor yet a traitor. I have no compunction about the consequences of this revolt. It will mean bloodshed on a tremendous scale—cruelty, suffering, destruction. I lay the responsibility for that at England's door. The English are a smug and hypocritical people. With what altruism they accepted the "burden" of this mandate over Palestine!—a country which they know will give them command of all the Eastern Mediterranean. I come from a proud people, and you have continually treated us as inferiors. To us you are an invader, just as the Turk was an invader. In the name of a government which we detest, and an order which we despise, you shoot and bomb and burn without mercy. Under your protection the most fertile parts of the land have been taken over from our ignorant peasants and handed to the Jews. Our interests have been ignored, our homes broken up. Gradually we are being pushed back by the Jewish immigration into the barren mountains. We have seen the Jews pouring into the country in disregard of your immigration schedules, arming themselves against us with your blessing. We know that they will not be content even when they have snatched the whole of Palestine. Some of them talk openly of the time when they will be strong enough to seize Transjordan too. We have used every peaceful means in our power to persuade you of the justice of our claims. You have sent out Royal Commissions and affirmed your good faith, and still the Jewish immigration goes on. It is to your interests to found a Jewish State, and your interests, as always, are more to you than justice."

"There may be truth in what you say," said Esther slowly. "I believe you are sincere and —I'm impressed. But what can I do? Why tell *me*?"

"I must still ask you to be patient for a little longer. I assure you that I have not had you brought here with a violence which I deplore in order to make a political speech to you or work off my indignation on you. In an hour or two our anger will take a more explosive and effective form. But before I tell you why I have brought you here, I am going to tell you something of our plans."

"Surely that's very indiscreet?"

"My dear Esther, unless you fall in with them you will, I'm afraid, never have the opportunity to talk about them—at least until it is too late. In the first place, I want to make it clear to you that this revolt will succeed. It differs from all previous outbreaks. This time we are fully armed. Gun for gun and bomb for bomb we can meet you, and we have an enormous preponderance of man-power. Over in that bureau is a document which your country would give thousands for. It is a complete list of over a hundred secret ammunition depots scattered through the mountains. We shall strike so swiftly and so powerfully that your aeroplanes will be rendered useless by our control of the aerodromes. In twenty-four hours your troops will be driven into the sea—unless . . ."

"Unless what?"

Hayson smiled. "I was hurrying along too fast. There is one thing, and one thing only, which can stop this revolt from happening at once. Let us, however, suppose for the moment that it is not stopped. In thirty-five minutes from now I shall leave this house—without you, I'm afraid—and walk over to your father's. Your father will be seized—as you were seized, quite easily. He will be persuaded to write or sign an urgent message to the British military authorities, saying that he has been kidnapped by Ali Kemal —you have heard of Kemal?—and carried into the Mountains of Moab near Petra. Actually he will be in Solomon's Quarries all the time."

"He would never sign such a thing."

"I said he would be persuaded," observed Hayson, and Esther felt her blood run cold at his tone. "I anticipate no difficulty at all. The letter will then be brought to the notice of the authorities, and it will be of such a character that its authenticity will not be questioned. It will say that the tribes are in revolt in Transjordan and preparing an attack on Palestine, that the position is desperate, and that the Arabs have sworn to kill him—in a most unpleasant way —in twenty-four hours if their demands for independence are not met—or words to that effect."

"You devil!" cried Esther.

"No, no," said Hayson; "you do me less than justice. As I say, your father will be safely in the quarries all the time. But see what will happen next. The British, furious that their man has been taken, dreading the political repercussions in England if he is killed, will at once send a strong body of troops and 'planes into Transjordan. When all the aeroplanes are off the ground we shall seize the aerodromes. Your reinforcements will still be in the Mediterranean. We shall watch the troops rushing in their lorries from Haifa and Jerusalem and Tel Aviv, taking their machine-guns and bombs with them, hastening into the mountains to save the life of their countryman and administer ruthless punishment to the kidnappers. We shall watch them, and how we shall laugh. Always it has been so easy for them in the past—they have had to deal only with sporadic unorganized attempts—never with armed intelligence. When they are miles away in the hills they will be attacked from strongly fortified positions and decimated by our ambushes. But *their* fate features insignificantly in our plot. *Their departure will be our signal.* As they ride away, the cities will revolt behind them. The Jews will be massacred. Jerusalem, with its great walls and its solid rock will be turned into an impregnable fortification. We shall sweep down over the plains to the sea, almost without encountering resistance. Your country will have only one weapon which we cannot equal—its navy and naval bombers. The navy may bombard the coast and land a great army under its guns, but by that time we shall have built an impregnable barrier inland away from the guns. It is planned to the last detail—and we shall win."

Hayson's face was flushed with a great enthusiasm, but his words fell slowly, confidently from his lips. He talked as one who is master of his circumstances and assured of his strength.

"Of course," he went on, watching Esther closely, "war is war. Once the revolt has started I cannot promise to control the natural anger of my countrymen. They will, I am afraid, subject your father to frightful indignities and no little physical distress before they kill him. Your own fate would be no longer a matter which I could control. Were I to show any mercy, I should be killed as a traitor myself. What would happen to you I am content to leave to your imagination—which I am sure is vivid. *But*—and this is what I have been leading up to all the time—there is a way out. I cannot guarantee to prevent the revolt, nor would I wish to do so, but I can postpone it until you and your father are safely away. Whether that happens depends on you, and you alone."

"I think I know just what you are going to say," said Esther very quietly.

"I am sure you do—to any intelligent woman it must be obvious. You see, Esther, you are a quite exceptionally beautiful and attractive woman. I want you as I have never wanted anything before. For ten years I have been filled with one purpose—to smash your country's power in Palestine—but—I am no stronger than Antony or Caesar. I know that, if this revolt succeeded, I could just take you for myself—have you as a forced mistress and win applause from my people for doing so. If I were wholly Arab, I might do that, for women are nothing in the East. Give me credit for rejecting that alternative. I know that I am bringing pressure upon your mind and body, but, believe me, after my fashion I love you as truly as anyone has ever loved. So much do I love you, so intensely do I want your love, that I am prepared to abandon the revolt to its fate if you say the word. I know I speak without emotion—there is no time for passion, and I have weighed this up already and come to this decision through much mental anguish."

He dropped down on the couch beside her. "Listen, Esther," he cried in burning tones, "come away with me. I have in my pocket at this moment two steamship passages to Italy. A boat leaves Port Said at ten to-night, and my car is ready. Before the revolt breaks we shall be across Sinai and over the Egyptian frontier. To-morrow we will be married on the boat. I have money in plenty—you can live where in the world you like, have everything you want. I swear to you that I will cherish you and be faithful to you for ever. Only say yes!"

"And my father?" asked Esther weakly.

"I have already prepared a letter to him. Not one which merely advises him, for his own safety, to leave, since I know, and you know, that he would ignore it. A letter which you must copy quickly and sign, telling him that I have abducted you, and urging him to follow you to the boat. I will arrange that he gets it early enough to ensure his escape—too late for him to catch the boat. Esther, my love, say yes. Time is pressing."

"I don't love you," said Esther slowly. "I would sooner die than come. If your love were as real as you say you would not put me to this torture. In every way the step you want to take is unworthy. You began to make me respect your sincerity as an Arab; even to make me admire you for your ability and courage—as an enemy. I despise your weakness now."

"Not weakness," broke in Hayson eagerly. "Sacrifice! The revolt will be postponed a few hours, perhaps, but it will happen. I am sacrificing, not my country, but myself—honour and prestige, the trust of my countrymen, the leadership with all that it may hold—perhaps my life. No doubt you have heard what happens to Arabs in Palestine who betray their trust. They are hunted down and killed. Our discipline is ruthless. Once a conspirator falls under suspicion of treachery or weakness, however slight, he is lost —and rightly, for only on that basis is revolution possible. Knowing that risk, I am prepared to face it."

"A gamble," murmured Esther, "with myself as the prize. For

life I should be tied to a man whom I feared and hated. If I tried to leave you I suppose you would kill me. You have made it clear enough how ruthless you can be. Your suggestion is one which does not consider me. There is no unselfishness in this tawdry thing which you call love—nothing that I could ever value. You insult me by supposing that I could ever be satisfied with it."

Hayson's face was suddenly wet with perspiration and paler than she had ever seen it.

"You little fool," he said, and now there was a new hardness about his mouth and eyes. "When it's too late you'll regret this stupidity and think better of my offer. I know what's in your mind—that blundering Englishman, Garve. You love him, don't you? You rely upon him? Well, where is he now? Racing off along a trail that's been specially laid for him. He'll be killed, of course. It's useless for you to expect help from him. Come, Esther, be sensible. Think, while there's time, of the alternatives before you." He tapped his breast pocket significantly. "Here is freedom, love, and admiration; a life of leisure and luxury, of travel and new sights, new skies, new climates, dress and jewels, social influence. This would not be the first time that a woman had married without great love and lived happily with such opportunities surrounding her."

"The picture doesn't attract me," said Esther coldly. "I don't trust you, and I should hate to live with you. That's my final word."

"How final," said Hayson, "even you, perhaps, hardly appreciate—if you insist on it. I cannot believe that you will be so foolish. Look ahead. Do you realize that, if you send me away, in a few hours you will be the plaything—the toy—of any hooligan who finds you? Do you realize that strange filthy hands will be fondling and enjoying that beautiful body of yours? Do you know that before many days are past you will be praying for death, if only it may come easily, and cursing yourself for your folly to-night?"

"If the future is black whichever way one looks," said Esther, "it is better not to look at all. There is always the possibility that something may go wrong with your plans." She spoke with courage, but her heart was like lead, and sudden tears of anguish filled her eyes. Within herself she felt that Hayson was right about the things to come. She was so helpless here. So entirely alone. If only Garve had been in Jerusalem there would still have seemed some hope. Without him, the city was empty. She was utterly miserable, and Hayson's very presence was repugnant to her. His coldly menacing attitude during this interview had filled her with such a loathing of him as she had never expected to feel towards any man. Yet the thought of her father was heavy upon her. It was a dreadful thing even to be told that one had the power in one's hands to save a beloved person from frightful suffering, and yet deliberately to refuse to use that power. If she lived and her father died at the hands of the Arabs, she would hear the groans of his tortured agony in her sleep at night, and would never know whether he had died peacefully or not. Always, inevitably, she would blame herself. Was it not better, perhaps, to give herself to Hayson? One day she might succeed in giving him the slip—it was unthinkable that he could keep her tied all her life. But to start with —to have to endure this man's passion at his will. He swore to be faithful, but she could not trust him or his Eastern blood. How likely it was that she would simply finish as a concubine—despised and discarded. She would always be afraid of his power and his will—in time, perhaps, she might give up the struggle and succumb to it altogether, so that mentally as well as physically she would be his chattel. Could anyone demand that sacrifice from her? In any case she did not trust Hayson's promises about her father. He wanted *her*, and would say anything to get her.

"Well," said Hayson impatiently, "I'm still waiting. In ten minutes I have to be away from here. Shall it be by car with you to Egypt, or alone to complete my plans at your father's house?"

Esther's knuckles showed white when she clenched her small hands in distress, but her words came firmly from her lips.

"I'll never go with you, Hayson. Never. You can do what you like with me—you have the power and opportunity; but, voluntarily, I'll never give myself to you."

"It's a pity," said Hayson; and now he suddenly resumed the tones of studied sarcasm which he had used at the beginning of their interview. It was as though, with an effort of will, he had slammed a door on his emotions, not without a certain feeling of relief, and become again the cold, efficient conspirator.

He smiled sardonically. "Perhaps, after all, you have saved my soul. I shall not now have earned the name of traitor." He affected to sigh. "Well, I'm afraid I must trouble you."

"For what?" asked Esther in sudden apprehension.

"I cannot leave you here free, young woman, nor yet take you with me, though if all goes well I may come back for you. There is only one alternative left, I fear, and for that I must apologize. It smacks of melodrama, but I must tie you up and cover your mouth so that you cannot cry out. I can take no risks, and if you were discovered, knowing so much, it might be fatal to our plans. I am therefore going to put you in a place where you are certain not to be discovered. Indeed, if by any mischance our plot fails and I am killed, it may be many many days before you are discovered. However, war is like that."

He seized a coil of stout cord which lay ready on the floor. "Before I start to put this on you I should like to know whether you are going to struggle or not. If you *are* going to struggle I shall have to hit you on the head with something first of all—but I am sure——"

Esther held out her hands passively. She had not lost hope yet, and there was more chance of successful action conscious than unconscious. Hayson made a workman-like job of the tying-up. Continually, as he worked and tugged, fastening her wrists behind her so that they were completely immobile, he apologized for his roughness, but his consideration did not lessen his efficiency. He was taking no chances.

Presently he stepped back a pace and surveyed his handiwork with satisfaction. Esther lay trussed and utterly helpless, her feet bound as tightly as her hands. Hayson tested the tension of the cord at her wrists to see that it was safe without actually cutting the flesh.

"I have never tied anyone up before," he declared. "I assure you it's not nearly so easy to do as to talk about. But I don't think you'll escape now."

He took from his pocket a large white handkerchief. "Even though you did scream I don't suppose anyone would hear you—not from where I'm going to put you—but I think I'd better cover up your mouth as an additional safeguard. Do you mind—if you open your lips slightly it will be easier."

Esther's eyes stared up at him helplessly. "I shall never forgive you for this," she murmured. It was useless to say more—useless, indeed, to say anything.

Hayson stood over her with the gag. "Even now," he told her, "there is still just time for you to change your mind."

"Never," said Esther, and there was an awful moan in her voice. "Never."

The gag descended mercilessly between her teeth, half choking her. With nimble fingers Hayson knotted it behind her head.

He bent and touched her breast with lascivious fingers, smiling. "I'm beginning to think that this hour might have been more profitably spent," he murmured.

He saw the moisture in her eyes, tiny tears collecting in the corners and welling over on to her cheeks. As though he feared the sight would be too much for him, he picked her up quickly and easily and carried her into his laboratory. In a corner was the dark room. He laid his bundle on the floor and went back into the lounge to get some cushions. He opened the dark-room door, spread the cushions quickly on the stone floor, and carried Esther to the improvised bed.

"The room is ventilated," he said calmly. "You won't suffocate. And if all goes well I shall come back for you. If not, good-bye."

Without touching her again he slammed the door, turned the key in the lock, and slipped it in his pocket. For a few minutes he busied himself about the house, preparing for his departure. Before he left he dropped a small torch and an automatic into his pocket and extinguished all lights.

Esther, from her prison within a prison, dimly heard the front door closing as he let himself out. She was fully conscious, and determined to remain so—as long as possible. Already she craved for water, knowing that there was none for her. For a time she struggled quietly to free her wrists, but already her arms were growing numb with lying on them, and presently she had to give up the attempt. She was powerless, and there was nothing to do but conserve what strength she had and wait. Wait for what? If Hayson were right, for the sound of guns and bombs and shouting in the streets, for the wail of Jews facing massacre, for Hayson's return. For the news that her father and Garve were dead. If that happened she was determined to shoot herself at the first opportunity that Hayson gave her. To live without Garve—to live as the forced mistress of Hayson—it was unthinkable. Her thoughts returned to the excitement of the evening before—those wonderful hours with Garve, the ambush. If only Garve had taken her with him—but it was futile to regret that now. Somehow, even in her extremity, the thought that Garve was free encouraged her to hope. She knew that as long as life was in him he would strive to find her. No doubt there was little enough he could do, but she trusted him to do something. Presently, from sheer exhaustion of mind and body, she slept.

16. Kidnapped!

Hayson strode quickly along the short stretch of road to the Willoughbys' drive, and in through the gate. He paused to cast a word or two of Arabic into the cactus, shortly acknowledged the reply, and marched boldly up to the front door. The Willoughbys' Arab servant opened to him, exchanged a quick glance of understanding, and showed him into the lounge. Willoughby himself was pacing up and down: Jackson was standing by the fireplace, knocking out his pipe.

"I hope I'm not intruding," said Hayson courteously. "Is anything wrong? I happened to be working late and was just thinking of turning in when I noticed your windows all alight. Nothing wrong with Esther, is there?"

"It was good of you to come over," said Willoughby. "As a matter of fact, there's a devil of a lot wrong. Have you heard about the ambush?"

"Ambush?" asked Hayson, and the startled surprise in his eyes was a masterpiece of simulation. "Good heavens, no! You don't mean, sir, that Esther—she's not hurt?"

"No, no—at least, we hope not. She and Garve were held up on the Jericho road, so the police informed me, but they got through all right. Fairfax, who's in charge at headquarters, told me on the phone over an hour ago that they were on their way home. It's only a few minutes by car, but they haven't come. I confess I'm worried."

Hayson nodded sympathetically. "What have you done about it?"

"All I can. I've told Fairfax and he sent out a patrol at once,

162

but they've reported that there's no sign of life in the city anywhere. They think Garve may have taken her to Tel Aviv—there's been a big explosion there to-night, you know."

"Really? I hadn't heard. I've been buried with my books all the evening. Well, that's possible, I should think."

"I'm sure she would have let me know," said Willoughby with weary irritability. "She promised to be back at the latest by two, and I told her I'd wait up for her. At the very least she would have left a message with Fairfax."

"One would have thought so. Have you—well, no, that's not possible."

Willoughby gave him a shrewd glance. "Garve's hotel? I rang them. He hasn't been back."

"I see. In that case it looks as though there's nothing we can do but wait, doesn't it? Do you mind if I stay—I doubt if I could sleep till I know what's happened."

"We'll be glad to have your company," said Willoughby heartily. "Have a drink."

"Thanks," said Hayson. Actually he was feeling in need of a stimulant, and his thanks rang true. He helped himself to whisky and added the faintest splash of soda.

"I suppose Baird has gone to Tel Aviv?" he asked casually.

"Yes. Hundreds dead, by all accounts. Heaven knows how these Arabs think it will help their case to blow up Jewish women and children."

"It's madness," said Hayson, and swallowed his whisky at a gulp. "They should know by now that terrorism never gets any concessions out of Britain."

His attitude was perfect—a judicious blend of respect, affection, and concern. He spoke as though it were understood by all decent people that the Arabs were badly led children who must be handled firmly. He had never denounced them—always, when he had talked of them, he had been firm, but liberal, like Willoughby himself. They understood each other.

Hayson glanced at his watch—it seemed to him that he had been glancing at his watch all night. It was nearly three o'clock. "We

163

ought to be getting news of some sort soon," he observed. His mind was not on his words. He was thinking, "Another two minutes."

"The curious thing is," declared Jackson, "that I could have sworn I heard a car stop outside the gate not much more than an hour ago. I was certain it was Miss Willoughby, but the car drove off, and she didn't come in. I wonder——"

What he wondered no one was ever to know. Without warning of any sort the lights went out. After that things happened so quickly that it was impossible to keep track of them. The door opened—there was a lot of movement in the big room—two shots, a groan and a fall—a sound as of someone choking, Hayson's voice, muffled, crying, "Let go, damn you"—words in Arabic rapped out as commands—an order to hurry. Then suddenly the lights went up again.

Hayson, with a gag in his mouth, was lying trussed up on the settee—though trussed less efficiently and ruthlessly than he had bound Esther. Opposite him, Willoughby was lying on the floor, also gagged, and helpless as a child. Three powerful Arabs stood over him, mocking his frantic glaring eyes. Two Arabs guarded Hayson. Jackson lay on the carpet by the fireplace, dying, while blood spurted from a great hole in his neck.

One of the Arabs went over to the fireplace and looked down at the pitiful sight. He stirred the body contemptuously with his foot. "He'll give no more trouble," he said.

Three of them seized Willoughby and carried him to the front door. Two others followed with Hayson. Abdul, whom the Willoughbys had trusted, opened the door for them. They waited a moment, and a car drove to the gate. Elsewhere the city was silent. Only a minute or two after the first attack the bound men were thrust unceremoniously into the back of the car with three Arabs on top of them, and were being raced along by the silent wall, past Damascus Gate to that point of the road which was nearest the entrance to the quarries. Just inside the cave, at the place where, in more peaceful times, the pedlar sat with his stone mallets and paper-weights for sale to tourists, an Arab stood on guard. A bayonet gleamed at the muzzle of his rifle: he was equipped for war.

The next fifteen minutes were a revelation to Willoughby. The Arab party advanced sure-footedly through the quarries, lighting their way with torches, wasting not a second. Without hesitation they singled out the passage which Garve and Hayson had taken, the one which gave such a convincing appearance of a cul-de-sac. Brusquely the helpless roped figures were forced through the narrow aperture and carried swiftly along the precipice edge. "Where ignorance is bliss," thought Hayson, momentarily envying Willoughby, yet trusting the Arabs who had made the journey so many times before. They were clearly conscious of the vital need for speed, and one who seemed to be in charge kept muttering exhortations to further effort. The eight-foot drop which Garve and Hayson had negotiated only with the greatest difficulty was almost taken in their stride by the Arabs. Fastening a rope round the waist of each captive in turn, they lowered the two bundles unceremoniously to the bottom. The last Arab clung to the ledge with his hands, and then let himself drop, alighting with the grace and ease of a cat. In a few minutes they were approaching the central chamber.

The aspect of the chamber had greatly altered since Hayson and Garve had last visited it. On the opposite side, and close against the precipice, twenty or thirty Arabs were seated on the ground. One or two of them wore European dress, and only their dark faces and tarbooshes proclaimed them Eastern. Others wore the robes of powerful sheikhs, and their fingers glittered with jewels. A little haze of smoke rose from the group, which was illuminated dimly by flares jammed into cracks in the rock. In the centre of the group sat an Arab sheikh, a little apart, like a leader, and when he spoke the others listened. His frame was powerful, his swarthy face strong and handsome.

With little ceremony the two captives were marched up to the group and forced to their knees. They remained gagged. The sheikh in the centre turned slowly towards the two men and his fine features broke in a bitter smile.

"Good-morning, gentlemen," he said in English. He looked at Hayson, then more closely at Willoughby. "We are indeed honoured to have two such distinguished guests—a leading light in English literary circles and a famous antiquarian. You must forgive us if our reception seems a little informal. But first let me introduce myself. I am known as Ali Kemal. I do not doubt that you have heard my name, though to my knowledge we have never had the mutual pleasure of meeting."

Kemal lighted a gold-tipped cigarette with heavily ringed fingers and returned to the attack.

"No doubt you will be wondering," he said in more businesslike tones, "why you have been brought here. I will tell you. In an hour from now I am leaving Jerusalem to raise a revolt against your Government throughout Transjordan. During the course of that revolt we may find ourselves in need of money. We feel that you two gentlemen may have some value to your country. We therefore propose to take you along with us. In the event of our failure, of course—but we needn't discuss that unpleasant and improbable contingency." He paused. "Have you ever been to Petra, Mr. Willoughby? It is a wild, remote, and inhospitable place—a place which perhaps your friend Mr. Hayson will appreciate more than you yourself, for it is full of interesting antiquities. As your Government will not know you are there, they will not be able to make any misguided attempts to release you."

Kemal drew thoughtfully at his cigarette and suddenly glanced across at Hayson, whose eyelids flickered.

Kemal smiled. "Your daughter, Mr. Willoughby, is already on her way to Petra. It is possible that she may prove an even more valuable hostage than yourself, and when the time comes for you to write to your Government at our dictation—without, of course, disclosing your whereabouts—the awkwardness of her situation will no doubt provide you with an added incentive."

He turned and gave an order in Arabic, and the captives were at once seized, carried across the cavern and placed in the mouth of one of the tunnels, their backs to opposite walls. There the Arabs left them.

Willoughby made one or two abortive efforts to loosen his bonds and his gag, but without the slightest success. He could see nothing at all, for the angle of the tunnel cut out all light from the central chamber. Something like despair seized his mind. That Esther should be in the hands of these ruffians! He dare not let his thoughts dwell on her—that agony of imagination was too great to bear. Thinking of his daughter would drive him crazy. If he could only help her—at whatever sacrifice—but at the moment there was nothing he could do. He might have argued with Kemal—temporized, promised, had his mouth been free—promised anything; but gagged, he had been powerless. Stoically he sat motionless and stared into the darkness.

Presently, however, he became aware that something was happening a few feet away from him. A scraping noise reached his ears, a noise which gave him hope. Hayson was trying to get loose, and, judging by the sounds, with some degree of success. His feet were rubbing on the rock as he turned and twisted. His struggles went on for perhaps five minutes. Then, to his joy, Willoughby heard a gasp from the wall opposite and Hayson spoke to him in an eager, sibilant whisper. "Mr. Willoughby—I've got my hands free and my gag. I think I can loosen my legs in a moment or two, but they're a bit cramped. Wait a minute."

The shuffling sounds began again, and in a surprisingly short time—surprising to Willoughby—Hayson came crawling over to him out of the shadows and began to work at his gag. It took him some minutes to loosen the knot, but eventually he unfastened it with the help of his teeth.

Willoughby gasped with relief, and Hayson gave a warning "Sh-sh!"

"The devils!" breathed Willoughby. "What are we going to do, Hayson? We must do something. You heard what they said—they've got Esther. God knows what they'll do to her."

"Sh-sh!" again Hayson cautioned him. "If we're found it's all up. Listen. If I can get your cords unfastened do you think you can get out the way we came in?"

"If it's the only way, I can try," said Willoughby. "But have we time? I think they fastened me up too carefully."

"Let's investigate," said Hayson. With a great show of energy he set to work on the knots, heaving and straining, cursing broken finger nails. "You're right," he said finally. "They've done their job too well. It would take an hour to free you."

"Never mind," Willoughby urged him. "The chief thing is to act quickly. Can you get out alone?"

"Yes," said Hayson. "I know every inch of the way. I can make it if there is no guard—if there is, I'll have to slip by somehow or fight."

"Good man. We must get a message to the military, Hayson. There's not a moment to lose."

"It ought to be written, sir—don't you think? I might be able to send it then by messenger if I get caught or wounded. Also it's an important matter—means diverting a whole lot of troops. They might not be willing to act on a verbal message from me."

"That's true—we can take no chances."

Hayson groped in his pockets. "I've a bit of pencil," he said finally, "no paper at all."

"Feel in my pocket," said Willoughby, hoarse with excitement. "There's a letter from my publishers—nothing important on it, but it will satisfy the authorities that the message comes from me. I think there's enough room for a few lines of writing. Got it?"

"Wait a minute," said Hayson. "I've got a flash-lamp."

Suddenly a faint red glow showed in the blackness of the passage—the bulb of the lamp behind Hayson's enveloping fingers.

"That's better," Hayson whispered. With difficulty he extracted a bundle of papers from Willoughby's breast pocket through the tightly encircling ropes. Swiftly he sorted them over, flashing the uncovered light on them.

"Careful with that light," Willoughby called in an agonized whisper. "For God's sake keep it covered or they'll spot us."

Hayson's fingers closed over the bulb again, and he cursed himself silently for his carelessness. Now that his plan was so near complete fulfilment it was more than ever necessary not to give Willoughby any cause for suspicion. The trouble was, his own hurry was greater even than it seemed, for time was getting perilously short.

"When I think of Esther I can hardly stop to be careful," he lied blatantly. "Ah—here's the letter. Acknowledging a communication—nothing that matters in that. Plenty of room for you to scribble a message too."

"Better try and get my hands loose somehow," said Willoughby. "They feel pretty numb."

"I'll have another shot," whispered Hayson. He set to work with a will, and success rewarded him. If he had known the secret of the knots he could not have freed the hands with more agility.

"Excellent, excellent," breathed Willoughby. "They're a bit cramped, but the blood's running back. You're a good man to have in a tight corner, Hayson. I hope we both get out. I'll remember this."

Hayson chafed Willoughby's fingers. "Better now? Here's the pencil—don't drop it. I'll shine a light on the paper. Ready? Shall I dictate? It'll be quicker."

"Carry on," said Willoughby. "I'll write——"

"Suppose we say, 'Ali Kemal has kidnapped myself, my daughter, and Hayson, and has taken us this morning to Petra. He is about to lead a revolt of the tribesmen throughout Transjordan——' "

"Just a minute," said Willoughby, "you're too fast—'has taken us this morning to Petra'—I suppose he *will* take us to Petra? We don't want the military going off on a wild goose chase."

It was a bad moment for Hayson, but he played his cards superbly. "Esther's there, Mr. Willoughby. At least, so Kemal says. We've no other information—we've *got* to take his word for it. It's that or nothing. Her life's at stake, and we've got to take a chance."

"Very well. I think you're right—'is about to lead a revolt of the tribesmen throughout Transjordan.' "

Hayson breathed again. "Better say, 'we understand large ransom motive for capture.' Got that? Shall we say, 'Suggest you take no notice of threats against our personal safety'?"

"Not 'suggest'—'insist,' " said Willoughby between his teeth.

Hayson smiled in the darkness—these Englishmen! One could hate their domination and yet admire their courage.

"'Insist you take no notice. Advise immediate dispatch'—that's not too strong, is it?—'advise immediate dispatch of all available troops to Petra'—got that?—'to smash resistance before revolt spreads.' That's enough, isn't it?"

Willoughby nodded. A drop of sweat fell from his forehead on to the paper. "I'll underline 'immediate,' though it won't be necessary. If I know the military, they'll be off the mark within five minutes of getting the paper." He added his signature, and Hayson grabbed the message from his fingers.

Willoughby sank back wearily against the rock wall. He was not a young man, and he had been violently handled. "Good luck, Hayson—God bless you."

Hayson gave a low whistle. An Arab came running with a flare and saluted. "Here's a message for the military," said Hayson sharply in Arabic. "We're ten minutes late—hurry! You know what to say."

The Arab saluted and was gone.

Willoughby was staring, unable to believe his eyes and ears. "What are you *doing*, Hayson? Are you insane?"

Hayson gently patted his shoulder. "Listen to me, Mr. Francis Willoughby. You've been duped—and I'm sorry for you, for I've learned to respect you as a man. I'm no Englishman—I'm a rebel and an Arab. No—don't say anything. You'll need your strength. The whole of to-night's proceedings were arranged. I shot Jackson—a pity, but war is war. They tied me up so that I should retain your confidence. I planned everything—naturally I am a little jubilant that it worked so well. I am as certain as you are that the military will act on your letter. All the Arabs in Palestine and Transjordan will rise behind your army. When it gets to Petra it will find nothing but ambushes. You are to stay here——"

"My daughter," whispered Willoughby weakly. "Esther, where is she?"

"I am glad to be able to tell you, Mr. Willoughby, that for the moment your daughter is safe in Jerusalem. I let Ali Kemal know by an arranged signal that she had not returned home—that our plans had worked out properly. He knew then that he could say she was on her way to Petra without your knowing better."

"Who's looking after her? Where's Garve?"

"Garve—Garve—Garve, always Garve," cried Hayson in sudden fury. "I neither know nor care —he's out of it. He's probably at Tel Aviv by now, and I hope his body rots there. As for Esther —when the revolt's over I shall look after her myself."

"Not if I live," cried Willoughby. "You're a traitor and a scoundrel—a plotting, lying traitor—you'll hang for this."

"Gently, Mr. Willoughby. You do not realize how greatly you are in my debt. I have relieved your mind of anxiety about Esther—or some of it —and we have no immediate intention of killing you. So far as is possible, I shall do my best to save your life—if only because I have accepted so often your liberal hospitality, and because I have a very great affection for your daughter. For the next few hours you are a prisoner of war, and will be treated as such. I will see that you have food, drink, and tobacco brought to you. But I warn you that any sign of weakness on my part, any suspicion that I am on too friendly terms with you, and my own life will be in danger. Already, though I lead, I am watched—already the sheikhs suspect me of intrigue with you. If they kill me you and Esther are lost. I advise you, therefore, to be discreet. Farewell for now."

Willoughby stared into the growing darkness, watching the retreating light. His thoughts were in a whirl. Dimly he felt that he should not have signed—that he should have known it was all a plot. Yet it had all been so natural—Hayson had acted his part so well. What a conspirator! What a leader!

If *only* he had not signed. He thought miserably of the troops crowding out of the city, straining to reach Petra on his instructions. And Esther—if only . . . if only . . .

"Esther, Esther," he groaned. The rocky tunnel seemed to take up the cry in mockery, and "Esther, Esther," was hurled back at him in waves of ever-diminishing sound.

17. Garve Turns Housebreaker

Garve's spirits, keyed to concert pitch by the fast night run and the sense of urgency which had increased as the distance lessened, drooped suddenly as the Ford came once more to a standstill outside the Willoughby residence. The windows were dark and dead, and so were those of Hayson's house in the background. This was anti-climax. To be up all night on a story was enjoyable enough, but to be hanging about in the early hours of the morning in a peacefully sleeping city, looking for trouble where none existed, was both boring and absurd.

Had Garve been a less thorough reporter he would either have set off again for Tel Aviv at this point or gone home to bed in disgust. In either case the history of Palestine would have been very different, though he would probably not have lived to have told it. So convincing was the aspect of the silent houses—so utterly improbable did it seem that anything nefarious had happened in them, that at one moment Garve's foot actually hesitated over the self-starter. Logic, and his professional training, prevented him. Unless his reasoning had been hopelessly faulty, this morning was the morning for action. It was true that no house had ever worn a more innocent appearance, yet silence could be anything but innocent. In any case, he had driven many miles at a furious rate to make sure, and make sure he would, even if it meant a burglary. He recalled several occasions in his early days as a reporter when by "making sure" against all probabilities he had landed a spectacular story.

He advanced cautiously up the drive. If nothing had happened, and all the inhabitants of the house were soundly asleep, there was no purpose in waking them. On the other hand, if there *were* anything unusual about the place, silence might be essential to safety. Garve knew from long experience how quickly and noiselessly the Arabs could move. He proceeded on the assumption that they were lying in wait for him. He walked up the middle of the drive, well clear of prickly pear and cactus, trusting in the bad light to prevent anyone taking a successful potshot at him.

The front door was tightly closed, and across the windows of the rooms on either side of it curtains had been drawn so carefully that there was not even a chink to peer through. Garve flashed his torch from side to side, and suddenly leaped. One of the lounge casement windows was slightly open. Garve knew the Willoughby household. Jackson, faithfully discharging his thankless duties, was a tyrant about windows. Every night, before retiring to rest in his room next to Willoughby's, he insisted on making a personal tour of inspection of the downstairs rooms to see that every window was fastened. Whether the windows were shut or open, intrusion by night was always a possibility, but if the intruder had first to break in, there was more chance of his being heard, particularly if he were more skilled in the art of assassination than of burglary. So at least Jackson had always argued, and he had acted accordingly.

Cautiously Garve opened the window wide and put a leg over the sill. There was, he considered, always a possibility that for once the window had been overlooked, and if Jackson heard anyone climbing in he was as likely as not to shoot first, and ask questions afterwards.

Inside the room Garve listened, motionless, in the darkness. Somewhere in the hall a big clock was ticking. There was no other sound of any sort. It was a new and eerie experience for Garve —breaking into a house at night. When he listened, the very walls seemed to be listening too. Try as he might, he could not make his movements noiseless. His shoes were strong and heavy, and at each step the toes gave a little tap on the floor. His very first movement caused a board to creak horribly.

"I'm a rotten burglar," thought Garve. "Better take my shoes off."

As he moved his right foot to get at the lace it made a curious sucking sound, as though it were coming away from treacle.

"Funny," said Garve under his breath. Shielding his torch, he let its dim rays fall upon the boards at his feet. For a moment he stared at the dark trickle incredulously; then he turned the full light of the torch upon it, and followed it across the floor to its source by the fireplace.

"Good God!" he ejaculated. There no longer seemed any need for caution. In two strides he was over by the body and staring horrified into Jackson's dead face. By the light of the torch it was chalk white, except where the blood had congealed round the gaping wound in the neck. Obviously he had bled to death, and quickly—it looked as though his jugular vein had been severed. Judging by the state of the room, the great dark patch on the carpet, the broad rivulet across the boards, his body had drained dry.

"Messy but merciful," thought Garve, and promptly turned his attention to the rest of the room. He was not surprised now to find signs of a struggle all about him. Many people had marched over these polished boards, which were dirty with the marks of feet and scattered gravel. Two wooden chairs were overturned, a vase of flowers lay in fragments against the window, and on the settee a tell-tale coil of rope had been left behind.

Garve proceeded grimly to search the room. He had only one thought in his mind now—to find Esther, dead or alive. He dared not contemplate her fate. He could telephone the police from here, but what could they do? Primarily it was vital to obtain more information. Clearly the house had been raided. The question was, who had been there, who had been taken, and where to?

A child could have deduced the answers to the first two questions. On the little occasional table the relics of a sociable gathering had been left untouched. Garve examined the ash-tray, which was eloquent. There was the heavy ash and moist dottle of a pipe—that would be Jackson's. Yes, Garve could see the pipe now, lying in the grate where it had fallen. There were eight cigarette stubs—seven of them were Virginian—those would be the ones that Willoughby had smoked—and one was gold-tipped and Turkish. Garve recognized it at once as Hayson's. So the man had been here—but not for long, for he had smoked only one cigarette. The question was, had Esther been there too? She might have smoked some of the Virginian, but she preferred Turkish, and Hayson would have offered her one.

Garve's torch passed on. There was whisky on the table, a soda siphon, a carafe of water, and several glasses. Three of them were dirty—used by Willoughby, Jackson, and Hayson. They all drank whisky, and Esther hated it. If she had been here she had drunk nothing.

But she must have been there—Garve had left her at the gate himself. But surely, if she had come in, they would all have gone to bed—after a last drink, anyway. If Willoughby was still up when the assailants arrived, as seemed likely since Jackson was shot down fully dressed, it was almost certain that Esther had *not* arrived at that time.

What time had the attack occurred? Garve stepped across and felt Jackson's body. Bloodless though it was, it was still warm. Garve picked up the pipe from the grate—why, even that was warm—just.

The events of the morning were falling into place. The attack had been quite recent, and the household had still been waiting up for Esther. What had happened to Esther between the time Garve had dropped her at the gate and now? And if Hayson had been here only a short time, what had he been doing when he wasn't here? If anything had happened to Esther, Hayson was almost certainly responsible. The problem was to find Hayson.

To find Hayson? But how? Night was racing on to morning, and he might be anywhere—in Jerusalem or out of it. As the leader of the impending revolt the probability was that he would stay in the city—but where?

Though time was desperately short, it was obviously essential in the first place to explore the Willoughby house, and make sure that murder had not been done in any of the other rooms. Garve ran through them quickly, flashing his torch now without fear. The servants' quarters were empty. Not a bed in the house had been slept in. Esther's bedroom, spick and span to the last detail, had clearly not been entered that night. Everywhere Garve drew a blank. The house was deserted. From the window of Esther's room Garve stared out thoughtfully across the rough garden that led to Hayson's. *His* windows, too, were dark and forbidding, and there was no reason to suppose that his house would be any less deserted than the Willoughbys'. Garve hesitated, uncertain what to do, and the fate of Jerusalem hung in the balance. What could he do? He must find Hayson, but it was impossible to comb the city. Behind those dark windows, perhaps, there might be some hint of his whereabouts, some evidence overlooked, something which, though it could not help the police to stop the revolt, might yet help them to suppress it. It was a long chance, but there was nothing else to do but look.

Garve felt more like a burglar than ever as he approached Hayson's house; but the thought of Jackson's bloodless body lying in the darkness behind him gave an edge to his determination. Hayson, however, had been more careful about his windows. Garve walked round the house, carefully scrutinizing each entrance, but without exception they were securely fastened.

Eventually he decided that the french doors from the loggia presented the least difficult problem to the unskilful housebreaker. It was quite clear that he could not hope to get in silently. He did not believe Hayson was in the house, but Hayson's servant might be. The only thing to do was to break the window and then see what happened.

It was the work of a moment to pick out from the boulder-strewn garden a piece of rock of the necessary length and heaviness. Using no more violence than he could help, Garve smote the pane of glass nearest the catch and it shattered completely. The fragments fell, in the main, inside the room on the carpet; but, even so, the noise of the blow and the splintering was startling. Garve listened tensely, his hand on his revolver. If he met any resistance now he was quite determined to shoot. The seconds passed and no sound came from the house. Garve listened, his ear at the broken pane, for the telltale creak of a board. Presently he ventured to insert his hand through the hole and turn the handle. The door swung outwards, easily and noiselessly. He stepped into the room.

His torch revealed nothing here—it was the lounge where he had sat with Hayson when they were discussing their visit to the quarries. Hayson's own study was obviously the place to ransack, but first Garve felt impelled to visit the upstairs rooms. This creeping about dark houses, expecting at any moment to feel the blade of a knife in one's back, was not a pastime which appealed to him. Once he had assured himself that the house was empty, he could search quickly and at peace. Room by room he worked through the building at the point of his gun till only the study was left. Yes; everyone had gone. He returned to Hayson's sanctum. His roving torch picked out the well-equipped laboratory running along one wall and the shelves of ancient pottery and other relics. Finally it came to rest on the bureau—the obvious place for concealing important papers. He examined the bureau carefully. It was of oak, and solidly built. No doubt Hayson had the key with him. In that case—Garve seized a heavy chair, balanced it a moment, swung it above his head, and brought it down on the lock with a crash which he felt must have roused the dead in the Kedron Valley. One of the legs of the chair snapped off, and the whole room shook, but the lock of the bureau seemed quite unaffected. Garve was getting desperate. The clock on the wall was loudly ticking out the seconds, and each tick hammered in his head. Careless now of the consequences, he placed the muzzle of his gun against the lock and fired. The noise of the shot was deafening. He waved the acrid smoke away and examined the bureau. The woodwork round the lock was blackened and splintered, but the lock still held. Again he lifted the chair, and the edge of the wooden seat fell flush on the lock. The top of the bureau rolled back and Hayson's papers were revealed.

Eagerly Garve went through them. It was clear enough that Hayson was a genuine antiquarian, whatever else he might be. There were letters from learned societies in London, requests that he should give lectures; congratulations from fellow-archaeologists on finds which were meaningless to Garve. Hayson had done little enough research in Palestine, but elsewhere he seemed to have been professionally active. Garve noticed with surprise how many of Hayson's own notes were kept in Arabic. The man must have a wonderful facility in the language.

Everything was neatly arranged as Garve would have expected, knowing Hayson's precision. Each pigeon-hole, each drawer, had its own label and its particular contents. Garve threw aside a mass of personal correspondence which he had the inclination, but not the time, to read, and delved into the last drawer.

At the bottom he struck oil. The long document, inscribed so carefully in Arabic characters, proved beyond doubt what Garve had only so far deduced—the complicity of Hayson in the plot. Garve could not read Arabic as easily as he could speak it, but it was clear to him that this was a list of the ammunition dumps. The exact location of each dump was described, together with the nature and the quantity of the arms. Garve gave a low whistle as he struggled through the text. Colossal! Incredible! No wonder the Arabs had had a feeling of confidence and jubilation during these last few months.

The bureau disclosed nothing further, and Garve could hardly hope for more. It was true that he had still no idea of Hayson's whereabouts, and that he was still powerless to help Esther; but this document alone was the key to the success or failure of the revolt. If the police or the military could only take possession of these dumps before the storm broke, the Arabs would be disarmed before they could strike a blow. Police headquarters. That was the next step. And quickly.

Stuffing the document into his breast pocket he was on the point of leaving when his eye fell on a roll of films which Hayson had left near the bureau. Films!—Now what was it Hayson had said about films? Something, surely. Ah yes—of course—the dark room. Garve walked over to the door and pulled the handle. It was locked.

"Funny," he thought, "locking a dark room and taking the key." He was anxious to get away, but his thoroughness triumphed. "It's dogged as does it," had been the slogan of his early reporting days—and what reporter could leave uninspected a locked room in the house of a conspirator. Blissfully ignorant of what lay inside, he raised his revolver again and fired through the lock. The first shot was enough. The door swung open of its own accord, and Esther's unconscious body lay sprawling at his feet.

He stepped back with an oath, startled, staring through the smoke, uncertain what had happened. Then he suddenly saw who it was, and was on his knees.

God, if he had shot her! With trembling fingers he examined her body. She was breathing. She was alive. There was no blood. It was all right —she must have been sitting or lying—could not have been as high as the keyhole. Raging anger seized him as he looked at her pallid cheeks, but he struggled to control himself.

"Keep cool," he muttered. "Keep cool." He groped for his knife and slashed the cords which bound her. Where her wrists had been tied red weals were growing purple under the bonds. No doubt she had struggled. First one white hand and then another fell limply to the floor as the cords were cut. He could see that her fingers were bloodless—the circulation had been stopped as by a tourniquet. Probably her feet were the same. He cursed and cursed, but went on working all the time. There—she was free.

He laid her out on the rug and rushed into the kitchen for brandy. He brought the bottle back with him, and water. Between her white lips he forced a few drops of the amber liquid, and bathed her forehead, using his handkerchief as a compress. She stirred, moaning slightly. She was coming round. He chafed her hands and feet.

She opened her eyes, shivered, and groaned. The blood was running back into her lips.

"There, there," said Garve, stroking her hair, whispering gently. "I know it's hurting—but it won't last long. Here, have some more brandy. Oh, my darling, thank God you're safe."

"Philip!" Esther softly breathed his name and smiled. "Philip, I knew you'd come—but it was such a long while. I—I went to sleep—but I got stiff and—and woke up again—and then I began to get dizzy and cold—I suppose I fainted."

"Don't talk for a minute," Garve urged. "You've had a bad time."

Esther was staring round her, still a little dazed. The colour was creeping back into her cheeks, however, and her eyes were alive again.

Garve could see that she was groping for recollection, and did not attempt to hurry her. His encouragement, in any case, was unnecessary, for suddenly she clutched wildly at his arm and struggled up into a sitting position, her face strained with eagerness.

"Hayson!" she cried. "I remember now. He wanted me to go away with him. He was going to kidnap father. Quick, we must go."

"Wait a minute," said Garve gently. "I want to move as quickly as you do, darling, but I must know all the facts. Sure you're feeling better now?"

"I shall be when I'm doing something."

"All right—tell me in as few words as you can what happened to you after I left you."

"I was seized by three men," Esther blurted out. "They were waiting in the shrubbery. They brought me to Hayson. He told me about the revolt. He's the leader—you know."

"I've just found his list of ammunition dumps," said Garve grimly. "Go on."

"He's an Arab. His name's Hussein."

Garve stared incredulously. "An Arab! Hayson—Hussein! Good God!" So that was it. The last piece of the puzzle had fallen into place. "Of course—his tanned skin, his dark eyes, his impassive manner, his Arabic. Well, he's the leader, and we've got to find him. Where is he, Esther?"

"In the quarries—so he said. We must see if my father is at home."

"He's not," Garve told her gravely. "There's no one there."

Esther was turning pale again, and he plied her with more sips of brandy.

"Then Hayson's carried out his plan," she said. "He told me he was going to kidnap father, and make him sign a paper saying he'd been taken by Ali Kemal to Petra, and asking the authorities to send a lot of troops after him so that the revolt could begin without any resistance. I'm afraid that sounds awfully mixed up."

"On the contrary," said Garve, "it's crystal clear—only too clear. The clever devil!"

"He nearly made me go with him, Philip. He'd actually bought two tickets on a boat from Port Said, he was so certain. He's got them with him now. He was willing to abandon the whole revolt."

Garve nodded. "I know the feeling. Just as I would have thrown up my job if I could have got you out of this before the crash. Now listen, Esther. There isn't going to be a crash. We're going to stop it. We *can* stop it—but you'll have to help."

"Oh, I *want* to help. Anything—anything."

"Listen—there are two things to be done. *You* must see the authorities at once. Everybody will try and keep you out; but if you tell them who you are you've more chance of getting through to them than I have. You'll take this list of ammunition dumps with you. They'll realize quickly enough that they'll have to put a guard on each—if it's not too late. Tell them about the plot to get the troops away. Tell them what you like, but don't leave them until they understand. If they've started sending forces to Petra, they must be brought back. Make that clear to them. It's up to you, Esther. Use your name, your womanly charm, any damn thing, but make them *act*."

"Leave it to me. How do I get to them?"

"I'll take you in the car and drop you outside. And this time I'll see there's nobody lurking in the bushes. How do you feel—are you fit enough?"

"I'm quite recovered—and—Philip—so happy to be with you again. What are *you* going to do?"

"Oh, I'm going to the quarries," said Garve nonchalantly.

"Philip—oh Philip. I knew that's what was in your mind. I'm so afraid—what can you do there? All the leaders—all the most desperate of the Arabs—will be there. You won't have a chance. You can't do anything if you go. Wait until you can get help from the police if you must go."

"Your father's down there," Garve reminded her gravely. "His life is in the utmost danger. I must go, Esther. In those quarries, if Hayson told you the truth, all the heads of this revolt are gathered. Without them the conspiracy is at an end, the rising will peter out. Once they are free and abroad in the country they can rouse their people, and civil war may last for years. It's now or never."

"But what are you going to do?"

"I'm going to try and meet Hayson with his own weapons—duplicity and cunning. And—yes, I've got it. Wait, I shan't be a minute."

He snatched up the telephone and asked for police headquarters.

"That you, Fairfax? Listen, man, this is Garve. Any sensational news? What's that—message from Mr. Francis Willoughby? Captured by Arabs? Right—I know all that. Now, listen, that message is a fake. No, I'm not going to argue; I'm telling you. What's that? I don't care what the authorities are doing—it's a fake. Miss Willoughby's on her way to tell them about it now. If you like you can warn them to expect her. What I want you to do—damn you, Fairfax, I know I'm a journalist, but your job and all our lives depend on this—it's a simple matter—no I can't come over, there's no *time*. Well, I'll tell you if you'll listen. Send a dozen men with two machine-guns to Hezekiah's Tunnel at the point where it comes out into the Virgin's Fountain. And send a similar guard to the top end of the quarries. Tell the men to arrest or kill any Arabs coming out of the tunnel or quarries during the next hour. . . . I don't care how many men you're short of—this is vital. You must get them stationed right away. I've got to ring off now, Fairfax, but don't fail me, for God's sake. Good-bye."

Garve hung up noisily. He shrugged his shoulders, seeing the question framed on Esther's lips. "Of course he doesn't understand a thing and doesn't see why he should take instructions from me—but, he's a good fellow, and I have a hunch that he will. Now then, old girl, ready?"

Esther nodded. "Please, Philip, be as careful as you can. I found you and lost you, and now I've found you again, and—I can't stand it much longer."

Garve was fumbling in Hayson's bureau. "If we get through this, Esther, we'll take the first boat back to England and be married right away." He found what he was looking for—a second gun that he had noticed in his previous search. The chambers were fully loaded, and he stuffed it into his pocket. "There—I'm a walking arsenal, and can't come to harm. Anyway there's a special providence—or have I said that before?" He gave Esther one great hug, and they both dashed for the car. The sky was growing light, and as they took their seats they heard the drone of engines above them, and saw dark wings sweeping eastwards into the sunrise.

"Bombers," said Garve tensely, "bound for Petra. It's your job, old girl, to get them back. Good luck."

18. Death Beneath Jerusalem

Garve waited outside military headquarters only till Esther had been safely escorted within, and then he drove back quickly to Damascus Gate. He was quite convinced that he had done the best thing possible in letting Esther do the explaining. As the daughter of the man who had been kidnapped she was in a special position, and the authorities would have to listen to her.

By comparison, Garve's own job was beset with difficulties. A plan was taking shape in his mind —a dangerous plan, full of pitfalls and hazards, a plan which might easily fail, but the only possible one in the circumstances. The need of the moment was to prevent the Arabs leaving the quarries—to keep them in there until Fairfax could bring up his party of police and cut off their line of retreat. That—and to prevent them from killing Willoughby.

The immediate problem, however, was how to get into the quarries at all. Every moment it was growing lighter—zero hour must be very near, for the Arabs in the quarries would undoubtedly want to leave before sunrise. If the entrance to the quarries were unguarded, well and good; but if, as Garve anticipated, there were sentries on duty, it might be impossible to enter without being detected. The opening to the caves was at the foot of the wall, and could be approached either along the wall or across thirty yards of open ground from the road.

As he drew near to the place Garve slowed the car almost to walking pace so that its engine should not attract attention. A dip in the road quite near the quarries offered an excellent and inconspicuous parking ground, and from there Garve walked back to a point opposite the entrance from which he could reconnoitre the position.

At once he saw that his fears had not been groundless. Just inside the entrance stood two armed Arabs conversing. Both were powerfully built, and each had a rifle and bayonet. They looked, thought Garve, alert and efficient. He cursed under his breath. At any moment the ringleaders of the revolt might file out of that narrow opening and disperse throughout Palestine. He must do something—*must* get in. He considered the possibilities. To attempt to surprise them was hopeless—the open ground forbade it, and the fact that there were two of them. Had there been only one, he would have risked creeping along by the wall and making a sudden assault. In present circumstances that would be suicidal. These Arabs had acute hearing, and were quick as lightning with a knife. Good shot though he was, Garve realized the impossibility of using his revolver on them from any point within safe range which would give him cover. Besides, he did not want to shoot lest the sound of firing should warn the Arabs inside.

Yet the minutes—vital, invaluable minutes—were slipping away. To go right round to Hezekiah's Tunnel and in by that entrance would take too long, and there might be a guard there too. It looked very much as though his fine schemes were going to come to nothing after all, and as though he would have to wait in this place till the police came.

But that was unthinkable. Surely, surely there must be a way. Any method, however desperate, was justifiable. If a frontal attack was impossible, was there no subterfuge that might succeed?

In a moment he knew there was a chance—an extravagant chance, a last throw. Quickly he slipped back to the car. It seemed a wicked piece of vandalism, but—war was war. From the floor at the back he dragged a two-gallon tin of petrol, and wrenched the cap loose with a spanner. Lavishly he splashed the liquid over the upholstery and woodwork at the front and back. He took the top off the petrol tank and loosened the nut at the bottom of the carburettor. Then, with the reek of petrol half choking him, he threw a lighted match through the rear window on to the seat.

As he rushed away he felt the hot blast of flame behind him. In a few seconds the car was a blazing inferno. Keeping well down in the shadow of the low stone wall at the roadside he raced back until he was level with the quarries. As he looked over the wall he could almost have shouted in exultation, for the two sentries were running across the open ground towards the car. They would think, he reflected grimly, that whoever had driven it there was inside, and since it was quite impossible to get anywhere near the flames, they would go on thinking so. Garve gave them a minute or two to get well down into the dip, and then slipped over the low wall and dashed across to the quarries.

He breathed again. Not merely had his ruse been perfectly successful, but he now stood between the conspirators and freedom. He might not seem to provide much of a barrier against thirty or forty desperate men, but the tunnels of the cavern were narrow and tortuous, with plenty of cover, and he had two guns. In such circumstances a single determined man might hold up an army. Had it not been for the presence of Willoughby in the cave he would have been inclined to take up a position at the top end of the precipice ledge, or, better still, at the narrow aperture which led out of the apparent cul-de-sac, and simply wait for reinforcements. The temptation was great, but Garve did not believe that the Arabs would want to bring Willoughby out alive. He had served his purpose, and in the daylight would be a dangerous encumbrance.

Only too clearly he realized that his difficulties were just beginning. It was not easy for him to recall the geography of the quarries, and he had only a small flash-lamp to help him on his way instead of the two powerful torches which had driven a great beam of light through the tunnels on his former visit with Hayson.

The problem which worried him most was how to find the right tunnel in the top chamber—the one which led to the aperture and the precipice ledge. He could recall no distinguishing marks about it, and was still in doubt as to what he should do when the difficulty was solved for him.

As he approached the entrance to the chamber, and for safety's sake momentarily switched off his flash-lamp, he saw that there was already a light ahead of him. He advanced with infinite caution till he was able to see round the edge of the passage wall into the chamber. A few yards away, illuminated by a flare, a third sentry leaned against the wall, his rifle grounded. Just behind him another tunnel broke the wall, and this, Garve concluded, was the one he was guarding and therefore the one which led below.

Garve no longer feared to shoot. He had come too far for the sound to be heard above, and if it were heard below it no longer mattered now that he was in the quarries, and could take up a position almost anywhere. It was rather like potting a sitting rabbit, but he thought of Jackson and hardened his heart. Taking careful aim—to miss might be disastrous—he fired at the man's head. The Arab spun round and dropped where he stood without a cry, and the noise of the explosion echoed and reverberated like thunder through the galleries. Garve waited till the noise had died down and stepped across to the sentry. As he had intended, the bullet had passed clean through his brain. He left the flare burning and hastened along the tunnel.

Yes; it was the right one. Again he switched off his lamp as he approached the narrow rock slit and peered round it cautiously before squeezing himself through. There was no-one about. The precipice no longer had any terrors for him, but he advanced cautiously towards the place where the tunnel suddenly dropped. Eight feet —that was nothing—when you knew its depth. He lowered himself over the edge, hung for a moment by his hands, and let go. He landed awkwardly in the dark, but without suffering serious damage.

He approached the central chamber in the dark, knowing that his only strength lay in seeing without being seen. The mouth of the passage where it debouched into the chamber was already visible as a faint glow ahead. Step by step he crept nearer, hugging the wall, when suddenly his cautiously extended boot collided with something soft and bulky on the floor. Instantly he dropped to his knees and pressed a round ring of steel hard into the middle of the bulk.

"Who the devil are you?" demanded a familiar voice.

"Willoughby!" Garve exclaimed. "What are you doing here alone? Are you all right?"

"Garve, you're the last man I expected to see." His voice rose excitedly. "There's a devilish plot on."

"Sh-sh! I know—don't worry. Esther's with the authorities now. With luck this trick will fail."

"Esther safe—ah!" There was such relief in Willoughby's voice that Garve felt rewarded already for the risk he had taken.

"I can't tell you about it now," Garve went on hurriedly. "You'll hear the whole story in time. Our job at the moment is to tackle these Arabs here. Do you know how many there are?"

"About forty," said Willoughby weakly. "But they haven't all got guns. If you could get these ropes off me, I might be able to help you. I'm as stiff as a ramrod at the moment—I seem to have been sitting here for hours, and it's a damned draughty passage. That fellow Hayson tricked me. Did you see any signs of troops leaving?"

"A few 'planes went over just now, flying east," Garve told him, sawing at his bonds with a knife that was far from razor-edged.

Willoughby groaned. "I was afraid so. The message I sent was strong enough to shift an army. Hayson told me Esther was already on her way to Petra."

"Did you put that in your message?" asked Garve suddenly, without ceasing to work at the ropes.

"I did."

"That's fine. Don't you see—the only danger was that Esther wouldn't be able to convince the authorities in time that your letter was an Arab trick. When they see her—see she's not at Petra —they won't need any convincing. They'll argue that if you were wrong about her, there's reasonable ground for supposing that you were misled about the whole thing. Once again our friend Hayson has been just a bit too clever. There—how's that?"

"I'll be ready to move in a few minutes. What's the plan of campaign? We can't fight all these blighters at once."

"No," said Garve grimly; "but we can keep them occupied—give them something to think about. Tell me, what's it like in the chamber? Have they much of a light?"

"A few flares—that's all."

"If we were to walk round the wall, should we be seen?"

"Not possibly—it's a big place, and the sides are as black as if there were no lights at all."

Garve nodded. "That's what I thought. Look here, I've got a spare gun. Can you use it?"

"If it's any good. I'm an old campaigner, you know."

Garve passed the weapon to him, and he weighed it in his hand. "It's a bit light, but I'll manage."

"I'm going to try and bluff them," said Garve. "It's our only hope. We're all right as long as they don't all try and rush us at once, and I don't think they will. It isn't any fun rushing into a dark place when you know there are guns there. We'll hold our fire until some one starts to come at us—then we've got to shoot to kill. They're a spirited crowd, but they won't feel so good when I've finished with Hayson. How about it, Willoughby; are you ready?"

"Lead on. By the way, Garve, one tip. If you do have to fire out of the darkness, move away from the spot directly you've pulled the trigger. They may shoot at the flash of your gun."

"I'll remember," said Garve. He led the way to the end of the tunnel in absolute silence, each man knowing that a premature sound might be the end of them. As Willoughby had said, the flares of the Arabs grouped against the opposite wall and the precipice did nothing to relieve the complete obscurity of the chamber's extremities. Hayson was talking, sitting on the floor with the others. He was talking in Arabic, and Garve soon gathered that he was issuing last-minute instructions. Ali Kemal was squatting by his side, no doubt the second in command. The flickering lights gave a ghostly aspect to the scene, but the cavern now seemed smaller than on Garve's first visit. He had suspected at the time, and was now certain, that his Odyssey across the floor had taken a very indirect course.

The Arabs were listening intently to their leader, and clearly had no expectation of an attack. They were relying on their three sentries above them, and no doubt on others below. They felt the quarries to be their own, and the natural dangers of the place a sufficient protection against intruders unacquainted with them.

Garve continued to lead the way, keeping close by the wall until he reached what he had always expected to be there—another passage running from the chamber at a point not very far from where the Arabs were sitting, but still sufficiently distant to be out of range of the flickering flares. Moreover, it was ideally suited to shelter a pair of snipers, for just inside its mouth it widened sharply, so that on either side was a natural bulwark. Garve took up a position on the left, and Willoughby on the right.

Now that the crucial moment had come in this great adventure, Garve felt far from heroic. The dice were heavily loaded against them in many ways, yet he recognized that had he been on the Arab side, and known the position, he would have been very far from happy as to the outcome of the approaching duel. The greatest danger, from Garve's point of view, was that the Arabs would scatter at the first indication that there was a stranger in the chamber. There might be a way, unknown to Garve, by which they could work round and take him in the rear, once they knew which passage he was in. Apart from that, they could only be dealt with effectively as long as they remained in a single illuminated group.

Garve gave one last look around the great chamber. Never, as long as he lived, would he forget this tense moment or this scene. The weird yellow light of the flares threw long ghostly shadows across the floor; the precipice lay, a threatening black line, in the background, losing itself in the darkness. Hayson, still calmly explaining his plan of action, sat like a Buddha.

Suddenly there was a slight stir among the conspirators, like the rustle that goes through a congregation at the last "Amen." Hayson had finished; they were going to disperse: it was now or never.

Garve had weighed his opening words like gold, for success or failure turned on their effect. In a loud voice he called out in Arabic: "Hayson—you are a traitor to the Arab cause."

Immediately the whole body of Arabs were on their feet, hands flashing to their weapons, cursing quickly, staring into the darkness, hardly able to believe that they had heard aright. Garve's fingers tightened on his gun.

"You all desire the independence of your country," he cried boldly. "I have positive and convincing proof that Hussein has betrayed you to the English. You are covered by guns from all sides, and the first man who moves from his position is dead. I have no wish to shoot you —any of you—and if you behave sensibly your lives will be safe."

"It's the Englishman Garve," shouted Hayson. "Follow me. We must kill him or we are lost."

"Ask him how I knew how to get here," Garve called again. "Who explained to me the secrets of the quarries? Who told me of the ammunition dump below us? Who told me of the entrance from Hezekiah's Tunnel? Fools—would you let him deceive you again?"

"Kill him," cried Hayson wildly. The crisis had come upon him too suddenly, too unexpectedly. For the first and only time he had lost his head. Garve's finger was on the trigger—only the pressure of a hair spring was needed to release the bullet —Hayson was advancing with thirty men behind him—when suddenly the ringed hand of Kemal fell upon his shoulder, heavy as the fate in store for him.

"Wait," said Kemal, and there was a dangerous suavity in his tone. "We cannot fight a voice in the darkness—and besides—I am interested to hear more."

Hayson swung round on him. "Do you trust the word of an English swine?" he cried. "Time presses, Kemal—the revolt waits on us."

"If the voice speaks with any truth,' retorted Kemal, "perhaps it had *better* wait."

"He's bluffing," cried Hayson. "He is alone —perhaps unarmed. Would you have our plans wrecked by the voice of a single enemy?"

Kemal faced Garve, who was seeing, but unseen. "Our leader says you are bluffing—do you hear?"

"I hear," said Garve. He raised his voice. "Number seven and number nine—fire into the air."

He pressed the trigger, and Willoughby fired a split second later. Both men stepped back.

"Those bullets," said Garve, "might now be lodged in your brain, Hayson—and yours, Kemal. I suggest that you all resume your seats, and we can then parley in greater comfort."

"I am agreeable," said Kemal; and Garve knew that fertile ground was prepared for the doubts that he was ready to scatter. Kemal was jealous of Hayson!

Only Hayson stood. His face twisted in diabolical rage, he screamed in English, "You'll die by the slowest of all deaths, Garve, for this."

"You forget," said Garve, "that your colleagues are very familiar with our language. Your threats to a witness will hardly be regarded as proof of your innocence. I give you five seconds to sit down and defend yourself. When I have counted five I shall instruct one of the men around these walls to shoot you dead. But I give you this promise—if, when I have finished, your friends declare you innocent, I will raise no finger to prevent your escape."

"Who speaks of escape?" Hayson scoffed. "You talk as though you have us in a trap."

"Exactly," said Garve. "Thanks to the information you have given us, there are soldiers above with machine-guns, and more soldiers with more machine-guns at the Virgin's Fountain. I can give you a safe conduct—and *only* I. Now, will you be seated? No? Then one—two—three—four—thank you, Hayson. That is your first sensible action since I have known you."

"The evidence!" cried Kemal impatiently. "I think after all you are only playing for time."

"Judge for yourselves," said Garve. "You know that Hayson, whom you have trusted, has been a frequent visitor at the house of Mr. Francis Willoughby. For reasons of his own, he has betrayed your movements and your plans, item by item, to Willoughby, to the police, and to myself."

"It's a lie," snarled Hayson.

"All the details of your plans are known to me —the date and time of the rising, the plot to kidnap Willoughby and make him write a message to the military, Petra—yes, even the whereabouts of all your ammunition dumps. Hayson gave me the list of them himself."

"It's a lie, I tell you," cried Hayson again. "Anything he has found out he has discovered without my knowledge or assistance."

"You will know best," observed Garve smoothly, "how many of you had complete knowledge of these things. The ammunition dumps, for instance—I speak from the memory of a conversation with Hayson—let me see. . . ." His mind went back to the document he had so recently perused, and he reeled off a list of the half-dozen places he could recall. "Perhaps," he added bitingly, "Hayson will say that he demonstrated his powers of leadership by committing this list to paper, and leaving the paper conspicuously about."

There was a moment's silence. Garve knew now that he had Hayson in the hollow of his palm. The man must explain about Esther or be silent.

"In big things and in small, Hayson betrayed you," Garve went on remorselessly. "He told me of the ammunition dump over by Bethany. He not only told me how to get into the quarries from Hezekiah's Tunnel, but he escorted me himself through the whole length of them, pointing out the dangers. He prepared an ambush for me on the Jericho road, but he warned me before-hand, and you know what happened, and how many Arabs were killed. The blood of those men lies at his door."

"If this is true," asked Kemal, "why is Hussein here to-night? If he has betrayed us to the English, why has he courted danger by coming here himself?"

"If he had stayed away," said Garve on the spur of the moment, "you would have taken fright and escaped before you could be taken. It was a condition of his bargain with the English that he should himself deliver you up, all together, so that the revolt could be smashed at its source."

"On whose behalf do *you* come here to warn us?" asked Hayson with a sneer.

"I am not a soldier, not a politician, but a journalist," said Garve. "I have seen something of Arab suffering in Palestine. I like and admire the Arabs. I believe they have much right on their side. I have come to prevent, if possible, the massacre of the finest of your leaders. I have come as a friend of all but Hayson."

"Every word that you utter is a lie," said Hayson. "If I had been in the pay of the English, would they have allowed me to bring Mr. Francis Willoughby down here to-night—would he be sitting now in that tunnel yonder, roped up, at our mercy. Do you know that we have only this moment agreed that he must be killed before we leave?"

"I know," said Garve solemnly, "that your decision was a perfectly safe one, since you yourself released him less than an hour ago, and put him on the road to safety."

Kemal sprang to his feet. "By Allah, is that true?" His hand was on his jewelled dagger. "If so——"

"Send someone to look," said Hayson, and in the light of the flares Garve could see the sweat falling from his face.

Kemal gave a swift order and an Arab went running off into the darkness. He was back in a matter of seconds, and his finger pointed accusingly at Hayson. "The captive has gone. His bonds are cut. . . ."

Now Hayson was on his feet as well, and with him the whole company.

"If Willoughby has gone," declared Hayson—and his voice sounded dry and cracked—"it is because Garve has released him. He is very clever—he is trying to persuade you to destroy your own leader, for he knows that without me the revolt must fail. For all these charges which he has made there are other explanations. I brought him to the quarries to kill him, because he was a danger to our cause. He was too clever and escaped. I said nothing to him about any ammunition dump—his curiosity is insatiable, and what knowledge he has he has obtained elsewhere. At this moment he is laughing at you, for he knows that there are no troops outside the quarries, though there may be if we delay any longer. What motive does he allege for this crime that he pretends I have perpetrated? I am wealthy —does he think that I would serve the English for gold? Does he believe that any promise the English could make to me would be sweeter in fulfilment than the joy I should get from seeing their throats cut?"

"Hussein is eloquent," said Garve slowly, "as well as very cunning. Up to a point he has been sincere enough. For years he has cultivated a hatred of the British, and looked forward to the day when he could revenge the wrongs of his countrymen. His leadership was, until he turned a traitor, able and efficient. He was not bought by the British for gold. There are some things sweeter even than wealth or revenge. Hussein loves the daughter of Mr. Francis Willoughby. For her he has been willing to throw away your lives and your hopes. You have seen her—perhaps at times you have even suspected it yourselves. He knew that if revolt broke out, her life might well be taken, and that, even if she survived, she would not willingly have anything more to do with him. Hussein has betrayed you for a woman's eyes."

"What have you to say?" demanded Kemal, turning on his leader. "Have you an answer to that?"

"Yes," said Hayson with great dignity. "It is true that I love this woman, though I detest the colour and the race which bred her. For her own qualities I love her. I repeat, however, that there was never any bargain—never any betrayal. I swear to you that I have disclosed nothing of our plans."

"Is it disloyal," asked Garve in a voice that cut like an icy wind, "to abandon at the last moment a revolt which you have prepared, for which you are responsible—to leave in the lurch your comrades who depend on you, whose lives must pay for failure—to leave them without a word, and steal away to a life of luxury with a woman of a race you hate. Tell me, Hayson, is that the sort of loyalty which would satisfy you?"

Hayson's face was ghastly pale under its tan, but he met without flinching the Arabs' accusing eyes. To the end he fought back, though the sense of his own guilt oppressed him, and at no time had he the air of an innocent man.

"Garve is himself in love with Willoughby's daughter," he said.

"He is jealous of me, and is using you, my friends, to make away with me. This story of his, that I contemplated abandoning my responsibilities and running away with this woman, is an unsubstantiated product of his own mind."

Kemal turned to the darkness. "This is the most serious of all your accusations. Have you proof?"

"The proof is on Hussein's person at this very moment," cried Garve. "Search in his pockets —there you will find two steamship tickets, bought yesterday to take him and Willoughby's daughter from Port Said."

It was a risk—Garve knew it—for Hayson might well have discarded such dangerous evidence. Yet somehow Garve believed that he would not even now have abandoned hope of taking Esther with him; that he would have kept the tickets against some unforeseen contingency.

There was a tense silence in the chamber. All the Arabs were watching Hayson's face, waiting.

"Well?" said Kemal. "At last we have evidence which we can test. If you still insist that you are innocent, Hussein—we must search you."

Hayson threw his head back in proud defiance and gazed without fear into the eyes of the men whom, half an hour ago, he had been instructing. They were solidly against him.

Hayson turned towards the dark wall of the chamber, and Garve wondered for a second if he were going to make a dash for freedom. Instead, without another word he whipped through the crowd of Arabs, and, before anyone could guess what he proposed to do, had flung himself over the precipice.

The suddenness of the action drew cries of horror from the Arabs, fading at once into listening silence. From the opaque depths came a heavy thud and a scream of pain as Hayson's body, hurtling downwards, struck a projecting fang of rock. Then in a moment came the dull splash of engulfing water, an echo of the splash, and nothing more.

The Arabs crowded to the edge and stared in futile horror into the backness. Garve grimly wiped his forehead on his jacket sleeve.

His score with Hayson was settled. It had been inevitable all along that Hayson should die, and the manner of his death had been easier than any the Arabs would have given him.

Moreover, with Hayson's unexpected end the morale of the conspirators was completely undermined. They had left so much to Hayson. Not one of them could say with certainty what was happening at that moment in the outside world. They had trusted Hayson, and now that trust was gone they were worse than uninformed.

Garve hastened to take advantage of their plight. "Ali Kemal," he called, "are you still prepared to parley? When I last interviewed you, you talked good sense. I believe you are still sensible. The choice before you all is death or surrender. If you fight here you will die at the hands of my men—if you try to fight your way out of the quarries you will be massacred by machine-gun fire. In other circumstances, death might be preferable to surrender. May I point out, however, that the revolt will not be helped by your deaths. The revolt is over. Your plan to mislead our troops has miscarried, your ammunition dumps by now are in our hands, your people are leaderless. If you surrender, you will live and carry on your country's struggle—perhaps by wiser and more effective means. What do you say, Kemal?"

Kemal turned, his dark, handsome face as impassive as carved mahogany. "How do we know that your talk of machine-guns is not all bluff?" he asked. "Perhaps, after all, we could walk out at this very moment unharmed into the Virgin's Fountain."

"Very well," said Garve, "call my bluff and try. I have warned you—if you're shot down don't blame me."

"What guarantee have we that if we surrender we shall not all be shot as rebels?"

"As to that," said Garve, "it is neither in my power nor in Willoughby's to make promises. You have been collectively responsible for mass terrorism and have engineered the deaths of innumerable innocent people. You have planned a revolt against the authority of Britain, and you will have to stand your trial. It may be that at this very moment the city is rising at your behest. What sort of mercy can you expect?"

"The people were told to do nothing until we left the quarries and gave specific orders," said Kemal sullenly. "If we leave as captives, you need have no fear, for there will be no revolt. In that case, what is our position with your Government?"

"I repeat that I can give no guarantee of safe conduct," said Garve sternly, "and you must know that as well as I. To the best of my knowledge, however, not one of you here has been directly concerned in any murder, and your leader has already paid the penalty for his actions. I suggest to you that if you leave the quarries without resistance, there is at least a chance that your lives may be spared. The alternative for you is certain death. Is the chance not worth taking?"

Kemal was conversing now in rapid Arabic with the other rebels. They all talked excitedly—arguing, replying. Occasionally a voice rose high enough to be intelligible to Garve, and he gathered that the two questions of loyalty and safety were being very thoroughly discussed. Eventually Kemal became again the focal point of the argument. Garve waited patiently, since every moment that passed made it more certain that Fairfax's men would have reached the Virgin's Fountain.

At last the conference finished and Kemal, drawing himself up proudly, turned to face Garve for the last time. "We have agreed upon our course," he said. "We are prepared to surrender to the authorities at the lower end of the quarries —if they are there."

"That is not good enough," said Garve stubbornly, "neither for you nor for me. If you leave the quarries armed, in the baseless hope that I am bluffing, there may be bloodshed before you discover I am right. I want no more fighting. Pile your arms, Kemal. My patience is almost exhausted."

Again the Arabs broke into excited talk, but this time the debate was brief. Kemal suddenly shrugged his shoulders and threw his knife and revolver on to the rocky floor. "We place ourselves in your hands," he said with simple dignity. One by one, the conspirators followed suit, until they stood only in their robes.

"Thank you," said Garve. "At last you have seen wisdom. Now—lead on—and no tricks. I am as familiar with the route as you, and *my* men will be following you."

Their spirit broken, the Arabs dragged the flares from their crevices and began to descend to the bottom level. Garve and Willoughby gave them a few minutes' start and then set off after them, moving cautiously.

"I think they know themselves to be beaten," said Garve, "but if they're feeling revengeful they might still set a trap for us."

"Tell me," demanded Willoughby curiously, "how much of your count against Hayson was true?"

"Only the last bit," said Garve, "may Heaven forgive me. As far as I know there was no treachery in his mind—he never expected that Esther would be in a position to report what he had told her. He was a deserter—or rather, a would-be deserter—not a traitor. All the same, though in many ways I was forced to respect him, I cannot help feeling that he fully deserved what he got. He was a most polished and unscrupulous liar himself, for his own ends, and it was fitting that he should have been destroyed by the weapon he chose."

"I must say," observed Willoughby, who showed no ill-effects after the exciting scene in the chamber, "that your own lack of veracity was redeemed by considerable ingenuity."

"You must remember I'm a newspaper man," said Garve unblushingly. "I have had long practice in shaping facts to suit circumstances."

He took Willoughby's arm in a grasp which he hoped felt filial. "Gently here—there's another precipice. We have to climb that ledge and drop down the other side. Can you manage it?"

"Just about," said Willoughby gamely, "though I must confess that when I came here in the hope that I should be stimulated I didn't anticipate that the stimulus would take such a subterranean form."

Willoughby was agile for his years, but his lame leg impeded his progress over the ledge, and he declared afterwards that its negotiation was one of the least pleasant experiences he had ever known. However, the passage was accomplished without incident, and in a few minutes the two men were skirting the ammunition dump, circling the bottom chamber, and dropping down into Hezekiah's Tunnel. As they turned to the left towards the opening, Garve's remaining fears were dispersed, for the broad figure of Fairfax was silhouetted against the morning sky. He was peering in at them, and as they hurried over the last few yards he came towards them, waving.

"We've taken them all," he cried as he drew nearer. "Every man jack, and sent them off under armed guard. Thirty-eight of them. Marvellous, Garve, marvellous."

"Did you have any trouble?"

"Not the slightest. I had two machine-guns trained on the opening, and if they'd shown any fight they'd have been mown down. As it was, they walked out in single file with their hands up. Wise birds—it'll mean years off their sentence."

"They must have been pretty cowed," said Garve. "They could have walked through the tunnel, if they'd had any spirit, and come out at Siloam's Pool. I forgot that."

"I didn't," said Fairfax complacently. "I had men up there too, but they weren't needed."

They climbed slowly from the tunnel to the Virgin's Fountain. "Miss Willoughby is up here," Fairfax told Garve with a grin. "The military tried to keep her away, but short of putting her under arrest there was nothing they could do, so they gave her an escort instead."

Esther was standing by the fountain talking to the two policemen who were to be left on guard at the tunnel. As soon as she saw the party emerging she waved and ran down to join them. The cool morning air had whipped some colour into her cheeks, and no one could have guessed that she had been up all night.

She threw herself into her father's arms and gave him a great hug of relief and affection. Then shyly she took Garve's hand possessively in hers.

"Darling," she murmured, "I'm so happy. I did my job too. The rescue orders were countermanded, and the planes have been wirelessed to return. There isn't any more danger now, is there?"

"I don't think so," said Garve soberly, almost overcome by her sweetness and the knowledge that she would be his wife. "According to Kemal, the people had to wait for a final instruction—and now they'll never get it. All the same, they saw the planes go, and the sooner they see them come back the better. But I refuse to worry any more." His arm slipped round her blatantly, and he turned to her father.

Willoughby had been watching them and listening to their affectionate conversation in some amazement, but now, as he caught his daughter's shy smile and Garve's broad grin, he suddenly understood.

"Well, I never," he said gruffly, gazing fondly at the young woman he had never been able to control. Then he blew his nose violently and said "Well, I never" again, as though all other speech had left him.

"May we have your blessing, sir?" said Garve softly, and after all they had been through it seemed a solemn moment.

Willoughby took Garve's hand in both his own. "I'm more than glad," he said. He bent to Esther and kissed her. "More than glad. If you don't kill her with excitement, my boy, you'll make her very happy. But—forgive an old man's curiosity—when did this happen?"

Esther laughed. "It was all your doing," she said. "Sending your only daughter to swim in the Dead Sea by moonlight with a strange man!"

"Ah!" said Willoughby—and in that "Ah!" was everything that could be said. He seemed tired, but very content, and the young people helped him up the hill.

"We must have a little celebration to-night," he said breathlessly, "or you'll be married before I can drink your health. He glanced wickedly at Esther. "What sort of an engagement are you contemplating—a year, two years?"

Esther stole a look at Garve. "We want to be married on the boat—going home," she said.

"I thought as much. And—when do we go home? What about your paper, Garve?"

"I'm finishing this job to-day," said Garve decidedly. "The story's over. I've got the finest exclusive I've had for years, and I'm going to telephone three columns to London if it costs a fortune. And when I've finished dictating I'll apply for honeymoon leave."

As the party breasted the last slope, Garve suddenly exclaimed and pointed to the eastern sky. "Look!" he cried, "they're coming back."

A number of tiny black specks were growing larger every second and the distant drone of aeroplane engines was now clearly audible. Eighteen black bombers were returning at full speed, and in a few minutes they were racing over the city. As they reached the walls they separated in a series of glorious swoops, circled, and flew low—so low that their evil-looking bomb-racks were conspicuous to all who cared to look. For five minutes they roared and turned and twisted, inspecting the ground for any sign of trouble, making it plain to all the population of Jerusalem that they had not gone to Petra after all.

The demonstration was awe-inspiring, convincing. Presently they flew off quickly towards the neighbouring aerodrome, their work done.

Esther drew a deep breath. "That settles it," she said. "A revolt has been arranged but will not take place."

Garve was more cautious. "Not yet, anyway," he said.

THE END